TOUCH·NOT·THE·CAT·BUT·A·GLOVE

Tom McKerley

Sugeid Schippeus

BLOODLINES

Touch Not the Cat

A Genealogy Mystery Novel

McKerley
& Schippers

First Published Great Britain 2011

by Summertime Publishing

ISBN: 978-1-904881-49-0

Design by Creationbooth www.creationbooth.com

www.touchnotthecat.com

ACKNOWLEDGMENTS

First and most of all we want to express our appreciation to Mr & Mrs Oliver Russell and Mr Guy Macpherson-Grant of the Ballindalloch Estate, for giving us the opportunity to use the name and location of Ballindalloch for Bloodlines - Touch Not the Cat.

We would like to stress that all characters in this book are a purely fictional product of our imaginations and have nothing in common whatsoever with any members of the Macpherson-Grant family in the present or the past.

This being our first fiction project, we are deeply indebted to our editor, Megan Kerr, book designer, Graham Booth, writers coach Jo Parfitt, "English Breeze" language teacher Hayley Johnson and Web designer, Remco Kalf, who have all educated and supported us on the process of writing the book.

The feedback of our test readers, Joyce McKerley, Remco Kalf, Connie Brocken, Cees van der Kroef and Marjory Marshall has been invaluable for the fine-tuning of the storyline and punctuation.

The amazing knowledge of intensive reader Marjory Marshall of The Bookmark bookshop in Grantown-on-Spey has been a great inspiration to include real facts and locations. The authors take full responsibility for any wrong or altered interpretations of factual information.

We also thank:

Alan L. Bain, President Emeritus of the American Scottish Foundation, based in New York, for encouraging, supporting and promoting our project.

The Garth Hotel in Grantown-on-Spey, for their very kind service and hospitality, with special thanks to Joan.

Molly Duckett of the Museum in Grantown-on-Spey, for her help on the history of the remarkable Grant family.

Fenella Corr of Ballindalloch Castle for accommodating our research.

(Ingrid would also like to recommend the chocolate cake baked according to a home recipe of Mrs Russell-Macpherson-Grant, served in the tearoom of Ballindalloch Castle)

Last but not least, we both want to thank our families for their patience and willingness to grant us the space to fulfill this project.

Thomas McKerley & Ingrid Schippers
July 22, 2011, The Hague, the Netherlands

PROLOGUE

"Cameron!" bellowed Detective Steve Hicks of the Raleigh Police Department, his deep voice dampened by the thick foliage of Wake Forest.

"We know you're here, give yourself up!"

The lean five-nine policeman in his mid-thirties moved like a hunter, taking slow deliberate steps, totally alert to his surrounding environment.

"We don't want anyone getting hurt," he tried again.

Hicks and his partner, Homicide Detective Cathy Stewart, were carefully picking their way through the woods some twenty yards apart, completely on their guard, their semi-automatic pistols held firmly in front of them.

The two cops were dressed in casual civilian clothes, with regulation arm and leg coverings, which served them well in the rough forest terrain.

A tip that Bobby Cameron had been seen camping out among the trees of Wake Forest had made Hicks and Stewart investigate further. It had taken them only a few minutes to find a small canvas tent lazily pitched beneath some trees, just off the edge of the woods. The tent was littered with empty energy drink cans, candy wrappers and a cheap sleeping bag.

"Great," Detective Stewart had muttered. "Nothing like a vicious criminal on a sugar high."

Now both detectives were inching their way forward over the moss and fallen leaves. The only sound they could make out was the gentle rain dropping on the thick, umbrella-like foliage above them.

"Cath!" Hicks suddenly whispered, instantly seizing Cathy's attention. He gestured with his index finger that she should circle a little further to the right. Cathy nodded in agreement. Her gun felt a lot heavier now and her palm was starting to sweat. Focusing on her breathing to stay calm, she continued to take slow small steps forward. Her eyes squinted, rapidly scanning as much ground as she could cover. Cathy had never shot anyone dead, she wondered if that was about to change.

Police sirens sounded in the distance. Cathy had wisely called for backup when they'd discovered the tent a few minutes ago. She hoped this was extra troops and smiled at the comforting feeling it gave her. She knew Cameron was one evil son of a bitch. Three days ago he had held up two gas stations in Raleigh. At one of them, he'd killed two people: a station attendant and a sixteen–year-old kid who had been driving alone for the first time with his new driver's license and just happened to be there.

"Drop the gun, bitch," commanded a soft voice behind her. "Drop it now."

Cathy froze. With a slow deliberate movement, she held the gun away from her body and tossed it a few feet to her right.

"Okay lady, turn around and face me. Nice 'n slow, you're doin' swell."

Cathy turned, trying desperately to control her shaking body. She could feel her stomach churn and felt the miserable urge to relieve her bowels. *Come on now, Cat*, she thought in an attempt to keep herself together, *they never show cops shitting their pants in crime series.*

It was the first time in her ten-year career that she had felt the warning fear so strongly of something about to go very wrong.

Cameron was kneeling behind a fallen tree, pointing his sawn-off shotgun directly at her. A broad-shouldered man in his late twenties with a neck almost the width of his jaw, an ugly crooked nose protruding from his face, he resembled his mug-shot exactly. Looking at him with as much indifference as she could muster, Cathy noticed Cameron was as nervous as she was. The single-barrel gun in his hands was shaking and his control seemed to waver.

"Step closer, I wanna see more of you," he ordered.

Cathy obeyed and walked slowly towards him. The muscles on his thick arms were straining to break free from the sleeves of his T-shirt and she noticed a purple tattoo on his right forearm.

"That's far enough," he growled. Cathy was now some five yards from him and, falling back on her training, did exactly what she was told, but very slowly, fighting to buy time.

"Too bad we don't have more time to play," Cameron slurred sadistically.

Where the hell is Hicks? Cathy thought, her heart thumping wildly in her chest.

"Two against one ain't fair, lady. Time to even things up. Sure hope you believe in Jesus."

In an instant there was a loud crack. Simultaneously, Cathy saw the red flame of the shotgun and felt the thud on her chest.

The spattering of lead pellets tore into her flesh, knocking her clean off her feet, landing her against a nearby tree. *Bang!* She heard a second shot and wondered if she had been hit again, but it all transcended into a haze.

Slumped against the tree trunk, she looked at her chest, dumbfounded. The white blouse quickly started to turn scarlet and she could smell the singed cloth. She stared unbelievingly. The surreal sound of Steve's alarmed voice came floating in from a distance, while she watched a butterfly land on her knee. *How beautiful and delicate,* she thought, observing the dark red wings with black edging. *So calming.* Then she noticed she was having difficulty breathing.

At that moment Catherine Stewart knew she was going to die.

CHAPTER 1

Wednesday 9 September 1885, Ballindalloch Castle, Banffshire, Scotland

"Why did your mother die, Alex?" The eight-year-old girl looked directly at Alexander Stewart, her blond curly hair dancing around her head in the mid-afternoon sunlight.

The way she posed the question made the boy, who was only two years older than the inquisitive girl, feel especially awkward, almost angry. It was anger however, he was not allowed to express. For even though he and the girl shared the same nursery now and were brought up in the same house, there were many things the girl was allowed to ask him, that he was not allowed to ask her in return.

"Perhaps you mean to ask *how* she passed away, Miss Katherine," he said evenly, hardly able to contain his feelings of hurt. The pain of his mother's passing was still vivid. Every morning he missed her soft, warm fingers going through his curly black hair to wake him up.

"Oh, I know *how* she passed away," the girl replied, "she died of a fever, but I wonder why? I mean, poor people who live in horrid conditions and who do not have enough to eat die of fevers, but your mother had enough to eat and lived in a proper house, so why did she have to die?"

The proper house, as Katherine so simply put it, was actually an ancient castle.

In her young and innocent world, nobody ever died. She had heard the servants whisper about a stillborn baby boy, but it never even occurred to her that she had lost a brother because she had never come to know him. Brought up in a lifestyle of plenty together with her five older brothers, Katherine was mainly focused on things she could have in life. Her daily schedule consisted of being woken up by servants each morning, bathed and dressed by a maid, and fed in the nursery. The family butler, Simpson, headed up the household staff and organized the meals and schedules. In his own way he took excellent care of the Macpherson children.

"You cannot see your father today, Miss Katherine," he would gently explain to the little girl. "He has guests."

She would often pass the day with servants and tutors without even having seen her parents, except perhaps for a short while during afternoon tea on the days that they were home. Only at main festivities, like birthdays and New Year's Eve, would the whole Macpherson family sit around the long mahogany table together and have an elegant dinner or a festive celebration. The only weekly family ritual was to go to church on Sunday. The castle and grounds would empty as everyone walked to Inveravon Parish Church, dressed in their best clothes. As leaders of the community the Macphersons occupied the row of pews closest to the pulpit, with Alexander and his father somewhere behind.

Katherine had known Alex for all of her life, it had only been recently that he had joined her and the other Macpherson children in their private living quarters.

Upon the tragic death of Alexander's mother, who had been one of the servants taking care of Katherine and her brothers,

Lady Macpherson had taken pity on the only child of their gamekeeper. With his father busy maintaining the Ballindalloch estate, Alexander often had to take care of himself and seemed lonely. He had to walk the two miles to Inveravon's public school six days a week, no matter the weather conditions. When Elizabeth had found the boy desolate and exhausted one morning on his way to school, she'd decided to speak to Alexander's father, Robert, and propose to take the boy into the Macpherson household to be properly raised. Alex was only to spend the evenings and holidays with his father. Robert Stewart had gratefully accepted the offer.

To Alexander, the arrangement only added to the confusion following his mother's death. Both his parents had always emphasized he was lucky to be raised on the Ballindalloch Estate, but should never forget his proper place in the household. It was a social difference Alexander Stewart had never fully grasped.

Growing up, he noticed he was sometimes quicker to understand the subtleties of life than some of the Macpherson boys. Also, the other children were never reprimanded in Alexander's presence, but he was told off on a number of occasions without any thought as to who was there.

This confusion turned Alexander into an introverted boy. He felt misunderstood and guarded himself against saying what he really felt; afraid his words would be discarded as nonsense or simply ignored. It brought him to believe he did not belong. Yet, somewhere deep inside him, lived a boy who stubbornly knew he was being underestimated. This was frustrating and sent prickles of anger up and down his spine at questions like the one Katherine had just asked him.

Still, Katherine was the only one from whom he could endure this sort of treatment. When one of the Macpherson boys addressed him, which they rarely did, except maybe for James, Alexander would sometimes not even answer and simply shy away. He was also all too happy that Laird Macpherson ignored him completely – except, of course, when he was spending time with Katherine. The master of the house would always find some chore for Alexander to do and send him away.

This contradiction of not belonging and yet feeling the pull of wanting to bond with Katherine, left him wandering between two worlds.

CHAPTER 2

The tall frame of David Stewart was sitting behind his desk in the study reading the most recent email Wayne Stewart had sent him. He had hooked up with Wayne through a website, "Genes Reunited". David had posted a request for information on his Stewart lineage, detailing what he had learned from his grandfather some years ago about their family's Scottish connection to an Alexander Stewart. It had been a deep and emotional exchange of memories with his grandfather at his father's funeral that had triggered David's need to find out more about his Stewart connections.

He learned his great-great-grandparents, Alexander and Sarah, sailed from Scotland and they married in Boston. Gramps had given David the wedding certificate, as a keepsake. It was on his desk.

CERTIFICATE OF MARRIAGE
– STATE OF MASSACHUSSETTS; BOSTON CITY

DATE: July 22, 1898

Place	Name	Age	Residence	Witness	Registrar
Park Street Church	Alexander Stewart	23	Waterside	Sean Devine	W. Hall
Boston Common	(single)		Backbay		
In the Form of the	(Journalist)		Boston MA		
Presbyterian Church	Sarah Gibson	29	Boston, MA	Annie Smith	
Of USA	M.s. Gillespie (widow)				
July 19ᵗʰ 1898	(Seamstress)				

He had discovered the details of Alexander's arrival in the USA, when he and Cathy went on a weekend break to New York and visited Ellis Island. The database however, had only provided basic details; name, age, sex, occupation, country of origin and date of arrival, 12 November, 1895.

Wayne's email stated *he* also descended from Alexander Stewart and Sarah Gibson. For evidence and information he had granted David access to his personal family tree on the website, which had helped him discover the place of birth of Alexander Stewart; Ballindalloch, in the County of Banffshire.

Had it not been for Wayne, David would never have been able to identify his ancestor among the hundreds of Stewarts born in Scotland in the early 1870's.

The discovery had started a flurry of correspondence between the two men. Wayne even suggested that David join him for "Tartan Week", an event organized since 1999, by three New-York-based American-Scottish organizations. Its prime purpose was to celebrate Scottish roots, using as a key subject the Scottish Declaration of Independence. This was drawn up and signed at Arbroath Abbey, Scotland, on 6 April in the year 1320. For this reason, "Tartan Week" always included that date.

Only few Americans knew that the Arbroath treaty had served as a model for the American Declaration of Independence and that almost half the signatories were of Scottish descent. David had smiled over Wayne's enthusiasm for his Scottish ancestry. He was keen to find out more about his own Scottish background, but it had never occurred to him to go to these events. He hadn't even visited any of the Scottish gatherings organized in North Carolina, so why go all the way to the Big Apple? As a result of his email exchanges with Wayne, he did become a member of the American Scottish Foundation.

Wayne's family tree, had given him some new information. David had known he descended from Robert, son of Alexander Stewart and Sarah Gibson. It was news to him though that they had another son, Michael, from whom Wayne descended. David noted with curiosity, this boy was born in or around 1893 in Boston – about five years before Alexander and Sarah were married and two years before they even arrived in Boston. He decided he'd look into that later.

So now all David had left to do was to print the birth certificates of these Stewarts of Ballindalloch. As he hit the print key on his laptop, the digital clock on the corner of the table read 11:30 pm. He stretched his long arms and legs and ran his fingers through his hair.

He was feeling rather pleased with his latest results. The noise of the HP printer filled the room as it spat out two documents.

Had his wife not been working a night shift at Raleigh PD, he would have gone to her to boast about his discovery.

But perhaps it was a good thing she wasn't home. She would find a way to ridicule it anyway.

He picked up the documents and stared at them.

Alexander Stewart, Male, born, Wednesday, 25th April, 1875, at Ballindalloch Estate, Banffshire. Father: Robert Stewart (Gamekeeper) Mother: Jane Stewart m.s. Black Registrar: A.J. Mackie

Robert Stewart, Male, born, Tuesday, 27th November, 1855, at Ballindalloch Estate, Banffshire. Father: John Stewart (Gamekeeper) Mother: Margaret Stewart m.s. Campbell Registrar: J. McLaughlan

So, the Highlands of Scotland are where my roots lay, he thought. The birth certificates made it conclusive.

In 1855, as he'd learned, a UK law was passed to make it mandatory that all births, deaths and marriages had to be registered. For anything earlier than 1855, the only possible resource for further research was old church registers. That gave David another good reason why he should visit Scotland.

Wayne Stewart had also mentioned that he'd actually visited the estate and its castle, as Ballindalloch had been opened to the public in 2005.

A Scottish castle, David thought. *Imagine that!* Although it was getting late, he needed to make one more check. He picked up his glass and drained the last of his Glenlivet. Using the Google search engine, he typed, *"Ballindalloch Castle"*. He clicked on the official home page and the screen opened;

WELCOME TO BALLINDALLOCH CASTLE
– Home of the Macphersons for over 400 years.

"What the…" he mumbled, leaning over towards the screen as if that would help clear his head. "Macpherson!" he said out loud into the empty room. He was stunned. *Wait till I tell Cathy about this. Maybe now she would take genealogy a little more seriously!*

Eager to find out more and fully awake now, David started to browse the website. It was clearly designed for the tourist industry. He read over a brief description of the history of the castle, going back to the 16th century, and noticed the section "Ghosts".

The alleged ghost tickling the tourist imagination was a Gordon Macpherson. According to the story, he mysteriously disappeared in 1895 while fishing in the Spey River that flows through the castle grounds. To this day, the website stated, Gordon was haunting Ballindalloch.

David wondered if his ancestor, Alexander, had still been there at the time of the disappearance. It was the same year that Alexander Stewart arrived in America.

When David finally went to bed, his mind overly active with all he'd uncovered, he convinced himself to keep his mouth shut and not mention anything to Cathy for the time being. First, he would call this castle and suggest a visit to consider Ballindalloch as part of a travel guide he was commissioned to write. That would give him the opportunity to find out if they had records going back to Robert and Alexander Stewart's time. Maybe the present laird could give him the name of the local church holding the Stewart family records.

His last thought before falling asleep was about a movie he had seen: *Six Degrees of Separation*. It was about a conman who charmed an Upper West Side family into believing he knew them very well through their son. The story line was based on the theory that between every two people on earth, there are never more than five people connecting them. *Basically, we're all related,* David figured, fading into his twilight zone between dream and slumber.

David woke to a quiet Sunday morning. Cathy was in bed, her back to him, asleep. She had come in after her night shift while he was still sleeping. Years of experience had taught her how to slip into bed unnoticed. He gently pushed off the duvet and climbed out of bed, trying his best not to disturb his wife.

A few minutes later, wearing only his boxers, he carried a piping hot black coffee into the study. He sat down and thought about calling Ballindalloch Castle – or should he first send an email?

It's 6:30 in the morning here, he thought. *12:30 in the afternoon there.* He picked up a print of the castle's home page with a picture of the present laird, an Angus Macpherson, looking back at him. David dialed the number listed under "Contact us". After just a few rings, he heard a voice answer with a very recognizable Scottish lilt.

"Ballindalloch Castle, who's calling please?"

In his most polite business tone to hide his little frisson of excitement, David asked, "May I speak to Mr Angus Macpherson please?"

"Hold on till I check if he is free. What's your name?" he was asked, without ceremony.

"David Stewart, phoning from the United States, looking for help on some family matters," was the best he could come up with.

"And how would you spell that?" asked the Scotsman.

"S-T-E-W-A-R-T," David said, remembering that Stuart was another common surname. He heard the old-fashioned sound of a phone being placed next to a receiver, and waited. When Angus Macpherson's rather loud but polite voice came on the line, David explained, "I'm calling for two reasons. First of all, I'm about to write a travel guide on Speyside and their whisky. I'm considering visiting your castle as I may want to include it as a tourist attraction." He paused to listen how Angus Macpherson would respond.

"Well then, you've certainly come to the right address, Mr Stewart," Angus boomed. "Ballindalloch opened her doors to the public a while ago and we get many American visitors. Also, we are indeed right in the middle of the Speyside whisky trail. In fact Cragganmore Distillery is but a spitting distance from here."

"*That* is very interesting, Mr Macpherson, I don't mind a good glass myself."

"The other reason I'm calling is actually of a more personal nature. I've been researching my family history and discovered I have an ancestor who was born at Ballindalloch – a Stewart."

"Have you now," the Scotsman at the other side of the ocean answered. "A Stewart you say. Would you know his first name and roughly when he was born?"

"Alexander Stewart, born in 1875."

"Really," the voice on the other end said. "Really now."

"Yes sir, I believe so, that is, if I have the correct year."

"It's amazing. I recall we had a Wayne Stewart visiting us from the States a while ago, also a descendent of this Alexander Stewart. Your ancestor is a popular fellow."

"Yes I know Wayne," David said. "In fact, he was the one who gave me the Ballindalloch details. Otherwise, I'd never have been able to figure out my Stewart's birth place."

"Let me see what I can dig up for you, Mr Stewart, so to speak. I must still have the information I gave to the other Mr Stewart somewhere."

"Thanks, that would be great, Mr Macpherson. You know, it's a bit funny my wife's maiden name is Macpherson, Catherine Macpherson. Quite a coincidence, huh?"

"I have to admit, Mr Stewart, there are quite a lot of us walking the face of this earth. But you know, if your wife is a Macpherson, she's considered a cousin, a clan member so to say. No matter where you live or where you come from, when you're a Macpherson, you're among cousins. There are several Macpherson clan gatherings worldwide, also in the USA."

"Yes, indeed, we have many Scottish games in North Carolina," responded David.

"We will be having our annual Macpherson clan gathering in Newtonmore," Angus continued, "some thirty miles from here, on the sixth of August. Tell you what, why don't you and your wife come visit us around that time? I can help you with information on Ballindalloch for your book and your Stewart's research, and your wife can meet lots of her Macpherson cousins. We will have many guests arriving for the event, so let me know in time if you will. Try to arrive here a couple of days before the gathering. If you email a picture of your wife, I'll put a small message in the program about her. We always do that with our overseas cousins who visit us."

"I'll suggest it to my wife, Mr Macpherson, although I'm not sure if she'll be able to free up time to join me. Also I have other meetings to plan. I know I need to be in London sometime in August."

"Well," Angus said, "if it clashes with your other appointments, your wife is more than welcome to attend on her own. You could meet up with her later. We'd take really good care of her, so you would have nothing to worry about."

David laughed, and then said, "my wife is quite an independent lady, sir, but I will ask her and let you know."

Angus, now sounding very keen to get Ballindalloch in this American guide, said, "If you decide to come over, fly into Dyce Airport at Aberdeen and I will make sure our driver picks you up. You and your wife will be our guests and once again, I would be delighted to help you with your guide."

The phone call left David contemplating how he could pull all this off, knowing Cathy would be her usual skeptical self.

A few days later, David received an email from Angus saying he had more information on the Stewarts.

It was too late to call Scotland, but the following morning, after Cathy left for work, David phoned the castle on the number listed in Angus's email.

Angus answered almost immediately.

"You have information for me?" David asked, excitedly.

"Yes, your Alexander Stewart was indeed the son of the gamekeeper of Ballindalloch. He lived here until 1895. He then moved to the USA and I don't know what happened to him after that. We do have old records that you're welcome to explore and other old documents that are in storage. We could also introduce you to the local church, and some of the school records might be interesting for you. Inveravon Church[1] and School[2] are but a fifteen-minute walk from the castle, using the Lady's Walk[3]. "By the way, I've also sent you and your wife a formal invitation to Ballindalloch Castle for the clan event.

You'll be our guests. And should your wife arrive earlier, the castle will be at her disposal as if it was her own."

When David finally finished the call, it was with an amazing sense of achievement.

His next big decision was; when and how to tell Cathy about the impending invitation?

CHAPTER 3

Tuesday 12 July 2011, 10.00 pm, Raleigh, North Carolina, USA

Cathy arrived at the downtown apartment just off Blue Ridge Road, close to the Museum of Art. The door of the first floor abode was open and barrier-taped. She ducked under the "do not cross" strip and went inside to the brightly lit room. She recognized the two forensics guys who were busy dusting for prints and snapping photographs. The body on the floor, lying on its side, looked petite. She couldn't see the face, which was angled towards the wall.

"Hi Tracey, Tom, what have we got here?" She walked towards them over the shiny wooden floor, careful to avoid smatterings of blood.

Tom, the older of the two men, took the lead, "Hi, Cat. We have a lady in her late seventies, attacked severely, I'd guess with some kind of blunt instrument. You can see at least three abrasions on the left side of her skull and face."

Tracey, a giant of a man with a gentle face and a soft deep voice that didn't seem to match his dominant appearance, pointed out to Cathy where blood had splattered around the front door of the small lounge.

"The perp probably hit her there the first time."

Cathy noticed an open black leather handbag lying in the corner, some of its contents scattered on the floor.

"Hi Cat," said Barbara, who had just walked in the room carrying a Starbucks coffee. The patrol officer was a short woman with bright red-dyed hair. Her eyebrow and nose showed marks from former piercings she'd had to surrender when she joined the force.

"Were you the first on the scene, Babs?"

"Yeah, we received a 911 about nine. I was here within fifteen minutes, but too late. I had a quick look around the joint for any possible weapon, but didn't find anything."

"Who made the 911, a neighbor?" asked Cathy as she glanced again at the body.

"Mrs Arnold herself," Barbara answered, pointing at the dead body. "The apartment next door is empty, but I spoke to a young couple on the second floor, and they confirmed her name. She lived on her own. They didn't hear anything out of the ordinary."

"Okay, Babs, go check with the other neighbors and let me know if you come up with anything."

Cathy squatted beside Mrs Arnold, who was lying on her right side. She was a small woman, fully dressed in a blue skirt that passed well beneath her knees. Her white blouse was dotted with blood stains. In a quick but strong flashback, Cathy was pulled into her own memory of a blood-stained blouse after Cameron had shot her.

"You okay, Cat?" Barbara's voice came through.

Cathy realized she had been staring at the blouse and tore her gaze away from the bloodstains, focusing on the rest of the victim. In her right hand, Mrs Arnold was clutching a telephone. Cathy looked at her grey hair mingled with blood and closed her eyes. An image of the old lady's face in shock when she was attacked appeared in her mind's eye. The horror of it was very vivid, almost as if she were still alive. It was paralyzing; Cathy struggled to open her eyes to get out of her trance. Finally she managed and started to blink rapidly.

"It was a hammer," she mumbled.

"What was that, Cat?" asked Tracey.

She stood up. "It was a fucking hammer, a claw hammer. I think it was a heart attack that killed her, not the blows. The perp was a young male, wearing a hood. You know the kind, a sport top with a hood. And he's left-handed."

Tracey couldn't help but smile at Cathy's matter-of-fact comment on something that was yet to be established.

"Well you could be right about the hammer," he said.

"Can I have your report tomorrow morning, Trace?"

"You betcha. It will be late morning, though."

Fuck, this is the last thing I needed. All this on top of the Hooper case, she thought.

Next morning, Cathy was scurrying around in the kitchen, trying to make herself coffee, but the meager four hours of sleep she had since her nightshift ended still played tricks on her. Frustrated, she slammed the door of the kitchen cupboard that held the instant espresso, making David wince behind his morning newspaper. He knew better by now than to interfere with his wife's mood swings. Had he known she'd wake up like this, he wouldn't have placed the invitation on the breakfast bar for her to spot. *Too late, cannot take it away now.* Cathy's hawk-like senses would notice immediately. In fact the silence coming from the kitchen told him she had probably just found it.

"I think this is for you, David," she said, looking at the contents she had removed from the envelope addressed to David Stewart and Catherine Macpherson, "unless you can explain why I would receive an invitation to some clan gathering."

"What invitation?" he asked, feigning ignorance.

"This!" she answered, waving the paper impatiently at him, making his newspaper move in the slight breeze. "I think it's an invite to a party in Europe. It's probably from one of your genealogy pals."

The formal-looking invitation from the Clan Chief Angus Macpherson looked highly professional. It had an embossed letterhead and was trimmed in tartan.

"That's the Macpherson tartan alright," David said, looking at the invite.

"Are you sure? It's different from the tartan my Pop use to show me."

"Some have several tartans, like a formal dress or say for hunting."

"Do you think they'd let me wear my jeans and sneakers if I wore socks in their formal dress tartan?" Cathy sniggered.

David ignored her smart-ass remark.

Maybe I shouldn't tease him about it so much, Cathy thought, but she really couldn't see the point of all this ancestry stuff.

The invite depicted a castle, reminding Cathy of a picture in one of her childhood books, *Fairy Tales by Grimm*, with lots of small towers emerging from a giant structure and numerous buildings knitted closely together.

"Ballindalloch Castle[4]", it read underneath, "The home of the Macphersons since 1546."

How would you pronounce that name in Scottish? Cathy wondered, *Ballindal*lotsch *or Ballindal*lock?

She shifted her attention to the separate handwritten letter that was in the envelope. It explained the background of the annual gathering. A third item, a flier, outlined the event's purpose which was to gather the Macpherson family members from all over the world in order to get better acquainted and celebrate the existence and history of their clan.

"What makes these people think we would want to attend their clan gathering, David? Hmm, I wonder …"

"Look, Cathy," David retorted impatiently, "Will you for once bury your cynicism and listen? Yes I did have contact with Ballindalloch, and yes maybe it would be a good idea for us to go there."

Cathy looked at him angrily and said, "Well then, you'd better give me one frikkin' good reason."

"Okay, I will!" David retaliated. "When I was researching Alexander Stewart, who is the very reason I am here today, if I may remind you, I discovered he was born at Ballindalloch. Coincidentally and here's why you should be interested, this castle also turned out to be a Macpherson home."

"So?" Cathy said, "There must be zillions of Macphersons worldwide, and besides, the family I care about are Americans! Jeez, Dave! How far do you want to go back, Adam and Eve?"

"Damn it, Cat. All I'm asking is that you give it some thought. When I made contact with Angus Macpherson, the present owner of Ballindalloch, and told him I was married to a Catherine Macpherson, his reaction was that this must be fate at play. He spontaneously invited us over. I didn't tell you about it because I'd anticipated this reaction from you! But I'm actually pretty excited about going to a Scottish castle where my ancestor was born."

"Ah, so Mr Stewart has decided already. Well, let me tell you, I'm not going all the way to Europe for a party, where I'll come across skirt-wearing men and be expected to take them seriously!"

"You're doing it again," David exclaimed in frustration. "Why is it so difficult for you to have some respect for my interests?"

A little embarrassed, Cathy walked away from the breakfast table, looking for the distraction of something to do in the kitchen. *That's a good question,* she thought, not for the first time.

"I don't know, David," she said after a while. "I just think all this family tree stuff is so boring. For some reason, those European roots just don't do it for me. Does that make sense? I have no other explanation for it."

Still irritated with her absolute refusal to at least consider going to the clan gathering, he didn't answer. Instead, he fished another item out of the envelope and held it up with both hands for Cathy to see. "Take a look at this."

It was a leaflet providing details about something called the "Highland Games," which were to be held in honor of the Macpherson clan gathering in the town of Newtonmore[5]. Immediately, her internal barometer switched to "ridiculous" again.

"Look at the picture of this massive, skirt-clad guy holding a tree trunk in front of his body," she pointed. "The guys at the Police Department will get a kick out of this one!"

"Okay," David said, angrily stuffing the invitation and leaflet back into the envelope and propelling it with precision aim to the side table near the kitchen door, where they usually kept their mail. "Your crazy judgmental attitude is throwing away a great chance for a break which, by the way, I think you badly need. You're practically living at the PD and your case load rules your life, not to mention the fact that it almost got you killed last year. Jeez, Cat, what does it take you to stop acting like a diesel engine and barging through life as if nothing else matters but work, work, work. Let me tell you, if I'm so irritating and work is the sole important thing in your life, then maybe we should call it quits. Because this *is* important to *me*! I want to know where I come from, why my family moved to the US, and what drove them away from Scotland."

David now had Cathy's full attention. She had been unpleasantly surprised by David's remark of "calling it quits". He'd never said anything like that before. What could be so important about his genealogy that he would go to such extremes? Wounded by his use of harsh words, and still feeling she had a right to her own opinion, Cathy gestured at the envelope and said, "How do you know it's not some Scotch money-making scam?"

"Scotch is a drink. I think you mean Scottish," David corrected despondently. "Hey, forget it." He threw his hands up in the air. "I knew you were going to react like this. Never mind, let's drop the whole idea. Anyway, you need to go or you'll be late for work."

"Exactly," she said sharply.

She picked up her bag and strapped her 9 mm semi-automatic to her body. He watched her doing so and felt a pang of regret and old pain. His Cathy was a very attractive woman, 5 feet 7 inches tall, with a slender athletic body. When she smiled, her dark complexion made her polar-white teeth glisten. He loathed the thought of her being scarred and felt a lump in his throat as he watched her check the gun and push it back into the holster.

"Don't know what time I'll be home, depends," she said and stepped out into the hall.

A split second later, the door opened. Cathy's arm appeared around the corner, picked up the invitation from the table, and disappeared again.

The possibility of going to Scotland lingered with Cathy all day, disturbing her usual decisive balance. She wondered if perhaps a trip overseas would be just the thing to get her and David back on track.

Maybe I'll contact this Angus Macpherson guy myself, she thought. "Okay, promise this stays strictly between us, Steve," she started, when she'd lured her partner out for a quick lunch. "I've received an invitation to a Macpherson clan gathering in the Highlands of Scotland, and I'm considering going. What do you think?" She handed the envelope to Steve.

He read the invite. When he glanced at the leaflet on the games, he said smiling, "Jeez Cathy, they could be a bunch of weirdoes. I saw this horror movie years ago about the Highlands in Scotland. They're all into open sex and dancing naked at night in the back yard."

"For Christ's sake, if that's your range of intellectual discussion today, then just forget it," she retorted, gathering the contents of the envelope, impatiently stuffing it back, much like David had done earlier in their kitchen.

She had to wonder if this was how she responded to David when he started talking about his Scottish roots.

A full day of filing paperwork and a lengthy meeting with her chief distracted her from further ponderings.

It wasn't until she got into her car around seven that evening that she thought of driving over to her parents' house, to present her dilemma there.

Like David and Cathy, her parents lived in the town of Wake Forest, a growing community with 28,000 residents, fifteen miles north of Raleigh. Over time, the town had become exclusive, accentuated by its beautiful historic homes and tree-lined streets.

When Cathy pulled into the driveway in her black unmarked Crown Vic, her father, James Macpherson, was sitting on the open porch of their tidy little bungalow, a combined brick-and-timber house built around the early seventies. James was wearing denim shorts and a check short-sleeved shirt. He was a lean man in his early sixties, still tall, with a handsome face and a reassuring appearance. Even now, simply looking at him gave Cathy a feeling of safety. He was a retired cop who had taught her a lot about police work that you couldn't read in an instruction manual or receive in training. James saw his daughter and waved as she stepped out into the hot humid evening from her air-conditioned car and walked towards the house.

"Hey, Pop," she said kissing him on the cheek. "I take it Mom's out?" She gave a knowing smirk. James was enjoying a cigarette, something he would never do when his wife was around. He smiled and explained that her mother had gone with friends to visit Eileen Turner, who had been in some kind of accident and was now proudly showing off her broken leg, providing her with the attention she always craved. They sat down on the porch steps.

"Let me show you something." she said. She dug the Macpherson letter out of her bag and handed it to her father.

James got his bifocals out of his shirt pocket and started to study the contents of the envelope, one by one.

"Hmm, a Macpherson clan gathering, that's interesting... Wonder why I didn't get one?"

"Because you're not married to David Stewart," she mumbled.

Her father looked at her profile for a moment while she sat on the deck step, her knees tucked under her chin, staring into the distance.

"Is he now researching the Macphersons?" James asked.

"No," replied an exasperated Cathy. "He discovered an ancestor from Scotland, Alexander Stewart, and believe it or not, Pop, he was born on the grounds of a Macpherson castle, the one on the invite. It drives me nuts and I don't know why." She sighed.

"Well…" James began cautiously, searching for the right words. He knew all too well his temperamental daughter was easy to ignite on this subject. "Maybe you should consider accepting the invitation and go meet some more Macphersons. To be honest, your mom and I have been worried about you ever since the shooting. A break from the force could do you good, you know."

She threw her father a warning look not to go there.

On his guard, he changed his strategy and, looking over the edge of his glasses, said, "Unless you think the invite is from a bunch of kooks. They might be into stuff like exhibitionism in the front yard, and howling during a full moon. I remember an old movie, the …"

"What's the problem with the men in my life today," Cathy exclaimed, jumping up from the porch steps. "Steve said almost exactly the same thing."

"Always knew I liked that guy," said James, giving his daughter a playful wink.

She rolled her eyes in exasperation. "Pop, I checked it out today on the internet, and Ballindalloch Castle is for real. It's been the home of a Macpherson family for over four hundred years."

James smiled affectionately at his daughter. "Your grandad, used to talk about his father, Eddie, who supposedly had some old pictures of a little town in Scotland. Never found any pictures, but then again, my pop was a great storyteller."

She could tell her father was intrigued with the invitation.

"Cathy," he said. "Mom and I think the shooting has taken more out of you than you realize. Maybe you should call this castle to make sure everything is above board, and if everything fits, go for it. That's my gut feeling. How great would it be if you'd uncover some family skeletons, Cat?" he added jokingly. "Come on; give me something to boast about to my buddies at the golf club!"

Cathy gave her dad a wry smile, kissed him on the cheek, and was already walking back towards her car when her father called after her, "Can't wait to tell your mom about this! Her family line probably goes back to some bears in the woods," James chuckled, playfully clawing at the air.

Cathy had to wonder if this Macpherson invitation was fate showing its hand like some kind of cosmic card game. Besides, she was trying to be honest with herself. Hadn't she already thought about going away for a week to a spa resort, once she and Steve had lightened up their case load? Also, her marriage had been in a serious dip. Both David and she were working long, odd hours, resulting in them passing like ships in the night.

Their sex life was nothing to crow about either. She couldn't even remember the last time they had actually made love. Perhaps if they went to Europe for a couple of weeks, it would help their relationship.

Her boss would agree, she knew that for sure. He had constantly been digging at her to take some time out.

Heading home, she felt her spirits lift a bit. During the drive she let her mind wander. Where and when had David and she taken such different turns? Had they missed the boat by not having children? Would having kids have helped their relationship remain more solid? They'd discovered some years earlier that she was unable to conceive. Since then, they had discussed adoption on numerous occasions. Neither of them were ever really committed and continued to simply focus on their work; Cathy in her demanding role as a homicide detective and David as a travel writer. Due to her unsociable working hours and David's constant travelling, they spent little quality time together.

She thought about the need to confront their situation. She was thirty-five years old now, seven years younger than David. It was time to make some big decisions. She certainly felt a deep connection with David and also believed that they still loved each other. However, their relationship desperately needed an upgrade and maybe it was time to do more than just *consider* adopting. A break in Scotland would give them time to discuss their future.

On the evenings when they were both at home, Cathy and David mostly ended their day in bed with a file to read. It used to be snuggling up and talking to each other about their day. Now the norm was to hole themselves up in bed and sift through their work.

"Have you given Scotland another thought?" David asked, sitting up in bed with his laptop resting on their "sweet dreams" duvet cover. "Reason I ask is, I've been offered to write a travel guide on Scotland. You know Ron McIntyre, from the NA Tourist Association? He mailed me. They're going to promote Scotland with some funding from the Scottish Tourist Board. Ron wants to give me the assignment."

Trying to hide his excitement, he continued. "I've suggested including the famous whisky trail in Speyside, where sixty percent of scotch is produced. That would bring me very close to Ballindalloch, you know."

Cathy remained quiet and kept reading her papers, feigning disinterest, not ready to make it too easy for David.

"I could tie this in with the invite to that clan gathering and combine it with some research on the Stewart family," David continued, pretending he didn't notice her deliberate silence.

"Well, I'm sure the whisky guide will suit you just fine," Cathy murmured, "provided you won't be too intoxicated to write anything."

"Very funny," David said, too put down by her attitude to even comment on it. "What about the clan gathering? Will you come with me or not?" he asked in a soft voice, not giving her the satisfaction of putting up a fight.

With a sigh, Cathy pulled her attention away from the documents she had been studying. "Aw, come on, David," she said. "What am I supposed to do at some gathering all the way in Scotland where everyone happens to carry the same family name?"

Changing into a more serious tone, he said, "Look at you and your never-ending work! Don't you ever think about taking it easy for a while?"

"Says Mr Travel Writer who is preparing his own trips in bed as he speaks," she replied.

"Yeah, but I was never shot for anything I've written." He leaned over, "I know you don't like to talk about it, but what happened last year has injured more than your body." Gently he slid his hand under the hairline of her neck, where he knew she liked to be touched.

"Not now, David," Cathy said lightly. In a split second she remembered her thoughts earlier that day about their marriage and regretted her obstinacy.

"Seriously, Cat," David pleaded with a wounded look on his face. "Look at how you reacted just now. We live and work in the same house but in separate worlds. I think it's time we both put in a little effort here. This trip is important to me and I think it will give a very interesting spin to use my own Scottish roots as a lead to write the travel guide. Just imagine how many descendants of immigrants could relate to that story! And for us, Cat, the fact that *my* ancestors were born in a castle that carries *your* family name. It's almost as if we're *meant* to do this together."

"I know," she mumbled, still feeling sensations where he had touched her. She couldn't help thinking how the invitation had occupied her mind as well, in spite of her defiance. She let out another deep sigh. Maybe David was right, and even though she told everyone who wanted to hear, and those who didn't, that she was over the Cameron shooting, she knew deep down that wasn't true. Maybe she was indeed running away from something.

"Okay," she said decisively, putting her files on the bedside table and sliding under the duvet. "I'll do it. I will go to Scotland with you, provided I can arrange backup for Steve."

"Thank you Cat," David said. He felt as if an enormous weight had just been lifted from his shoulders. "Can't tell you how much I appreciate this. Now you don't need to worry about a thing; I'll make all our travel arrangements."

Cathy was already regretting her commitment. From under the duvet she said, muffled, "Maybe we'll turn out to be related."

CHAPTER 4

Thursday 13 June 1895, Inveravon Church and Burial Grounds, Ballindalloch, Scotland

"We are gathered here today to bid our final farewell to Elizabeth Macpherson." The rich baritone voice of Reverend MacDonald boomed against the intensifying wind.

"We will remember her as the giving, compassionate and much respected Lady of Ballindalloch."

"We will remember how she supported the Laird and Chief of the Macpherson clan."

"We will remember how she brought seven Macpherson children into this world and was blessed to raise six of them, God rest the soul of Gordon Junior, with whom his mother is now joined again."

"It will be remembered how she helped the less fortunate and always took pity on those in need of help."

"It will be remembered how the Lady Macpherson raised Alexander Stewart as one of her own."

A large crowd stood assembled on the little yard of Inveravon Church, so many that there was not enough room for all, causing people to stand outside the wall lining the church grounds.

Gordon Macpherson stood at the foot of his wife's coffin, which had been placed in front of the family mausoleum opposite the little church. His eyes were searching the crowd. For reasons he could not entirely understand himself, for they had quarreled almost all their lives, Gordon wished his younger brother William could be here now. But as it was, the letter announcing Elizabeth's passing would not reach Chicago for at least another month. Gordon had thought of sending a telegram, but decided against it, granting his brother, who had been very fond of his sister-in-law, some more time in oblivious ignorance of what had befallen Elizabeth.

Dark storm clouds gathered above the mourners. Gordon's jaw was set and his eyes were now cast resolutely towards the ground. His long black overcoat showed the curves of his short broad body with the harsh Highland wind pushing him in the back, almost as if it was urging him to take one more step forward.

Even though he was only in his late fifties, Gordon's face looked haggard with deep folds around his nose and mouth, and crow's feet darting from his eyes.

He wished that Reverend MacDonald would bring his eulogy to a close, even though he knew the final farewell that was soon to follow by placing the coffin in the family tomb with his ancestors, would be almost too much for him to bear. Gordon willed the tears to stay in his eyes. He needed to set an example of strength for all there to see.

How he was going to survive without Elizabeth, was still far beyond him. His wife who, always modest without outshining his position as Laird of Ballindalloch, had meant so much, not only to the people of Speyside, but especially to the Macpherson clan.

Gordon looked up to see his children standing in a semi-circle around the heavy, brass-handled coffin, each holding a single rose from the castle garden, Elizabeth's garden, to be placed on her coffin as their final farewell. Alexander Stewart stood side by side with Katherine, who now even went so far as to lean her head against Alexander's shoulder, while he put his arm around her protectively.

In spite of his grief, Gordon felt the hot flash of anger rise in his throat. How dare the gamekeeper's son take the liberty of comforting his youngest child like that in front him and everyone else?

One of the first things he needed to do, Gordon knew, was to settle certain family matters as soon as the shock of Elizabeth's sudden death had subsided.

CHAPTER 5

Patience was not a virtue Cathy had in abundance.

It showed when the stewardess gently shook the shoulder of the lean, dark-haired woman who had fallen asleep with the in-flight magazine teetering on her lap. Reluctantly, Cathy Stewart tore herself away from her dream. "Fuck it."

The flight attendant raised a disapproving eyebrow, but smiled wearily, the kind of smile given to a toddler to get it to co-operate.

"Will you please buckle up?" she said. "We're about to land. It's for your own safety."

Cathy did as she was told and made no further comment, reminding herself that she needed to be more prudent with her outbursts. Ever since the Cameron incident, Cathy's dreams had become very vivid, leaving her sometimes with moods in which she found it hard to contain her actions. She stretched her body as much as possible within the confines of the economy seat. She could still feel the resistance of the scar tissue where Cameron's pellets had splattered her chest and left lifelong marks on the body she was once so proud of. She wasn't sure if she would ever totally overcome the effects of the experience. Even the memory of sitting up in the hospital bed three days after the shooting, reading about her own death in a police report still unnerved her. Normally, Cathy would be the homicide detective in charge of writing such a report. That time however, in painfully explicit detail, she'd been the one reading the description of the events that led her to being shot.

Her partner Steve had gunned down Cameron just a few seconds later, causing instant death. Steve's swift reaction of immediately hoisting Cathy's limp body from the soggy ground into their police car and driving like a bat out of hell to Duke Raleigh hospital, some twelve miles away, had drastically altered the outcome of the shooting.

The thud of the landing gear unfolding from the belly of the airplane jolted Cathy back to the present. She sank back in her seat and attempted to focus her thoughts on something else, but it was no use. Time after time, something would remind her of the events that took place that damp, early fall day and the details would start playing in her head all over again. She still remembered how freeing it had felt to simply slide into the abyss of nothingness, away from the pain. There had been no fear, no resistance at all from her side to slip into the folds of death.

Ironically, it had been the very fact of her "dying" that had saved her from actual death, even though it wasn't mentioned as such in the police report. She had reconstructed the events herself later on, after putting various detailed medical questions to her doctors, in the no-nonsense questions of a seasoned detective typical of Cathy. She found out that her heart, no longer pumping blood through the arteries, had given her body a chance to hold on to what little reserves it had left, until the doctors could put her on life support and bring her vitals back up. In the race against time it had all been a near miss, with six shotgun pellets to remove, a collapsed left lung to be restored, and entrance wounds to be closed as aesthetically as possible. The fact that she remembered floating above the bustling doctors and "seeing" her own body lying on the emergency room table, she ascribed to near-death experience.

She'd once read some book about that. It seemed pretty far-fetched then, but now she looked on such things in a new light, just like her experience with dreams and even feelings of foresight. All these tendencies had been there to begin with, but although she had read about these phenomena to satisfy her curiosity, she had always managed to steer away from what she called *psychic fantasy.* It suited her practical mind much better. The whole Cameron experience however, had shaken her internal controls... partly because of what had brought her back.

It hadn't just been the doctors. She knew that with uneasy certainty. Something had drawn her, like a recoiling spring, back into her body. She clearly remembered *knowing* she still had some important task to complete, but what, she didn't know. This was gravely unsettling, as she always preferred to know what was going to be next.

Okay, enough now, Cathy thought, it was time to buckle up. She peered through the small oval window of the plane. Aberdeen airport started to come into view. She picked up her handbag from under the seat in front of her, making sure before landing that her passport and destination information were all in order and easy to reach.

The plane landed suddenly and a split second later the pilot hit the reverse thrust of the jets, pushing all the passengers slightly forward in their seats. Cathy looked out the rain-swept window at her first view of Scotland. It was a gloomy, wet summer day; she couldn't see much. It was almost as if Scotland didn't want to give itself away just yet. Or, maybe it was Cathy not really wanting to go on with what she'd started.

She was one of the first passengers to step out from the plane into the Scottish breeze, her long dark hair blowing across her face. She shivered as she pulled the collar of her trench coat around her neck against the stiff Highland wind and walked towards the small airport terminal.

Welcome to Scotland, Catherine Macpherson, she thought. Casually looking around her, she continued walking with the crowd. The gentle rolling hills in the distance captured her gaze. She stopped abruptly, forcing other passengers to walk around her.

So, this is where I'm supposed to have come from? Yeah right! She shook her head. She felt exhausted and wondered what on earth had made her decide to give in to her husband's plea for them to visit the country of their supposed ancestors.

CHAPTER 6

Monday 28 October 1895, Ballindalloch, Banffshire, Scotland

Fascinated, Katherine Macpherson watched the rabbit disappear behind the arched root of a majestic oak tree that stuck out from the earth like a giant's toe out of an old shoe. She had hunted the rabbit down past the grazing fields into the forest, guiding her horse over fallen tree trunks and small ditches, on occasion flattening her flexible body over the horse's mane to avoid being struck by a branch sticking out over their path.

Any outsider would have wondered why this smartly dressed eighteen-year-old lady of obvious means, riding her vibrant purebred horse, would want to spend her time chasing a mere rabbit on a sun-filled late autumn afternoon, and risk being injured. To Katherine her behavior was crystal clear.

She wanted out. Out of the restrictions of her upper-class life, out of the bonds birth had given her by making her the only daughter of the ruling Macpherson Laird of Ballindalloch. The row with her father that had made her leave the house only an hour before had made it conclusive.

If only my mother was still here. She could and would not do what the Ballindalloch Laird expected of her. These were changing times, where women started to choose their own path, refusing to be puppets on the family string any longer.

Like the Alice she had once read about, Katherine had followed the rabbit hoping it would take her away from the confining world in which she had been brought up.

Had her mother known when she gifted Katherine the book for Christmas a number of years ago, *Alice's Adventures in Wonderland,* by a Mr Lewis Carroll, it would appeal to her daughter's spirit with such conviction, she would probably have refrained from giving it.

To Elizabeth it had been an attempt to steer her strong-willed and quick-witted daughter away from the dangerous new times which were being brought to the doorstep of Ballindalloch Castle. Elizabeth had hoped that by granting her daughter permission to read the book, Katherine would come to understand that real life was to be preferred over fantasies which could only bring a young girl trouble. Little did she know that instead of calming the girl's temperament, it had confirmed Katherine's inner knowing that there was more to life than Ballindalloch.

But then, of course, Elizabeth Macpherson had never read *Alice's Adventures.* She had really not read that many books at all. Not because she did not want to, for she *could* understand her daughter's passion for books. Elizabeth had enjoyed reading the novels of Jane Austen, even though she had been apprehensive about the possibility of her husband finding out about the content. He would surely not approve of a woman writing about such intimate social matters, even if the rest of society was raving about the novels. Gordon Macpherson strongly felt that women should not pursue intellectual or social activities outside the boundaries of family life. Writing novels, in his opinion was an occupation reserved for men, who at least had a balanced point of view of what mattered and what not.

It must surely have been a curse to him that his only

daughter out of seven children, had always displayed, even as a young child, such wit, intelligence, and desire to explore.

"Katherine, you always ask too many questions," Gordon had reprimanded his daughter once, when she was only five years old. "Little girls are not supposed to ask questions, they are only expected to do as they are told."

Gordon's inability to see and acknowledge his daughter's exceptionally bright mind, as well as his insistence on sticking with his own set of beliefs and values had already clouded their father-daughter relationship at an early stage. It had in fact caused the young Katherine to pose even more questions, though not to her father.

"Why do women always have to do as they are told?" she asked her mother one morning, while being dressed by one of the servants. "Why can men do everything they like and why are servants not allowed to do things they like?"

The maid braiding her hair had given a little tug at a strand, as if to warn Miss Katherine, things like that were not to be spoken of. Her mother had reacted with a raised voice. "Katherine!" she had cried out, as if catching her daughter's hand in a biscuit barrel. "Those are no thoughts for a little lady. Children should be seen, not heard."

Fortunately for Katherine her mother, unlike her father, never really got angry when Katherine posed these unlikely questions. Katherine could even feel her mother's hesitation at some of the answers, as if Elizabeth Macpherson wasn't quite sure if the response she was giving was the correct one. This unspoken bond between her and her mother always made Katherine feel safe and appreciated.

The relationship with her father, however, had always been an entirely different matter. This morning acceptable boundaries had been overstepped by both sides.

"If you want me to love and respect you, you should give me reason to do so," Katherine had shouted at her father. In return Gordon Macpherson had spit out all his frustrations on what he called "unruly behavior, not suitable for a young lady". He had accused Katherine of being totally disrespectful of the rules and regulations he had set and had denounced her preposterous habit of spending her days either in his library or riding the terrains surrounding the castle, regardless of the weather conditions, time of day, or the company she kept, as well as her obvious liaison with the gamekeeper's son, Alexander.

The Laird would have preferred to see his beautiful daughter occupy herself socially, entertaining the daughters of respectable families in the county or their sons even and ultimately marry a son of a business associate.

Watching his daughter turn into an intellectual had been a sour experience for the old-fashioned Laird.

In her early teenage years, Gordon had already caught her reading foreign novels, studying scientists like the crazy fellow Darwin with his ridiculous and blasphemous theories on the Origins of Species. He'd forbidden Katherine to ever set foot in the library again, but that had made her lock herself in her room, refusing to eat.

Finally his wife had persuaded her husband to allow their child her pursuits. She had known her daughter well enough to know she would persist and sooner starve to death than comply with her father's wishes.

The library was Katherine's most cherished space in her life. Her father forbidding her to go in there was like being denied air to breathe. She loved the silent presence of knowledge. She could almost feel it calling out to her when she sat behind the big brown reading table at the centre of the library. Simply watching the grand collection of books was enough to make her feel content.

As there was no one in the castle to recommend any specific books to her, except maybe for Alexander, who shared Katherine's passion for reading and writing, Katherine had designed her own way of choosing books.

At random she would choose a starting point at one of the many bookcases that lined three walls of the library.

Using the library steps if needed, she would open one of the glass doors, close her eyes, and gently trace the rows of books with her fingertips, until she felt a book call out to her. She'd then open her eyes, take the book out of its place on the bookshelf in a careful and respectful manner, place it on the table, and leaf through it to see what message it had to relay to her.

Either most books in the library were simply really good or her own personal hide-and-seek game indeed led her to the most interesting books. Whichever was true, she most often found herself enthralled.

Inevitably, it would lead her outside the small world of Ballindalloch Castle.

This time no rabbit or Alice was there to save her. Her father had been clear this morning; "You will forget all about the Stewart boy and any notion about university. You will marry one of the Grant sons or nobody at all. The choice is yours."

Katherine wondered sitting on the oak tree root;
What sort of choice was that?

If only she could be like Alice and drink a potion to make her bigger or smaller so she could go through portals that would take her away to other worlds.

She knew people in Speyside would be talking about her, as they had done so often before. She also knew she had, as her father had put it, "sorely disgraced" the Macpherson name for long enough.

Ever since her mother's death in June, there was no one left to be Katherine's advocate and help her escape from what now seemed like an inevitable fate. If she did her duty by marrying a Grant, Katherine knew she would never be allowed to study at the University of Edinburgh. The dream of going to university was futile. Although a law had been passed two years earlier that women could have higher education, they were not allowed to practice their knowledge and skills in any official profession. It outraged Katherine every time she thought about it. How deceitful it was to allow women to study law, for example, but not permit them to be lawyers.

The social circles in which the Macphersons moved, were already talking about her. As long as Katherine could remember she had attracted gossip. As a child, idle talk came about because she was as tall as her brothers and competed with them in education assignments and sports, especially rowing and canoeing on the river and when she "came out" at the age of sixteen it was rumored that she much preferred to spend time in the library over attending social gatherings.

The rumor-mongering continued, as she had been seen on more than one occasion dressed in her brother's riding attire when she was out horseback riding. She felt uncomfortable in the traditional, confining female riding habit and side saddle, feeling she was at a disadvantage when racing her brothers or Alexander.

Her boldness gave her great confidence that made people wary of her.

"It's just their insecurity, Katherine," her mother had told her once when Katherine questioned why people talked about her so negatively.

Jolted back to her present reality, Katherine's mind and reason told her that there was no tossing off the harness of cultural expectation. Her clenched fists betrayed her anger. She despised her father when he tried to establish his control by sheer rule of force.

CHAPTER 7

Thursday 4 August 2011, 2:05 pm, Dyce Airport, Aberdeen, Scotland

Not exactly the spa resort vacation I had in mind, Cathy thought, as she walked towards the baggage claim area to collect her luggage. *But there's no turning back now.* She'd only visited the United Kingdom once before and that had been England – a few days in London as part of a European tour; her parents' gift for Cathy's graduation from college.

When she walked into the arrivals hall, dragging her suitcase behind her, she switched on her cell phone to let her husband know she'd arrived safely. David had left for London two days earlier to attend some business meetings and then make his way to Scotland. He planned to join her on Sunday morning at the castle.

She smiled at the memory of his utter surprise when she'd finally accepted the option to go ahead to Ballindalloch on her own. She was actually glad David had to go to London first. It would give her time to adjust at her own pace and do her own thing. The only downside was the thought of attending the Macpherson gathering and Highland Games on Saturday without him. Maybe she could use his absence as a plausible excuse to get out of it.

She hoped she could find an internet connection and catch up with Steve to see if any progress had been made on the Hooper and Arnold cases they'd been investigating. Cathy was still holding her cell phone and looking around her at the busy people-traffic in the hall, when a hand reached out and rested gently on her shoulder. A deep rough voice with a heavy Scottish accent said, "No time for that now, missus, we need to be on our way, it's a terrible day out there."

Unimpressed by somebody telling her what she could not do and irritated by the possessive gesture of the hand on her shoulder, Cathy turned to face the tall Scotsman who had addressed her.

"Mr Christie, I presume?" she said in a tone that she usually reserved for suspects at the PD.

"Call me Christie," the Scotsman answered flatly and without further ceremony, grabbed her case and started to stride towards the exit.

"How did you recognize me?" she asked, trying to keep pace with the man's long strides.

"You're a Macpherson, aren't you? I've been living around Macphersons all my life. I can recognize them from a mile away."

"That's crazy; I've never been here before!"

"Still," Christie muttered, "You look like a Macpherson, no doubt about that."

Without saying another word, he marched into the open-air parking lot, leaving Cathy bewildered about his manners and with little other choice than to follow him. He seemed to be in a contented mood, whistling while pulling the suitcase. His long black overcoat and thick silver hair were blowing in the wind. After only a few minutes, they reached Christie's car. He loaded her case in the trunk of what was an old and tired Land Rover.

"Get out of the breeze, missus; we don't want you catching a cold, now do we."

As he switched on the ignition and crunched the gearshift to find reverse, he looked at her in the back mirror. "It's going to take us about an hour and a half, so don't you be needing the toilet. Just put your head back, because I know you must be tired."

Cathy was feeling uncomfortable with Mr Christie, the tiredness from the journey not helping. She guessed he must be at least seventy years old, but still in good shape. His rugged complexion and broad shoulders, as well as his being over six feet tall, made him look like an ex-Marine – or whatever they had in Scotland, soldier or Highland warrior.

"Thank you, Mr Christie," she offered with a touch of sarcasm. "I'll do my best to simply enjoy the scenery."

Stretching her long legs in front of her and, in an afterthought, even kicking off her shoes, she was determined to make herself comfortable and not let any harsh Scottish manners influence her mood. She could fend for herself when she needed to.

Time dragged by in the dingy car, windshield wipers flopping side to side to keep a light rain shower at bay. The inside of the car was dusty and untidy, but at least it was warm. It was unbalancing, to be driving on the left-hand side of the road. It emphasized the feeling of alienation that was creeping over her. Trying to shake off that discomfort, she focused on the lush green views of the countryside. One of the few times he actually spoke, Christie volunteered that Speyside produced sixty percent of the malt whisky made in Scotland. Cathy didn't bother to explain she already knew that through David. The A96 was a winding, seemingly never-ending two-lane country road busy with traffic. Many cars were pulling trailers and hampering other drivers. Not exactly highway standards.

Closing her eyes, she thought of the argument she and David had over the invite to the castle. At first, she'd accused him of being deceitful, going behind her back. He'd said the main reason for the visit was his Stewart family research and travel guide. The Macpherson invite was purely something for her to pass the time.

Christie's sneeze snapped her out of her thoughts and she realized they had actually stopped to allow a herd of cattle cross the road. They were like no other she had ever seen, jet-black, hardy, and hornless. She asked what kind of cattle they were and he explained that they were Aberdeen Angus[6].

"You'll see more at the castle grounds, missus. The Ballindalloch cattle herd is the oldest Aberdeen Angus in the world. They descend from native cattle further north, going back to the 12th century."

Nice item to include in David's tourist guide, Cathy thought.

The Highland scenery of hills, ablaze with purple on either side of the road, she had to admit was stunning. Apart from his lecture on the cattle that carried the same name as her host to be, Christie hardly uttered a word during the journey, other than what she suspected were some Gaelic curses at other motorists.

An hour into the journey, Cathy noticed they were now on route A95. Finally, local signs for Ballindalloch started to appear and, soon after that, a sign for the castle itself. As they were nearing their destination, Cathy grew more attentive, gazing out of the window, even feeling a little impatient when another delay stalled their drive. It was road works. Cathy's annoyance softened when she saw a young man in a yellow florescent overcoat controlling the traffic through the single lane, holding up a cardboard sign with "STOP" handwritten on it. Eventually he turned the sign and "GO" appeared. Cathy smiled at the simple, almost comical process.

The area of Ballindalloch was dominated by peaceful woodlands, mainly noble pine trees. *What a beautiful and perfect countryside for horseback-riding,* Cathy thought, immediately wondering why she would think that. She had never sat on a horse in her life.

In many ways, the landscape reminded her of home. *Maybe because of the trees*, she thought. Raleigh was known as the "City of Oaks" after the abundance of oak trees in and around it. She also noticed several small hotels, so she assumed it must be a popular part of the country for tourists. David would have plenty to write about here.

Finally they reached the castle. Christie drove onto a side road and nudged the car up to a security gate. He rolled down his window and punched in a number on a box secured to a wooden hut. A second later, the security arm lifted and allowed the car to continue down a steep gradient road, twisting and turning. Within a few minutes, she could see a grand walled garden to her left. Turning left into the main approach of the castle, they moved slowly over a road of red stone chips and Cathy captured her first view of Ballindalloch Castle.

Her initial thought was "awesome," as the great edifice stood proud, flanked by three circular towers. Even against the graying sky, it seemed like a Disney Land setting. On top of one of the turrets of the castle was the Scottish saltire fluttering in the wind, a light blue flag with a white cross. Beyond the castle, a lawn spread out for what seemed miles, the grass lush and manicured. Further in the distance, the horizon was hidden by thick woodland.

The castle grew bigger as the car slowly approached and then the realization of why she was here hit her. *Oh David, it would have been better after all if you had been here.*

CHAPTER 8

Tuesday 29 October 1895 Ballindalloch, Banffshire, Scotland

It was Katherine Macpherson's dream to expand her horizon beyond Ballindalloch. She could not share this with anyone else in the family, especially her brothers. They were all clever, but did not seem to feel the need to change anything in their lives.

But then they are men, Katherine would say to herself. *They can do as they like.*

"Gamekeeper sons have to watch where they tread as well, you know," Alexander boldly replied to her once, when she complained that she wished to study medicine, but was not allowed as she was "only a woman".

The comment made her study Alexander more closely, secretly admiring his courage to voice his own discontent. In a way, she felt that Alexander Stewart was closer to her and knew more about who she really was than any of her real family. Alex, at least, understood what it was like to have secret thoughts and ambitions. It created a special bond between the two young people.

Katherine was also the only person who knew about Alexander's dream to break the chain of three generations of the Macpherson-Stewart gamekeeper tradition and become a journalist. Not even Alexander's father knew about this. It was this mutual desire to breach with tradition that united them.

As usual, where it concerned matters about Katherine, it was Katherine's mother who had condoned the friendship and her father who strongly disapproved. Up to her death Elizabeth always defended Alexander and Katherine's companionship.

She had raised Alexander Stewart among the six Macpherson children, almost as if he were her own. Secretly, she sometimes thought of Alexander as a replacement for her stillborn baby boy. This way, she could feel complete with seven children.

Her husband had strongly objected. He felt the line of division between the two social layers was too thin to be tampered with.

He often reminded himself not to rely too much on his gamekeeper. Robert Stewart had served the Macphersons ever since the death of his father and former gamekeeper of Ballindalloch before him. Having been raised on the grounds, Robert had spent many a day with his father. He knew the necessary routines and lands better than Gordon himself. Sometimes this made Gordon uncomfortable. He would find fault in the gamekeeper's work and point out some inadequacy to prevent him from thinking he had total control over the Ballindalloch lands. For all those who had business dealings with the estate, however, Robert Stewart was perceived as the true manager and Gordon grudgingly knew that.

Alexander being raised among the Macpherson children should not give his gamekeeper any wrong ideas, besides this Alexander was far too forthcoming for Gordon's taste. The boy had been caught several times in the library reading a book instead of doing chores around the castle or helping his father.

Not so long ago, Gordon had witnessed Katherine and Alexander in the library together. They had been sitting next to each other at the reading table, their heads almost touching, bent over some book, laughing and talking about something that had eluded him completely. Even startling himself, he had raised his voice to a volume that could be heard in the kitchen quarters across the hall.

"Is there nothing else you idle people can think of doing! Alexander! Go to your father and ask him for a more suitable task rather than occupying my library."

What unsettled Gordon most was that neither of the young people had shown any sign of remorse. They had simply glared at him and had slowly closed the book they were reading. Katherine had walked past her father out of the library with her head held high, without even looking at him. Alexander had only nodded his head, towering over the five foot eight inch Gordon with his own six feet of height, bluntly staring the laird in the eye for a short moment on his way out, leaving Gordon bewildered.

I should not allow those youngsters to unsettle me, he thought. *They should respect who I am and what I have achieved for the family.* Had he not successfully exploited the growing whisky trade over the past years? It was about time this long business acquaintance was rewarded with the marriage of his daughter to one of Grant's boys. A Grant lad would surely know how to control Katherine's behavior.

Gordon often wondered who she inherited her fiery temperament from. Not from him, that was for sure. He believed her nature would stand her in good stead as the wife of a Grant. Her dowry would be well capable of supporting a future husband socially from behind the scenes. Both families had secured significant wealth and power and Katherine would make sure this continued for their offspring.

Therefore, Gordon Macpherson decided it was time for Alexander to leave Ballindalloch. Since he was convinced the gamekeeper's son would resist, a plan started to hatch in his head.

CHAPTER 9

Thursday 4 August 2011, 4:00 pm, Ballindalloch Castle, Banffshire, Scotland

It was four o'clock in the afternoon when Cathy arrived at the castle. Her body clock felt shaken by the six-hour time difference, but something else was also causing disorder in her mind. It was the ancient feel of the place, despite the many cars parked in the driveway. *Without them, this would be like entering a world long gone,* Cathy thought. *It's as if I've been taken on to some movie set.*

Two small dogs were running towards the car, yapping nervously around Mr Christie when he stepped out. They were scraggy-looking animals, one black, one white, wearing tartan collars. Their small tails pointed proudly up in the air.

Wow, they sure stepped straight off a whisky label, Cathy thought.

"Here you go, missus" Christie said, now opening the passenger door. He shouted something incomprehensible at the dogs which made them scurry away. Stepping out of the car, she trod on the damp, wet gravel and flinched. Christie somewhat smugly pointed to her shoes inside the car. Embarrassed, she quickly pulled them on.

Suddenly, she felt the hairs on her neck rise. She looked up to see if it was Christie scrutinizing her, but he was already busying himself getting her luggage out of the car. She gazed at the long wide castle wall that stretched out before her and the flower bed running along the full length of the building. Carefully selected and beautifully kept flowers mirrored a typical English flower garden, of the kind she could never create or even maintain herself. A row of small windows on the first floor drew her attention. Cathy felt as if someone was watching her from behind the shaded glass, like a one-way police mirror in an interrogation room.

The jet-lag, which she knew gave an underestimated blow to the senses, must be doing its work now, she reckoned. With a deep sigh, she pulled herself together.

"What about my luggage, Mr Christie?"

"Don't you be worrying about that, missus. Go see to yourself and meet the family; I'll take the case up to your bedroom. You take good care of yourself," he ordered in his rough Scottish brogue.

She could have sworn she saw a smile on his face when he said that.

Angus Macpherson was sitting in his oak-panelled study just off the main hallway of the castle when he heard a female American voice talking to old Billy the doorman.

Shuffling his papers together, he quickly stuffed them in the bottom drawer to his left and locked it with a large desk key. He dropped the key into his pocket. *Our American guest has arrived on schedule,* he surmised.

He walked into the hall to greet her. Reaching out his hand, he boomed in a jovial manner, "Catherine Macpherson, welcome to our home, I am Angus." Cathy looked at the rather small square-shaped man with a florid complexion, dressed in an undersized formal jacket and bright tartan trousers. "Come, come," he said, draping a podgy arm around her shoulder, ushering her into an impressive library.

Books from floor to ceiling lined three of the walls, all in closed cabinets with glass doors. The fourth side of the room held a window displaying a wonderful view of the flower garden. Three younger men sat dotted around the library. As she stepped in, they all stood up with almost military precision. Angus introduced them as his sons.

One by one, they shook hands with Cathy. First was Angus Junior, tall and slim with red hair and a pale complexion. He seemed comfortable with himself. Next was George, somewhat smaller and already going bald, stocky and slightly nervous looking, and then John, who seemed to be the eldest of the three, a tall slender man unlike his father and brother George. Cathy guessed they were all in or around their thirties. She also immediately recognized a lazy sophistication about John, as if the world could do what it wanted while John would decide his own fate. She liked men like that. Her partner Steve Hicks was similar – basically uncontainable, yet more involved with what was happening around him than most other men. John's handshake, unsurprisingly, was the strongest of the three.

Angus explained briefly to Cathy how he wished his wife, Mary Jane, could still have been here to welcome their guests, but that she had recently passed away after a long illness. Cathy could sense the pain of her death was still strong. Angus added that his wife had always been popular with the people at the games and would be greatly missed at this year's clan gathering.

Then, changing his tone, he said, "But my dear, let's turn to a more uplifting topic. It really is an honor to have you with us.

Your husband, David, sent me a picture of you some weeks ago. I've taken the liberty of placing it in the gathering program. I hope you do not mind, dear. It's not every year we get a new cousin all the way from the States."

The smile on Cathy's face froze as she looked at Angus. She made a mental note to question David about sending the picture. He sure was a lucky man not to be here right now. But she also resented how Angus had simply used the picture without even consulting her. She had spoken to him on the phone! He could have asked her consent. Was he one of those old-fashioned patronizing family patriarchs, who simply went about their business, not bothering to ask the opinion of the people they were impacting? She hated that. She wasn't even family, just carrying the same surname. Noticing Cathy's silence and awkward smile, Angus turned his back to her to hide a frown and a feeling of unease with the American lady. He focused on pouring a Cragganmore single malt whisky into two large chunky crystal glasses that stood displayed on a drinks cabinet. He hadn't really thought beforehand about what Catherine Macpherson would be like. He had simply wanted to entertain and hopefully impress the wife of the travel journalist who would write something complimentary about his castle in the travel guide. Observing Catherine now, Angus wondered how easy this lady would be to impress.

Trying to stimulate the atmosphere, he turned back to her. "Here you go," he said, handing her the glass with a generous amount of whisky. "I hope you can appreciate this, as I think we need to celebrate this special gathering in style with some local produce. It's distilled only a few minutes from here," he added smiling.

"Let's see if my alleged Scottish genes will co-operate on this one," she said jokingly, raising the glass to her lips.

In fact, she had to admit that she was truly amazed at how normal it felt to sit in a Scottish castle surrounded by Macphersons. She thought about the hours of work David put into his Stewart research and here she was, freeloading Macphersons with no effort on her part.

Angus's sons had all been quiet and attentive so far. John stepped in to help his father steer his way through the hospitality show.

"Speaking of genes," John said, "Have you researched your family background at all? We have had family from Ballindalloch going to the USA. In theory, you could descend from one of them."

"John, there must be thousands of Macphersons in the USA..." George jumped in.

"I've never done any research myself," Cathy said, remembering how she had joined David on a trip to New York some years ago. They had done a boat tour to the Statue of Liberty and the old immigration building on Ellis Island. David had spent a lot of time in the research center on the island. She, meanwhile, had bided her time watching some entertainment show somewhere else in the building, about the life of *Bela Lugosi*, one of America's immigrants who went from being a Hungarian refugee to living the Hollywood dream as one of the most famous Draculas the world ever knew. The show had been fun, but other than that, she hadn't really enjoyed the excursion. It had been crowded with masses of people going on and off ferries with little protection against the pouring rain. She had been forced to buy one of the cheap plastic rain capes they sold on board, depicting the Statue of Liberty on the back. She had actually brought it with her to Ballindalloch, as it made a handy travel bag item and she'd heard the weather conditions could change rapidly in the Scottish Highlands.

"I'm not really interested in all that family tree stuff, unlike my husband David, he's a fanatic," she said to John. "But anyway, it's very kind of you to invite me here."

"I'll give you a tour of the castle grounds tomorrow," John said, "before the tourists start arriving at ten. That will give you more time and space to enjoy it better. Is your husband not joining you?"

"Yes, David plans to arrive on Sunday," she answered. "I'll look forward to your tour of the grounds, John."

"Maybe you'll even get to see our ghost," George cut in.

Cathy couldn't help notice how Angus gave George a quick glance. John, saw his father's unease, and satisfied Cathy's inquisitive eyes by saying, "You definitely don't have to take this sort of thing seriously, but some of us Celts claim they have seen ghosts in the castle."

"You mean Gordon Macpherson?" Cathy asked, astonishing all present.

Before giving David the final green light to have her tickets booked, Cathy had done some research and read about the apparition.

"I met your ghost on the castle's website," she said. "He went missing while fishing in a nearby river, I believe?"

"Well," John said, glancing at his father for a moment. "In fact, he mysteriously disappeared in 1895. Some say he was murdered, some say he had an accident. In any case, be it a ghost or a shadow he left behind, he's caused quite a bit of trouble in our family over the years that much is certainly true."

"Don't you be listening to these horror stories, my dear," said a handsome elderly man who had just entered the room. He walked directly to her and held out his hand in greeting.

"I am Thomas Macpherson and you must be Catherine."

Cathy felt a jolt of recognition. The likeness between this man and her father was uncanny, even though Thomas Macpherson was at least twenty years older. *This is what my Pop will look like when he is in his eighties.*

"You can call me Uncle Thomas if you want."

Astonished, Cathy hesitantly shook his hand and was even more taken-aback when he sat down next to her on the couch, as if he'd known her for years. Thomas flashed a challenging smile and asked, "Have this lot been confusing you with all sorts of Macpherson tittle-tattle?"

It took Cathy a few seconds to compose herself.

"We were just talking about a Gordon Macpherson and the trouble he continues to cause, right John?" She looked at John for confirmation.

"Yes," John said, "We were discussing family genes. I was about to tell Catherine, Gordon disappeared and has haunted the castle ever since."

Thomas did not say a word, but he did keep eye contact with Cathy.

"Well," she volunteered, "As I said before, it's my husband who's the genealogy buff. Mind you, no offence meant, I am proud of being an American."

Thomas leaned towards her and said, "My dear, there is no such thing as being an American unless you are a Red Indian."

Cathy almost gasped. Not just what the old man had said, but the tone he used to deliver his comment. His face was dead pan. He didn't even flinch. She wasn't sure if she should get angry or start laughing, but was too flabbergasted to make up her mind. *Is this a typical Scottish welcome?* she wondered pursing her lips.

The others were silent. The pause of conversation was obvious and awkward.

Angus coughed, and put in an effort to save the situation by changing the topic. "Don't listen to ghost stories, my dear. The only things you need to be afraid of here are the midges."

In a welcome release of tension, everyone laughed, nodding their heads in agreement. Cathy, now recovered, admitted she hadn't read anything about midges on the castle website.

"It's like a mosquito with boots on, like a Rambo mosquito." George chuckled at his way of describing a midge to an American.

Cathy decided to go with the flow. "I'm sure I can handle both the midges and the ghosts."

"I'll look forward to meeting your husband on Sunday," Angus said, "I'll be happy to show him the estate. It's a shame he'll miss the games on Saturday, though."

"I'm not even sure if I will go to the Highland games," Cathy admitted "Maybe I'll prefer the quiet surroundings of a country walk instead. The grounds look so beautiful. Is the whole area around the castle open to the public?"

"Yes," Angus answered. "We opened four years ago to help with the costs to maintain the castle and grounds. Managing a four-hundred-and-fifty-year-old estate doesn't go unnoticed in the wallet." He patted his right pocket as if it were the place he secured all his money. "But only part of the castle itself is open to the public, and you'll be in our private guest quarters, my dear, so don't you worry. Oh, by the way, we are having some work done on the drainage system outside. Sorry about that. They start on Monday morning, so I hope it doesn't disturb you and your husband too much."

With a wave of her hand, she dismissed any possible problems. "I am sure David and I will be fine."

Angus went on to mention with some pride that they get about 20,000 visitors a year at the castle. "We get income from salmon fishing, as the River Spey and Avon flow through our estate. The confluence of the rivers is in Ballindalloch, you know. There's also generous income from grouse shooting. Our gamekeeper does a wonderful job preserving the natural habitat for these sports. There are plenty of good reasons for Ballindalloch Castle to be referred to as the Pearl of the North. You and David might want to try angling or shooting, free of charge of course. But I do hope you will join us at the games on Saturday. Enough talk now, let's prepare for something to eat before you retire tonight."

"Will you be joining the meal, Mr Macpherson?" Cathy asked Thomas, reluctant to call a man she just met "uncle".

"Which Mr Macpherson would you be addressing my dear?" Thomas asked in a friendly way.

Cathy felt herself blush slightly.

He broke the ice by laughing and saying, "For sure, lass, I'll see you later in the dining room."

Angus stood up, walked to the door, and shouted on Billy. "The doorman will show you to your room, your luggage will be waiting for you there, and we'll see you at tea. We can chat more about the games then and maybe convince you to attend."

Tea... Cathy thought. *What happened to dinner?*

Old Billy was a skinny crooked man in his seventies, bald, and with an extremely tired-looking face. He walked very slowly with Cathy up the carpeted stairway. She couldn't help notice his dreadful limp. After several winding steps and corridors, they arrived at what was to be her bedroom. Billy opened the door and waited for Cathy to step in first. The drapes were drawn and the single lamp burning made the room dark and mysterious. She could just make out her suitcase propped against the wall at the far end. She turned to thank Billy, but he had already started to hobble down the hall, to return to his post at the main entrance of the castle.

Suddenly, Cathy felt very much alone.

CHAPTER 10

Back in her bedroom, Cathy closed the thick squeaky oak door,
kicked off her shoes, and tossed her suitcase onto the bed,
zipping it open in one efficient movement.

A tiny antique wardrobe, shorter than Cathy's five-foot
-seven, stood waiting for her to hang her clothes. *It has a
certain Cinderella quality,* she thought as she looked around,
allowing the feel of the room to sink in. Even though it was
actually quite spacious, the low ceiling and small windows
made the room seem smaller.

*The castle really owns everything within its walls,
impenetrable to outside influences,* Cathy thought.

It surprised her how that felt somewhat suffocating. She
wondered what it would have been like a hundred years ago.
With nowhere to go except the castle and the grounds, she'd
feel like a prisoner if she had to live here.

She felt totally secluded from the world. This was
compounded by not knowing what was happening to David.
She always had an inkling of where he was, what he was doing,
even when he was traveling, but this time her mind was totally
blank as to his whereabouts. She had tried to call him earlier

from Christie's car, but was unable to get a connection on her cell phone.

She picked her phone out of her travel bag and, although it looked like she still had no signal, tried David's number anyway. The silence that followed was conclusive. Trying to shake the eerie feeling that clouded over her, she sat on the edge of the four-poster bed to reassemble her thoughts. *I might as well unpack,* she thought, and slid off the bed. One by one, she began picking pieces of clothing from her suitcase, giving them a thorough shake before hanging them on the wooden hangers in the wardrobe. Unlike hotels, with the top part of coat hangers connected to a metal bar so guests would not steal them, these were real coat hangers, which made the unpacking much more pleasant.

As she emptied her suitcase, a certain familiarity crept over her, as if she had been in this room before, doing exactly what she was doing now. She closed her eyes, trying to shake the feeling of *déjà vu.* Back home, surrounded by familiar people, she could deal with this illusionary stuff. Here, being on her own, interfered with her desire for control and increased her feeling of isolation. Comforting herself, she thought, *I must be jet-lagged, or maybe the whisky has gone to my head.* She took a few deep breaths in and out all the way down to her belly, as she had been taught at her yoga class back home, making the exhalations slightly longer than the inhalations. For a split second she wished she was at the Raleigh PD, for normality's sake, back in control. Even though it could be a tough profession, she was always more capable of containing and explaining her feelings at work, compared to her time away from the job.

The sound of a man's voice penetrating the wooden door distracted her. He was calling her name. She opened the door of her room and peeked out into the hall, first to the left, then right, but saw nobody.

"Angus? John?" she called out.

Feeling the hair on the back of her neck tingle, she closed the door very gently. "We don't want to rattle any old ghosts, do we now Cathy," she said to humor herself, mimicking a Scottish accent.

Taking five minutes to freshen up, she gathered the energy to get through the rest of the evening. She could feel her heart rate was up from being tired, but was still determined to make a good impression on the Macphersons. Contrary to her initial thoughts and Uncle Thomas's peculiar welcome, she was warming towards the castle and its inhabitants. A previously unrecognized curiosity started to emerge.

Cathy took her time making her way downstairs, trying to get a picture in her head of the castle's layout and the location of her room in relation to the rest of the building. *In case of fire,* she told herself, but a small inner voice whispered that she was looking for more than that. For some reason, her police mode had been switched on.

Coming down the main staircase, she stopped abruptly a few steps short of the black and white tiles that covered the hall floor. Something had caught her attention. Her lips parted slightly and she felt a shiver run down her spine. She was aware of a few people mingling in the hall, but her attention had been immediately drawn to the sensation that overcame her. She suddenly noticed that the surrounding air felt cold against her skin, as if she had just walked into a much cooler part of the castle. Her mind flashed back to the Cameron shooting and the moment when she had walked through the forest holding her gun in front of her, *feeling* something was about to happen.

There was a sense of urgency in the air around her, as if she were late for an appointment or as if someone was impatiently waiting for her.

"You must be Catherine." A croaking female voice interrupted her thoughts. Turning, Cathy found herself staring at two elderly women, both faces framed in lilac colored hair, dressed in similar tartan skirts with black handbags hanging from the crook of their arms. They reminded Cathy of *Thomson and Thomson*, the twin detectives in the *Tin-Tin* comic books, who always dressed exactly the same for every occasion to blend in with the crowd. It was only the bowler hats that were missing.

"Yes, I'm Cathy," she replied, only too happy some pleasant energy had entered her atmosphere.

"Angus told us about you, dear. I can see you are a Macpherson, for sure. I am Maggie and this is Euphemia, my older sister. You need to shout at her, she's as deaf as a doorpost."

"Is everything alright, my dear? You look a wee bit pale," Maggie said, with a look of slight concern on her face.

"I had a bit of a weird feeling just now," Cathy answered. "And I'm cold. I must be more tired from the trip than I realized. I only arrived a few hours ago."

"A *strange* feeling you say? And you feel shivery?" Maggie answered. "I hope it isn't our Gordon Macpherson being inhospitable, my dear. He tends to show up at family gatherings."

Cathy assessed Maggie's remark with her policewoman intuition and said, "Wow, your family really does take this ghost seriously! This is the second time since my arrival that someone introduced him to me. It might make me wonder if he's actually real," she tried to jest, hoping it would chase away her feeling of unease.

Maggie stepped closer, making Cathy catch a whiff of her lavender-scented body. "Gordon was the laird until his disappearance in 1895, you know. He is most certainly real."

"Are you telling me there really is a ghost here?" Cathy asked, mimicking Maggie's serious tone.

Cathy noticed how Maggie was trying to hide her face from her sister Euphemia and thought. *She must be a great lip reader.*

"Aye, I believe I've actually seen him on one occasion," Maggie whispered bringing her head closer to Cathy. He's been walking the castle for years; a tormented soul he is! Some say he drowned in the Spey, while fishing, right here in his own grounds. Others say that he was murdered by the Stewart boy. In any case, his body was never found and that's probably why the poor soul is tormented."

"The Stewart boy?" Cathy echoed. "Would that be Alexander Stewart?" David had mentioned the name of his Scottish ancestor often enough for her to remember it.

"The Macpherson men have a habit of disappearing you know," Maggie said, ignoring the fact that Cathy knew the name of Gordon's alleged murderer. "Gordon's father, Edward, he boarded a train in Edinburgh just after Christmas. It was in 1879, I believe; he was making his way to Dundee. There was a force ten gale when the train was crossing the Tay Bridge.[78]" Maggie emphasized the strength of the storm by drawing a wide circle in the air with her arms, the black purse still dangling on her right elbow. "The train never arrived, you know, the bridge collapsed and seventy-five souls perished. Forty-four of them were never recovered. Edward was one of them."

"Does he also haunt the castle, this Edward?" Cathy managed to ask in between the flow of Maggie's words, with her thoughts still on her husband's ancestor being named as a possible murderer.

"No," Maggie promptly answered, "And nor does Malcolm Macpherson. *He* miraculously disappeared while trading whisky in America during the prohibition years. They say he was smuggling from Canada into America and that his death was ordered by Al Capone himself. Yes, we have had some famous disappearances in our family, but Gordon is the only one who returns every now and then."

"Catherine dear, don't let my sister upset you with all her stories. You look pale, lass," Euphemia volunteered, cutting into the conversation for the first time. Giving Maggie an angry look, she hissed through her teeth, "Now what have you been telling her?" Turning back to Cathy she asked, "Do you need to sit down for a wee while?"

Ceremoniously, Euphemia guided Cathy to a chair in the hall. Cathy played along, feeling an instant liking for the old woman, but was wise not to lean on her, for they would certainly both have stumbled.

"I'm okay, Euphemia, thank you. It's just that my husband is a Stewart and his ancestor Alexander was born here," Cathy said quietly.

"Is that so?" said Euphemia, her eyes looking cunning as they searched Cathy's face.

It occurred to Cathy that Euphemia might be hard of hearing, but she was certainly a better listener than her sister.

"Well, dear, I think you should put those stories out of that pretty head of yours and join us for something to eat before we all fade away."

She took Cathy by the arm again and Maggie appeared on Cathy's other side. Together, they almost hoisted her off the chair. Safely tucked between the two sisters, Cathy was led towards the dining room grinning at the situation she was in. *Alexander Stewart, a murderer… Wait till you hear this, David Stewart!*

CHAPTER 11

Wednesday 30 October 1895, Ballindalloch, Banffshire, Scotland

Alexander and Katherine were enjoying their horse ride nearby the castle, when the changeable highland weather announced a thunderstorm. The sky blackened as the first big drops of rain caused an intermittent rhythm of sound on the leaves of the overhanging trees.

"To our cottage, Katie, quick," Alexander called out.

Instantly Katherine understood his line of thought. "What a wonderful idea," she chirped, "It's been ages!"

The old deserted farmhouse Katie and Alex had used as their explorers den in earlier childhood days, stood waiting on a small clearing amidst the trees. Hastily, they secured their horses to iron rings under the overhanging roof and slipped through the old door into the peaceful space, Katie taking the lead. The rain was hammering on the roof like thousands of little pebbles being tossed out of the sky. It was indeed an extraordinary heavy storm. Yet the sturdy old roof held its fortress, turning their shelter into an agreeable and intimate hide out.

While wiping off the raindrops that had been able to catch them, Katie was immediately drawn towards the welcoming atmosphere of the little house.

"Isn't it a shame that nobody lives here anymore?" she said. "It has always felt such a lovely place to be. In fact I wouldn't mind living here myself, wouldn't you?" Katherine added, swirling around to face Alex. "We could make a fire and cook ourselves a dinner, read all the books we wanted and talk about anything we liked. Wouldn't that be wonderful? "

The tiny cottage consisted of a square-shaped living area with a fire place that used to house a cauldron. The iron hook that held the vessel could still be seen protruding from the chimney. Half way between the floor and the ceiling was an alcove that had served as a set-in bed, with a simple ladder leaning against it.

Katie and Alex stared at each other, a pregnant silence hanging between them. They had shared many a dream in this place and talked about their mutual wish to look over the edges of their existence. Suddenly Alex saw tears well up in Katherine's eyes.

"Oh, Alex what are we going to do?" she whispered.

"I'd rather live in this dingy house or somewhere in Leith with you, than to find myself married to one of those boring, know it all, peacock Grant boys."

Alarmed, Alex stepped towards her. An avalanche of contradicting feelings overwhelmed him. Next to his parents, nobody had ever been as important to him as Katherine Macpherson. With her, he had always seemed complete.

Until recently he had been able to keep the disturbing thoughts of Katherine getting married at bay, knowing such an alliance would make a continuation of their friendship difficult. Yet it was not his ambition to live in Leith, one of the very modest parts of Edinburgh, with Katie either. His dream was to travel outside the borders of his dreaded existence as gamekeeper of Ballindalloch, and write about what moved the people. Alexander knew he had the ability to observe the world as it was, without being distracted by too much richness or poverty to cloud his view. He knew he could contribute to the changing times they were living in.

He also understood Katherine's desire to step outside of her boundaries. If she'd be allowed to go to university and study medicine, she would make a great physician, he was sure of that. Alex noticed a curl had detached from Katherine's hairpin and had fallen over her cheek. In a tender gesture he wiped away a tear that was rolling down her face and gently pushed the wandering braid of hair back in its place. Their eyes locked. Alex detected the stubborn determinedness he knew so well of Katie. It made him smile.

In response Katie's mouth moved to his. He knew he was not supposed to let this happen, but could not resist wanting to feel the touch of her lips on his. Hesitantly their tongues found each other. Alex almost staggered as a wave of uncontrollable longing swept through his body. The bold way in which she kissed him, pushed all rational thought aside, their kiss drawing them into each other like magnets. They both knew they should stop, yet wouldn't.

With time disappearing into the corners of their consciousness, they didn't know how long they stood there kissing. When they did stop, they held on to each other their fingers intertwined, heads almost touching.

"Please don't leave me alone Alex, don't let me be married-off," Katherine whispered. I need our friendship more than I need a husband. I want us to be together forever. Please make time stand still right here and now."

Everything that happened next would have been impossible to stop. Clumsily but without any hesitation their hands searched for each other underneath their clothes, as if the joining of their bodies was their only means of survival. The feel of Katie's skin underneath his hands surrounded Alex's reason like a mist. The motions that followed were as inevitable as his need to breathe. Their bodies found each other, while they lowered themselves onto the floor all pretence or hesitation evaporating into the space that surrounded them.

Only a short cry of Katie cut through the air, followed by a deep groan from Alexander, as his sexual tension slowly subsided.

CHAPTER 12

Thursday 4 August 2011, 6:40 pm Ballindalloch Castle, Banffshire, Scotland

Walking into the cavernous dining room between Maggie and Euphemia, Cathy wondered if the "Stewart boy", as Maggie had called him, really was David's ancestor. Maggie hadn't responded to her remark at all. Maybe she'd misunderstood. Would Maggie know she was married to a Stewart? Would Angus have told her?

She forced a smile at Angus who was already seated at the table. For some reason, she didn't want him to know about her thoughts. An open fire burned in a large, beautifully carved wooden fireplace. Cathy could smell the crackling logs in the air and was drawn towards the warmth of the flames. Standing with her back to the room she held the palms of her hands against the reassuring heat of the fire, rubbing them every now and again as if to spread the warmth to her arms and further into her body.

"Come ladies and sit down," Angus bellowed. "I see you've already made a couple of friends, Catherine. Don't listen to any of their old stories and gossip, I've had to put up with them for years." He laughed.

Maggie waved a fist at him in jest.

"For those who have not yet met our cousin from the United States, could I have a moment please to introduce Catherine Macpherson from North Carolina," Angus announced, interrupting the chatter at the dinner table.

Cathy smiled at everyone, feeling uncomfortable, and was thankful when Angus gestured that she should sit at the left upper corner of the table. Like a true gentleman, he stood up and positioned her chair to help her get comfortable. *The guys at Raleigh PD should learn how to do this,* Cathy thought, smiling, enjoying being treated as a lady.

The large dining table was covered with a cotton cream-colored tablecloth and silver cutlery. A floral centerpiece and what looked like Macpherson tartan napkins provided color. On her right sat Maggie and then Euphemia. Angus was seated adjacent to Cathy at the head of the table. Opposite her to Angus's left, she found the friendly face of Thomas Macpherson. He nodded at her benevolently, but did not volunteer any conversation. She noticed again how handsome he looked.

She made a polite "who is who at the table" inquiry with Maggie and Euphemia. She learned from Maggie that she and Euphemia were great-aunts of Angus. "Effy", as Euphemia was sometimes called by her sister, only smiled occasionally – presumably not hearing what was being said, but Cathy had begun to doubt that.

Among the group Cathy also recognized Angus's sons and Maggie mentioned that the slim, rather bony lady at the far end was Angus's sister, Jean.

They were served what was referred to as a "high tea", although very unlike Cathy's concept of such a meal. To her, high teas were expensive gatherings in chic hotels with mounds of salmon and cucumber sandwiches, scones, and teacakes. It intrigued her when the first dish served was a steak.

A group of thirteen, Cathy counted, had sat down to the high tea. Sitting opposite her, Uncle Thomas seemed a little anxious, not saying anything, but every now and then they made eye contact. Nobody else seemed to care about his silence.

Angus explained to Cathy that hundreds of people would attend the Newtonmore Games, as it was freely open to the general public, but there were admission costs, of course, £5 for an adult – which, he commented, was a cheap day out! For the clan dinner on Saturday evening at the castle, he said, he expected around thirty guests would attend and they would arrive at various times between now and Saturday.

From where she was seated, Cathy observed, through the open door, a couple of people arriving in the hall. A tall man, dressed in a kilt, pulled a bulky suitcase, followed by a woman carrying a travel case. Something about them made Cathy glance again, but she couldn't quite figure out what was intriguing her. Then she chuckled, realizing what it was that struck her as odd. The couple that had arrived was of African lineage. Back home in the US she wouldn't think twice about it, but here in Scotland and wearing a kilt? She also noticed that his kilt was a different pattern and color from the Macpherson tartan that she had quickly become familiar with.

Euphemia, who seemed to be observing every little aspect of her behavior, answered the question without it being asked. "That's the Stewart tartan, my dear. He is Wayne Stewart and his wife Eleanor. They've been here before. His ancestor was born here."

Euphemia looked at Cathy smugly, as if waiting for her to respond. The penny dropped.

"Not the Stewart boy again!" Cathy exclaimed. "He must have been quite a man. Sorry, Euphemia, but you're losing me here."

She glanced at Uncle Thomas, hoping for some help, but he just shrugged his shoulders and sipped his tea.

Maggie laughed out loud at Cathy's remark tossing her head back. "Aye, well, the Stewarts have done a few remarkable things, I must say."

"From what I know," said Maggie, taking over the conversation, looking around her, and dropping her voice, "Alexander and his wife fostered a young black boy and that wee lad was Wayne's family line."

"Jeez, that must have been unusual. In fact, very brave of them to do that in those days," Cathy remarked.

"Aye," Maggie went on. "Maybe it had something to do with him being a fostered child himself. You see the Stewart boy was raised here at the castle along with the Macpherson children."

"You know where the name Macpherson comes from, Catherine?" Angus asked breaking up Cathy's animated conversation with Maggie.

"It's an old Gaelic name," Cathy responded.

In a schoolteacher tone, Angus replied, "Well done dear, it's from the twelfth century, Mac-a-Phearsain, meaning 'son of the parson'. You see, at that time, celibacy of the priesthood was not enforced."

Euphemia quickly added, "Nothing much has changed then," making those within earshot laugh loudly.

Cathy smiled, now knowing for sure Euphemia's deafness was only a stage act.

"The clan motto," Angus went on, ignoring Euphemia's riposte, "is 'Touch not a cat but a glove.' Do you know what that means?"

Cathy smiled, "No Angus, I don't. I get a feeling you are about to tell me though." She was actually enjoying the exchange with Angus.

"The motto's meaning is – touch not the cat when it is without a glove," Angus replied proudly. He added, "the glove of the wildcat is the soft under-part of his paw, and when it assumes a warlike attitude, the paw is spread, or ungloved, revealing very dangerous claws. The motto is a warning to those who would be so imprudent as to engage in battle when the claw of the wildcat is ungloved."

Cathy could tell from everyone's faces they had heard Angus show off his Macpherson knowledge before. Some were even yawning. Angus got all enthusiastic and even brought some picture books to the dining table to show her pictures of previous clan gatherings over the years. He passed a picture from 1988 and, tired, she stared at it without really knowing what to look for. With her fingernail, she absentmindedly tried to remove a white spot on the picture without success. It was on the far right, just behind the two rows of people posing for the camera.

"Who or what is that *not* in the picture?" Cathy joked, remembering that white spots on pictures often hide supernatural images. "The castle ghost?"

Angus glanced at the picture and seemed annoyed with himself. Quickly, he removed the book from her inspecting eyes.

"Well then, Catherine," he said. "Are you looking forward to the gathering? Maybe I should tell you what to expect, especially at the games at Newtonmore. I do hope you'll come along."

She sat back in her chair wondering what the etiquette would be about leaving the table now. While he continued talking, she tried to concentrate. Consciously taking a full intake of breath to help stifle the growing need to yawn, she heard his voice as if from a distance. Fatigue was kicking in from the journey as well as the stress of the many new impressions. Only occasional words from Angus were now comprehensible. "Chief of the Clan… all Macphersons are cousins… chief is a father figure to all the clan… first among equals…"

In an effort to stay awake, she decided to take advantage of the talkative mood he was in.

"If you don't mind me bringing it up again, Angus, what's the story on our cousin Gordon Macpherson?" she asked, purposely using the word "cousin" to show she'd been paying attention.

Cathy knew a thing or two about angling, as her father had taken his tomboy teenage daughter with him quite often. It hadn't been salmon fishing, but fishing nonetheless. She had memories of the stilling effect of standing in the tranquil almost meditative water, tuning in for the kill.

"Aha, you've obviously been talking to a few of the Macphersons, Catherine," Angus exclaimed, glancing at Maggie, who just grinned back. It was apparent he would rather discuss something else. "This topic comes up from time to time around the dinner table. He is, after all, our castle ghost, as you discovered on our website." He turned his gaze away from Cathy and looking at the table cloth instead, brushing away imaginary crumbs. "The official position of the authorities at the time was that it was presumed that he drowned while fishing in the Spey. But my own view is more, let's say, open to conjecture. The poor soul could have been a victim of foul play."

At the far side of the table, Jean Douglas Macpherson, Angus's sister, slowly placed her knife and fork on her plate and folded her hands over them like a roof, her elbows at each side of the plate. Cathy noticed her neck had reddened and her face flushed crimson at Angus's words.

Staring over the full length of the table directly at her brother, as if nobody else was there, she said, "Angus, dear, I know you are head of this family, but you should not give your personal views to a stranger like Catherine. It was a long time ago. Nobody really knows what happened and I would not have Catherine thinking there were ever any murders in this house." Taking a deep breath, she continued, "You know how treacherous the Spey can be, Angus."

"That's true, I had to be dragged out of the river once, two miles downstream, when I was a wee boy," Angus replied looking at Cathy.

"Gordon died there in a tragic fishing accident and was probably hit by those hazardous timber rafts that went to Garmouth," Jean added with conviction. "And there are many bends, drops, and marshes where a body could get snared and left to, well, you know what I mean."

It felt to Cathy they were putting on a show for her, as many around the table seemed rather subdued. Angus did not respond. Instead, he grabbed a decanter from the table and poured the golden liquid into his teacup. Cathy noticed that Uncle Thomas's water glass was lying on its side, the tablecloth wet from the spilled water. Uncle T, as she had started to call him in her mind, had quietly left the table. He was quickly winning her sympathy. There was an intelligence and reassurance about him that she found intriguing and certainly absent from Angus. She watched Angus lean over in Jean's direction as if he wanted to cover the full length of the table.

"Catherine is no stranger, Jeanie," he said more softly. "She is a Macpherson, please remember that. Anyway, to be honest, it doesn't matter a jot if old Gordon popped his clogs in the river or indeed met with some other foul deed. It helps keep the tourists interested." He winked at Cathy. He seemed happier now that he had managed to get the last word on the matter.

Jean raised both her carefully styled eyebrows, tossed her napkin next to her plate in an angry gesture, pushed her chair back more noisily than necessary, and left the table. Angus gestured to his son John to follow her.

A disappearance of someone so important to the community must have caused quite a stir at the time. Strange, though, to have such a heated debate now on something that happened over a hundred years ago. Cathy's police-trained mind also heard an undertone of something else in Angus's comments. It was as if he had been provoking Jean, who, for whatever reason, would not accept that a laird and chief of the Macphersons could have been murdered. Maybe it suited Angus's ego that his position, although prestigious, also carried some risks.

Everyone around the table was silent. *Maybe they don't like discussing Gordon at all,* thought Cathy, as she recalled it was her who started the conversation. She stood up and looked at Angus, announcing that she'd try and call her husband and then get some well-earned sleep.

Placing a hand on her arm, as if to delay her and reassure himself that she wasn't upset, Angus said, "John will show you around the castle grounds tomorrow. And by the way, breakfast is served promptly at eight, my dear. Hope you sleep well."

Glad to leave the now oppressive atmosphere, Cathy walked into the main hall leading to the front door.

"… and why not, if I may ask? Do you think Angus can keep this a secret forever?" she heard a woman whisper.

The echoes of the old castle were playing tricks on her. The vaulted ceiling reflected the words as if the woman was standing in the same spot as Cathy. However, she realized the whisper was from further down the hall leading to the bedrooms. For a moment, she was tempted to tiptoe down the hall to see if she could hear more, but decided against it and headed for the front door.

Stepping outside into the evening Highland air she tried her cell phone again and, as expected, found no signal. *David should be somewhere in London – or maybe even Scotland by now,* she thought. She did not know what hotels he had booked. It had become quite a challenge to get in touch with each other. She wondered if perhaps he'd tried to call the castle at all.

It was almost a quarter past eight when she walked slowly along the gravel path that would take her towards the river.

From his bedroom window, Thomas watched the American lady walk towards the Spey. The eighty-year-old veteran of the family yawned. He always went to bed early these days, but especially tonight. Dinner had ended with a sour taste, thanks to the quarrel between Angus and Jean. He had grown weary of the Gordon mystery, and wondered what had kept him from speaking up all these years.

Still looking at Catherine in the distance, he chuckled to himself. *She has spunk, I'll give her that,* he thought, *Asking about Gordon so casually and directly. I bet she didn't expect to get such an emotional outburst.* Jean always got her knickers in a twist trying to protect the good name of the family.

Thomas undressed, put on his night clothes and slippers and walked into his en-suite bathroom.

"One day, you'll tell the truth, you old bugger," he said to his reflection in the bathroom mirror. Where had the time gone? It was almost seventy years ago and he wished it had never happened.

If only I had married and settled somewhere else, everything would have been different. Climbing into bed, his thoughts returned to their American guest and how she truly looked like an identical twin of *her*. With a wry smile, he realized that Angus would probably never have invited Catherine had he known in advance what she was like. He switched off his bedside lamp, but found it difficult to settle.

Maybe Catherine was here to put things at rest. Thomas hoped and prayed it would be so. Somebody had to.

CHAPTER 13

Wednesday 30 October 1895, Ballindalloch, Banffshire, Scotland

"Let's go back to the stables," Katherine said, kissing Alex lightly on the cheek. She pushed herself away from his body and started to re-arrange her clothes.

The air between them was silent. They had both known this was bound to happen, yet had never shared their thoughts on it.

"You and I will always be each other's first," Alex said softly.

"As we always have been," Katie answered without looking at him.

They both felt confused. Fumbling with their clothing as they got up, they tried to retreat back to normalcy.

"Katie," Alex said, taking hold of her hand, "I don't know what will happen next, but know I will always be loyal to you. Even if we can't live in this cottage or in Leith, we have each other. That is more important to me than anything else in the world. You are the most extraordinary girl, Katherine Macpherson." Alex pulled her towards him one more time circling his long arms around her in a protective gesture.

"Come on Alexander Stewart, we need to go before people find cause to gossip about us again," Katie said, trying to dull the awkwardness of the situation. Outside the sun was showing its face again to the earth. Some small puddles of water were still visible.

Without wasting any more time Katherine mounted her white mare and set off. Alex quickly followed on the impressive black stallion, Stretcher, the horse that, even though it was not officially his, felt like his own.

"Come on Alexander Stewart, I'll race you to the stables," Katherine cried out louder than necessary. Hesitating for a moment Alex gave her a heads start. He couldn't bring himself to compete with her as he normally would. He followed her just fast enough to keep pace.

Within five minutes, they were at the castle stables, Katherine a few seconds before Alex. "You're a cheat," she said, tossing her ponytail over her shoulder with a swift movement of her head. "You let me win! That's not a fair challenge."

He smiled wearily as he watched her dismount from the horse. He was just about to try and say something that would console her obvious desire to run away from what just happened between them, when Gordon Macpherson appeared from the stable.

"Katherine, what's going on here?" he asked with a cold stare at Alexander.

Alex felt his stomach knot up. It felt as if Gordon knew what had happened at the cottage.

"Good afternoon, sir," he said quietly, but his address was ignored.

"Nothing, Father," Katherine said. "Alexander and I just went riding and..."

Gordon interrupted her and ordered, "Go to the house, Katherine. I need a private word with Alexander about the gardens." Now looking up at Alex, he bawled, "Get off the horse when I'm talking to you!"

She frowned at her father and then looked back at Alexander apologetically. Mouthing that she would see him later, she handed the reins of her mare to the young stable boy Callum who had appeared from the stables. She trudged towards the castle.

"Let's step inside for a word in your ear," Gordon snarled, opening the stable door.

Alex flung a long leg over Stretcher's back, dismounting at his own pace, taking his time to guide the horse towards the stable. He wished he would have been given some more time to prepare his reaction towards Gordon.

A few weeks before, in a monologue that had left little room for response, Gordon had told Alexander that he and Katherine were spending too much time together. Alexander had defended their friendship by speaking up about how they genuinely cared for each other. At that Gordon had walked away, extremely angry, without further comment.

Alexander and Gordon were now in the stable standing close to the tack room. The sunlight was blazing through an open shutter into Alex's eyes and he blinked rapidly, trying to focus on Gordon. The damp aroma of mildew mixing with particles of dust motes in the air, made the stable feel stuffy and uncomfortable.

"So what work needs done in the gardens, sir?" Alex asked, hoping the laird wouldn't notice his unease.

"Forget the garden you know I need to talk to you about Katherine! How can she marry someone if she continues wasting her time with you," Gordon growled, letting go of any decorum. "Get off your high horse, Alexander Stewart. Don't forget my late wife, God bless her, only took you into our home because she felt sorry for you. That does not give you any rights in our family. I trust you are listening. It's time you packed your bags and started a life of your own."

Gordon's reproach hit him hard, his mind frantically seeking for the right words to retaliate. He hoped that Callum was not in ear-shot of this row. It made it even more difficult for Alex to think properly.

He glared at Gordon, "Do I get to have any say in this, sir?"

"In a word," Gordon retorted, "No! I want you out of here, the sooner the better for all concerned. You will have to create your own opportunities instead of living off mine."

"What about Katherine?" Alexander asked. "Have you any concern for what she wants?"

Gordon, his eyes blazing with rage, clearly insulted by the blunt question of the gamekeeper's son, stepped forward, lowered his voice and almost gently, had it not been for the undertone of threat, said, "You will go one way or another. Do not underestimate me! And you will *not*, I repeat *not*, say a word to anybody about this conversation, especially Katherine. And in case you get it into your deceitful head that your father might have anything to say in this, you're wrong. Even if he had, he'd probably agree with me anyway. So, if not for your sake, then obey me for your father's sake, to make sure he keeps his job. At least *he* knows his place!"

Alex now felt an apoplectic rage emerging, but knew to contain it. How dare Gordon Macpherson threaten his father's position like this? Three generations of Stewarts had faithfully served the Macpherson family. Surely he would not send his father away because of the wrong doings of his son!

As if reading his thoughts, Gordon added, "If you make

this difficult for me, then be sure, as God is my maker, I will think of something to make you leave!"

Angrily, Gordon pulled the door of the stable open, clattering it against the wall, causing Stretcher to whine and take a few nervous steps.

As he marched out of the stable, a shaken Alexander was left behind, the harsh reality of the situation now setting in.

Quickly Alex unsaddled his horse and steered him to the safety of his stall. He took a few minutes to brush down the stallion buying time to compose himself. Then he went in search of his father. As he walked past the castle, he could see Katherine staring out of her bedroom window. She waved her hand. He waved back, but quickly dropped his head and walked towards the small Stewart lodge on the west of the castle grounds.

He found his father outside their modest home, sitting on a bench reading the previous day's newspaper. Donald Simpson always passed on old newspapers to his friend.

Like Alexander, Robert Stewart was tall, with a stocky frame and dark complexion. He had a full head of dark brown hair, but like his well groomed beard, some grey streaks were starting to show.

"What bothers you, son?" he asked, recognizing something was wrong.

Alex immediately blurted the details of his discussion with Gordon and kept repeating, the laird wanted him to leave Ballindalloch. His father, listening without saying a word, allowed Alex to ramble on and finally gestured that they go inside.

"Let's have some tea," Robert said.

Filling a copper kettle with water, while Alex sat down at the scullery table, Robert stared out of the window and said softly, "I'm really disappointed with Macpherson."

Alex looked up in surprise. He had been expecting his father to say something like, "I told you to leave Miss Katherine alone." Also, his father never left out the title of *Mister* when he referred to the laird.

"He should have discussed this with me," his father mumbled, still with his back to Alexander. Turning around, holding the kettle, he looked at his son and asked, "Do you wish to be a gamekeeper like me for the rest of your day's son? I've seen your writings and how you are always reading books. The English tutor, Mrs Roxburgh, told me you have a remarkable talent for the written word, Alex." Placing his free hand on Alex's shoulder, he continued. "It might be time for you to start a new life away from here and change the Stewart tradition. Every family's history has bloodlines going from rich to poor, and failure to success. Maybe it's your destiny to change our family's fate, even though it might not be an easy journey. I know it hurts right now to even think of leaving all you care for. But an uncle of mine used to remind me of the Stewart family motto – *veriscit vulnere virtus.* "Courage grows strong at a wound."

Alex smiled. His father always surprised him with his unexpected knowledge.

"Maybe it's time you started to make use of your education, Alex." Robert continued. "I've seen you look at the skies longingly in the evenings, brooding, and I know you're smart. Go out there and get what you want out of life. It's not here for you."

Even though his father's response was very understanding, Alexander decided not to burden him any more with the trouble he had brought upon their small family. His father had obviously resigned to his own world and fate, finding satisfaction in the niches he had created for himself.

"Leave it for now, think about what I have said," his father suggested. "I promise I'll speak to Gordon and sort out this mess. But one thing Alex, stop spending time with Miss Katherine, it invites trouble."

A worried Alexander, with Gordon's harsh words still ringing in his ears, reluctantly agreed to this, never daring to disclose to his father what had really been going on between he and Katherine.

CHAPTER 14

**Saturday 2 November 1895, Grantown-on-Spey,
Morayshire, Scotland**

"Simpson, get my horse and carriage ready; I have business to attend to in Grantown," Gordon commanded his butler.

"Certainly, sir, what time will you be leaving?"

"Now, tell the coachman to make haste, it is important."

Quickly, but at a pace that still complimented his status, Simpson took off in the direction of the kitchen where he knew the coachman, Mr MacLean, would be having his breakfast. Fifteen minutes later, Gordon stepped into his carriage and asked the coachman to get the best out of the two horses.

MacLean and the horses did well even though the hills were cloaked by early morning mist and the wheels of the coach creaked and groaned as they sank into the ruts on the muddy road. Arriving forty-five minutes later, the High Street of Grantown was already bustling with market traders preparing for the day ahead. Following his instructions, the coach driver turned the east corner of the main square, passed the Grant Hotel, and halted the sweating horses in front of the police station. Even before the coach had fully stopped, Gordon opened the door and jumped out. Sergeant Robbie Grant, recognizing the Ballindalloch coach, hurried to greet him.

"Good morning, Mister Macpherson, how can I be of service?" the policeman asked as Gordon barged inside.

"Take me to your office, Sergeant," Gordon grunted without looking at the man. "I wish to report a theft."

CHAPTER 15

Cathy's head was spinning from everything she had heard since her arrival only a few hours earlier.

Why the hell hasn't David called me? she thought. *You'd think he would want to know I've arrived safely!*

David always took his time with everything, which was one of the marital irritations between them. Cathy had a much bigger need for instant gratification.

Heading for the river, she took the path that had been indicated to her from the library window earlier that afternoon.

John had told her it was a short distance from the castle and she should follow the signposts that directed the river-walk for the tourists. She turned and looked back at the castle and shivered as she reflected on her strange experience walking down the staircase on her way to dinner. *Old castle ghosts indeed,* she thought defiantly.

Black cattle similar to the herd she had seen earlier during the car-ride from the airport, were lying on the grass on both sides of the path leading to the river. They were separated from the castle grounds by two simple wooden gates, one leading to the castle, the other to the Spey. There were no other people in sight as she approached the river. She could hear the noise of the rushing water.

Reaching the path by the riverbank, which was lined with trees on her right as far as she could see, Cathy inhaled the cool fresh air, and stared at the water. The current was extremely fast and noisy. She watched the torrents bounce over and around rocks that emerged from the water surface at various points. "Well, hello River Spey," she muttered.

Why had Jean been so adamant to have her believe that a fishing accident had killed Gordon Macpherson and why was everyone else so quiet, except for Angus? It had been a bizarre discussion at the dinner table, almost a show. Was it really possible that a Laird of Ballindalloch and experienced angler on his own fishing grounds would drown in waters he knew better than anyone else? Nurturing these thoughts, Cathy left the path and carefully walked down the small incline towards the river's edge.

About a hundred yards ahead of her, she could see the choppy white waters where the Spey and the Avon, clearly merged. It was there that Gordon Macpherson apparently lost his balance while salmon fishing. She ambled towards the confluence along the cobblestones that lined the bank of the Spey. The waters were not so deep here, maybe three or four feet deep at the most. She reckoned the river should have been no different in 1895, even in a rainy season. The fast flowing river would probably wash away any sediment from the stony surface, so it wouldn't be that slippery.

Cathy sat down on the white cobbled stones on the riverbank and studied the river. The constant noise of the rushing water filled the air around her. *There has to be more to this story*, she thought.

CHAPTER 16

Saturday 2 November 1895 Ballindalloch, Banffshire, Scotland

A note pinned to the front door of their lodge summoned Alex to come to the castle's study at noon that day. When he arrived, Alex noticed the study door had been left slightly ajar. He could see Gordon sitting behind his big oak desk, through the gap. Purely a tactical move, Alex realized, as Gordon kept him waiting long after Alex firmly knocked on the door.

"You may come in now," Gordon eventually said, glancing at his pocket watch.

As he entered the room, Alex noticed a bulky brown envelope on Gordon's desk, sticking out from under a clutter of papers.

"Shut the door and sit down," Gordon ordered.

Alexander closed the door quietly and then sat on a chair that had been placed opposite Gordon at the center of the desk. He fixed his eyes on the older man.

"Let me get straight to the point," Gordon said, ceremoniously placing his fountain pen in its brass holder. "We have had a theft in the castle. Precious jewels that belonged to my late wife, God rest her soul, have gone missing. I'm glad she is not here to witness this. It would have saddened her dearly to see artifacts disappear that have been in our family for over four generations."

Gordon looked at Alex, "As you may well understand, I had no choice of course, but to report this to the police. Would you know anything about this theft, boy?" he asked, slightly tilting his head backward.

"No, sir," Alex said, keeping his nerves at bay. "Why would I know anything about such a dastardly deed?"

"I'll tell you why," Gordon replied, a bit disappointed by the younger man's calm composure. "Only Simpson, Mrs Craddock, our dear housekeeper, your father and I have keys to the room that held these pieces. Now it certainly wouldn't be Mrs Craddock who took them. I am sure you would agree with me there? Speak up, man," he snarled as he leaned across his desk, staring at Alex.

It did not take Alex long to figure out what was happening. He had to struggle to keep his composure, but somehow managed to maintain his focus.

"Are you trying to convince me it was my father, sir? Or are you implying it must have been me? You know full well it was neither. Whatever game you are playing, sir, I would like to understand the rules."

"The rules are simple," Gordon replied, leaning even more forward while narrowing his eyes. "You have a choice to make Alexander Stewart, before the authorities arrive to start their investigation. What do you suggest I tell them? I think it would be wise if either you or your father leave Ballindalloch this afternoon."

The silence in the study was deafening. For a moment it seemed to Alex that the world had stopped turning and that all life stood still. Alex knew very well he wasn't given a choice. Gordon was talking about *him* and using his loyalty to his father as a tool.

"As the Stewarts traditionally served the Macphersons well for many years," Gordon's voice cut in, "I am willing to support your family to a certain degree. I will help one of you to start a new life. I cannot be fairer than that."

His lips tight together and his heartbeat racing, Alex watched Gordon lean back in his desk chair and gently tap his fingers of both hands on the desk. After another pause for effect, Gordon said, "I have booked a passage for one person on the SS State of Nebraska. The ship is leaving Glasgow tomorrow at noon, bound for New York."

Unexpectedly, Gordon's right hand smacked down on the large wrinkled envelope Alexander had noticed when he first came into the study.

"This envelope," he said softly, "contains the calling card of an acquaintance in the town of New York. He can help you find work in the whisky trade, provided you work hard and do not grant yourself any unwarranted liberties like you did here."

Alexander stood up in a fury. He leaned his long frame across the desk, gripped the collars of Gordon's jacket, pushing him back in his chair, and raged, "Gordon Macpherson, you are not fit to be the head of any family. You are a liar, a cheat, and you will regret this!"

Gordon, his jacket still in Alexander's firm grip, smiled as he softly whispered, "Are you going to assault me, boy? Be violent? Please do! What better way to get rid of you. It would only add to your already blemished reputation and raise the stakes of you being found guilty of theft. Who would believe anything *you* would have to say against my word after such an appalling display of bad behavior?"

Alexander stared into Gordon's dark, triumphant eyes and felt despair rise in his throat. A voice in his head warned him not to allow hatred of the laird cloud his judgment.

"You leave me with little choice," Alex managed to say, releasing Gordon from his grip, amazed at his own actions. His guilt about what had happened with Katherine in the old cottage only a few days before, immobilized him completely. He may not have committed the crime Gordon accused him of, but he was guilty of gross misconduct that still weighed heavily on his shoulders. Maybe Gordon even knew and felt he had a right to dispense of Alexander in this foul way.

"I will go," he said hardly audible to Gordon, "on the condition you look after my father and Katherine through all of this."

Realizing he had just pushed the strong young man to his limits and relishing his success, Gordon had to restrain himself to stay composed. Only a slight stammer betrayed his excitement over having won this battle.

"A c-coach has been arranged to meet you at the main gate in one hour's time to take you to the station. And take this," he said. "You will need it. The papers are in your name."

Gordon handed Alexander the brown envelope. "Forget the coach," he snarled at Gordon, "I will walk to the station on my own two feet. And don't you forget that in the eyes of God all men are equal. You may be able to mislead the constable, but not our Lord. Curse you and the ground you walk on."

On these words Alex turned away from Gordon, and walked out of the room with long strides, leaving the door wide open.

More shocked than he cared to admit, Gordon walked over to a small table, which held a decanter of whisky. He poured himself a large glass, taking a big gulp immediately.

Alex was surprised by his own verbal outburst especially as the harsh truth of what was happening was still incomprehensible. It simply couldn't be true. It must all be a bad dream, some distorted misunderstanding.

When he closed the heavy oak door of Ballindalloch Castle behind him, he was not yet able to recognize that he was also closing a chapter in his life.

After the damaging exchange in the study, Alex headed home and packed a modest bag with some basic clothes and on impulse, his favorite book, *The Adventures of Sherlock Holmes*. In a rush he started to write a small note to his father. Alex found it hard to refer to Gordon as "Mr Macpherson," but decided to be formal for his father's sake.

Dear Father,

I have been ordered by Mr Macpherson to leave Ballindalloch within the hour.

The reasons why shall unfold over the next few days, but Father, we will know these reasons hold no bearing.

I have been given a ship's passage to America.

I promise to write and explain what happened. I do hope your strength and faith will be enough to help you through this difficult time.

I shall let you know my whereabouts as soon as possible.

Your faithful son,

Alex

He was aware of the little time he had, as it would take him a full day at least to get to Glasgow.

"Gordon, you fox," Alex muttered to himself as he started to realize more and more how the laird had carefully planned all of this beforehand. He had waited for the day that the afternoon train from Ballindalloch to Grantown was running. Carrying his travel bag, Alex quickly went past the castle's kitchen quarters. He found Mrs Craddock, a rather plump, pleasantly wrinkled woman with thick grey hair tied in a haphazard bun, preparing some food. The normalcy of what she was doing struck Alex as out of place, as his own situation was momentarily so surreal.

"Have you seen Miss Katherine, Mrs Craddock?" Alex asked the woman, who he knew had always thought well of him.

"I'm afraid not, Alex," she said, in her melodious tone. "I'm told Miss Katherine was to go away for a few days to Edinburgh, but do not know exactly where. Maybe she's visiting relatives or friends. Is everything alright lad?"

Alex let out a deep sigh and shook his head, feeling his heart sink. Gordon had obviously thought of everything, right down to the finest details. For a moment Alex contemplated leaving a note in Katie's room. Turning around on his heels, he sped towards the main hall only to find Gordon had predicted his actions. Leaning casually against one of the wooden panels of the main staircase leading to the bedrooms, Gordon had obviously been waiting for Alexander.

"Going to Katherine's room now, are we? Up to find some more family treasures?" Gordon inquired with a forced smile, betraying himself by nervously taking a few steps back.

Alex could have attacked Gordon there and then. Instead, despair rose from his throat. He uttered a loud cry and ran out of the house as if being chased by the devil himself.

CHAPTER 17

Thursday 4 August 2011, 11:55 pm, Ballindalloch Castle, Banffshire, Scotland

Angus tossed and turned in his sleep. His blankets had fallen to the floor and his round belly was peeking from under his pajama jacket as his body lay curled up, trying to contain its warmth. Beneath his eyelids, his eyes moved rapidly from side to side. His breath was shallow and quick. Although his consciousness was in another dimension, his physical body was producing all sorts of danger signals. His muscles were tense and muffled sounds were coming from his throat.

Suddenly he cried out loud and bolted upright with his eyes wide open. With difficulty he tore himself away from his dream, looking around as if afraid that whatever it was that had hunted him down in the nightmare, had followed him into the present space. That was exactly the case, he realized, as he fell back onto the pillows with a big sigh.

Both in his dreams and in real life, the ghost of Gordon Macpherson was chasing him with personal malice. Lately, it had evolved into a recurring dream. He would be running outside the castle on the gravel path leading to the main door, to find that he had forgotten to put his shoes on and could only run slowly as some enormous force of gravity pulled him down.

His feet were bleeding as the jagged little stones pierced the skin of the soles of his feet. Alarmed, he knew he had to run away from Gordon.

There was always a sense of urgency in his dreams. Angus knew that Gordon needed to complete something, like finding the last piece in a puzzle. The terror and panic would reach a crescendo ending in darkness when Angus inevitably fell in a black pit and woke up with the shock of hitting the bottom. He could literally feel his physical body slam back against the mattress of his bed.

His heart still pounding, Angus bent over the side of his bed to retrieve his blankets. He pulled them back up and rearranged them in a makeshift way. Feeling restless, he got up and walked to the small rosewood cabinet at the other end of his bedroom, opened the paneled glass door, and took out a decanter of whisky. He poured himself a stiff measure and drank it in one gulp, grateful for the hot burning sensation of forty per cent alcohol sliding down his throat.

When will this stop? What does he want from me? Angus wondered. He could still feel the presence of Gordon around him. Suddenly furious and desperate, he flung his empty crystal glass against the wall, shattering it into pieces. With angry strides, he walked over to his bed and tore the bed sheets off. Wrapping them around himself like a cloak, he plunged into the padded chair behind his desk.

Maybe here, away from the bed, Gordon would leave him alone, Angus prayed.

CHAPTER 18

Cathy woke with a start. The bedroom was in total darkness, with the drawn heavy velvet curtains blocking the morning light. With her biorhythm still confused by the six-hour time difference, it took her a few seconds to work out where she was. She didn't have a clue what time it was either. Her watch lay next to her bed on the night table and told her it was 2 am, but she realized she had forgotten to adjust it.

"Two in the morning is exactly what it *feels* like," she muttered to herself, while a big yawn tried to capture fresh energy into her body.

From outside, the noise of a car engine being started and voices raised in argument trickled into her awareness. Reluctantly, with feline movements, Cathy took her time to stretch, folded her hands behind her head, and reflected on yesterday's events.

It was an unusual feeling to realize she had just slept her first night in Scotland, as it actually felt like she'd been here for much longer. Not having heard from David yet didn't seem to be that important anymore. Despite all the conflicting impressions of yesterday, she was beginning to feel quite comfortable with the Macphersons and Scotland. In particular, Uncle Thomas and John had caught her fancy, though for two entirely different reasons.

CHAPTER 19

Friday 5 August 2011, 9:25 am, Ballindalloch Castle, Banffshire, Scotland

Dressed in casual clothes and sturdy walking boots, her camera dangling on a strap around her neck, Cathy walked out the main door of the castle, welcomed by a delightful summer morning. Old Billy was polishing the brass panels of the doors. When she wished him a good morning, she received a nod of his head in return.

Does he ever sleep? she wondered.

Angus stood in the driveway smoking a cigarette, talking to a young man in his late twenties. She walked over to join them.

"It's a fine morning, Catherine," Angus greeted her. "Let me introduce you to Hamish, our piper, who will welcome the guests that are staying at the castle. We were just discussing what music he should play. Hamish, this is our American cousin, Catherine."

"Good morning, very pleased to meet you Hamish," Cathy said, shaking his hand. He was a tall muscular man with wiry black hair and a fine bold face.

"I missed you at breakfast, it's gone nine." Angus said.

"I rarely have breakfast, Angus, only coffee. And I assume I can still have that, even if it's after nine?"

"Are you making fun of me, Catherine?" Angus said, almost flirtatiously. "Ask Billy about your coffee and he will see to it. I'll catch you later. Maybe you could give me some ideas what to include in your husband's travel guide."

Without commenting on David's assignment, which Angus seemed eager to discuss, she wandered back towards the castle and glanced at her cell phone in hope. She might as well have looked at her shoes; still no signal.

Billy brought her coffee in the library. "Mr John will be here directly to see you. I hope the coffee is strong enough," he muttered and limped back towards the hall.

She sat down on a brown leather chair beside a large, round, dark-wood table. The coffee was in a delicate china cup, white, with a rose pattern around the rim and a matching saucer. She tasted it. It was putrid. Just as she was pouring it into a potted plant beside her chair, John walked in and caught her in the act.

"I take it the coffee was a hit then," he joked, the steam still rising from the plant pot.

She chuckled and said, "I'm sorry, but I think the plant will enjoy it more than I will." Her eyebrows arched as John caught her off guard, when he bent over to give her a morning hug.

"It's a lovely morning for a walk," John said, quickly covering up the moment of unexpected familiarity.

They strolled outside, past the public tearoom, and into a long tunnel of ivy that stretched for almost one hundred yards. Emerging from the other side, the sun enveloped them in sudden resplendent light. The sky was blue with just a few puffy white wandering clouds.

"Wow, the castle and the lands look awesome in the daylight," she exclaimed. A feeling of longing overcame her, a yearning to explore the surrounding lands as the countryside seemed to beckon her. She was genuinely impressed with Ballindalloch. Everything about the place was impeccable and she could easily understand why it attracted so many visitors.

"Tell me some more about the family and the castle, John."

"That's over four hundred and fifty years of history to cover, where would you like me to start?"

While they walked through the gardens closest to the castle, John began to talk about Ballindalloch originally being a fortalice. However, in 1845, the building had been enlarged in the castellated style it still retained. John diverted the conversation to what she thought about Ballindalloch and how different it must be from her normal surroundings.

"That's true," Cathy said, "but it also feels sort of familiar. I have to admit I never expected that to happen." They approached a huge walled-garden. John opened a squeaky black wrought-iron gate.

"Wow, this is something else," Cathy cried out. It made her stand still just taking in the view, deciding where to go first, with John patiently observing the effect it had on her.

When she started to walk, John made sure to stay two or three steps behind her, to give her a chance to absorb it all in her own time and space. An array of colors and fragrance of the flowers were bursting all around her. Lilies, Dahlias, Rhododendrons, Begonia and Petunia blossomed. An abundance of shrubs were lined in rows with great precision some gripping the perimeter of the walls, still shining with the morning dew. A superb rock garden with tumbling spring water caught Cathy's attention and she gasped in awe.

"These gardens are so incredibly well kept," she said, turning to face John.

"Fantastic, is it not? The rock garden was laid in 1937 by the fifth baronet."

Cathy smiled, not asking who the fifth baronet was. She savored the haven of aromas and colors. Out of the corner of her eye, she observed John. He was wearing washed-out jeans, a dark blue sweater, a brown suede jacket, and boots that had not seen polish for a while. Cathy thought he looked better in casual clothes than in the formal clothes he was wearing the day before.

She was a bit taken aback by a small pang of guilt that shot through her when John said, "It's a pity your husband is not here, Catherine, to enjoy it with you. Do you have children, if I may ask? "

"No kids. Too busy working, I guess. Are you married, John?" she shot back at him. "Too busy working, I guess," he imitated, smiling. "Both my brothers are hitched and have kids, but I think I will stick to being an uncle for now. What do you do that keeps you so busy?"

"I'm a cop," she said.

"Police? Wow. What kind of cop are you?"

"I'm a homicide detective, have been for a few years."

She started walking towards the rear wall of the garden just ahead of him now snapping shots with her *Kodak*.

John quickly caught up.

"It must be exciting and quite a dangerous job."

Ignoring his comment, she asked, "What do you do for a living? Do you live here?"

"Oh my God, no, I'm only here till Monday. I was born and raised here and will eventually move to Ballindalloch when I become laird. But right now I work and live in the capital."

"London?" she asked.

John smiled patiently, "Of Scotland. Edinburgh. I have an apartment in the south-west of the city. An area called Morningside."

Cathy liked John's accent. She recognized his Scottish lilt. He was obviously a well-educated man.

"So what do you do there?" she pursued.

"I'm in financial investments. I work for RBS. Quite boring, compared to you, eh?"

"RBS?"

"Royal Bank of Scotland. Our headquarters is in Edinburgh."

"I've heard Edinburgh is a beautiful city," she remarked. "What about Maggie and Euphemia, do they live here?"

"No, they're all here for the clan gathering. Only my father and Uncle Thomas live here, along with some of the staff."

She faced the handsome Scotsman, the morning sun dazzling her. Over John's right shoulder, a gorgeous bed of red roses about twenty yards further on caught her attention.

"John, those are beautiful," she said, pointing at them.

"I suppose they are. They're called Ballindalloch Roses."

"I've always loved roses, though I'm not much of a gardener myself."

"Me neither," John admitted. They made their way towards the center of the garden. A plaque commemorated how the walled garden was redesigned in 1996. That seemed almost unbelievable to Cathy as the garden, like the rest of the castle grounds, looked as if they would have been the same for hundreds of years.

Secluded from everyone else at the castle within the confines of the walls, she felt as if she had stepped back in time. With a wistful sigh, she sat down on an old wooden bench.

CHAPTER 20

Saturday 2 November 1895 Ballindalloch, Banffshire, Scotland

Nervously walking the narrow country tracks, Alex opened the envelope Gordon had given him. Inside were two train tickets, one from Ballindalloch to Grantown-on-Spey and a connection to Perth. The other ticket was for Perth to Glasgow and a ships passage from Glasgow to New York on the SS State of Nebraska. There was a pre-paid *Allan & State Line* Certificate of Passage dated 28 October. Alex didn't recognize the signature of the payee who had paid the total of seventy five dollars. He found dollars in bills of ones, fives, and tens. A quick count told him it amounted to two hundred dollars. He wondered how much that would be in pounds. A note gave the name of a coachman who would meet Alex at Glasgow Central Station to take him to the port.

America! The bastard actually meant it. America! Alex hardly had time to let the horrendous reality sink in. He couldn't leave, it was impossible, not after what had happened between he and Katherine; even if he wasn't sure of how to envision a future with her.

Tears welled up in his eyes. *Katie what have we done. We've ruined any chance we ever had.* Panic overtook Alex's rational thinking. Confused he tried to make sense of his options. On the one hand this was what he had dreamt of; to explore the world outside Ballindalloch. But now to leave all he loved made him feel as if he couldn't breathe, with his new life stretching out before him like a daunting prospect.

For a moment, he thought about not meeting the coachman and just hide away somewhere in Glasgow, find a place to sleep, and a job. Staring at the tickets, his inner conflict grew to enormous proportions. He loved Katherine, loved his father and his life at Ballindalloch, but his dreams were beckoning; a spectrum of possibilities. America could well meet the expectations of these ambitions.

What would be his future if he stayed in Glasgow or Ballindalloch? There would always be rumors, people whispering behind his back. Saying how he'd had the fortunate fate to be raised among the rich and then had taken the bold liberty to try and grasp what was not his to take. And he would be at risk of Gordon hunting him down, should he ever find out Alex didn't leave Scotland.

Going back to Ballindalloch was no option. Even if he could prove his innocence on the theft, there was still the matter of his relationship with Katherine. As a couple, they would never be accepted, not by the Macphersons or by the good people in the county. Even if he exposed Gordon as a liar he would be held responsible for blemishing the Macpherson name. No matter what, Alex could never win and the consequences for everybody involved would be horrendous. Anyway, Gordon was probably right. The authorities would always take the word of someone with obvious wealth and position over that of a labor class man; that was the way the world turned. If he went back, three years of imprisonment at Craiginches could easily await him. What good would that do Katie and his father?

Gradually, Alexander was coming round to test the destiny fate had tossed his way.

"If only," Alex muttered to himself, "If only Katherine could be here with me now."

Making his way to the station, using the Church Walk as a shortcut he reached the ancient stone circle at Lagmore, and sat down on a fallen stone to assemble his chaotic feelings.

The sky was heavy and grey. He could feel the first drops of rain on his head. It made him think of Katherine and how they had sheltered from a storm only a few days before.

Uttering a deep sigh, he strained to lift himself from the stone and looked up into the sky. *Dear Lord, give me a sign*, he thought, *what am I to do?* It was as if a voice in his head gave the answer. He promised himself he would go to America. With his right hand leaning against one of the ancient stones of the circle, he swore he would return to Ballindalloch in due time.

His father would keep him informed and bring Gordon to reason, Alex was sure of that. For now, it would be best to do what the laird wanted.

With some good fortune he'd be back within half a year. He pulled his collar up high against the increasing rain and with a heavy heart continued downhill towards Ballindalloch Train Station.

CHAPTER 21

Friday 5 August 2011, 11.00 am, Ballindalloch Castle, Banffshire, Scotland

"Catherine, I think you are here for a reason," John said, hushed, looking all around him as if he suspected someone was eavesdropping. He sat down next to Cathy on the bench in the walled garden.

"For a reason. What do you mean?" she asked, clipped. In the distance, a piper started to play, the sound carrying easily into the gardens.

"That's Hamish the piper," he said, looking in the direction of the castle. Some guests must be arriving."

"Let's cut to the chase here, John," she said, holding him with her gaze. "Tell me what you mean by saying that I'm here for a reason."

He looked at her for a fleeting moment and hesitated, sharpening her curiosity. "I don't know, Catherine, it's just a feeling I have," he answered, staring ahead of him.

"Does it have to do with Gordon Macpherson?" she asked.

"What makes you say that?"

"Well, it seems to be the only subject you guys talk about around here. Maybe you should call Ghostbusters."

"You shouldn't make fun of this, Catherine! It's not like we have a floating white sheet with eye holes chasing us, you know! The spirit of Gordon Macpherson *does* haunt the castle, and torments my family, and honestly it makes my father ill with worry."

John stood up from the bench and paced up and down in front of her, making large gestures with his hands as he spoke. "Cathy, you've already witnessed how things that happened over a hundred years ago still affect our family to this day. I mean, think about what was said over dinner last night."

She was pleased that John had stopped calling her Catherine, but at the same time sighed at having to listen to ghost stories. *Jeez, spooks in a Scottish castle.*

"John, I am sure your father only wants me here to make sure my husband writes great things about Ballindalloch in his travel guide, but," Cathy said, slipping into police mode, "I've already decided to do some more legwork on the Gordon story. I'm a police woman. I love what I do. I've been reading *Sherlock Holmes* since I was in diapers."

He smiled at her response, but was clearly waiting for more.

"So," Cathy said, "Let's see what we've got here, Dr. Watson... We have a Gordon Macpherson who drowned in the Spey while fishing or a Gordon that was murdered. Either way, his body was never found."

"Oh, I don't think he drowned," John said, confirming what Cathy had already thought, "The laird would know his fishing grounds like the back of his hand. Based on what I've heard over the years, the only person with the slightest motive to harm Gordon would have been an Alexander Stewart. He fled to the USA that same year."

Deciding to keep quiet about her husband's connection to this Alexander Stewart, Cathy continued her line of questioning.

"So where would he leave from to get to the US?" she asked, producing the notebook she always carried with her.

"He must have sailed from Glasgow." As an afterthought, he added, "By the way, Glasgow is on the central west coast."

"And how would he get the tickets? I mean, you couldn't just buy a one-way ticket, Ballindalloch to the States, that easily in those days, right? So how would he have gotten to Glasgow from here?"

"He would have traveled by train, from the local station."

"Local?" she asked.

"Yes, Ballindalloch Station. But it closed down years ago, long before I was born. It's beside Cragganmore Distillery."

"Okay, no time like the present. Let's go, we have to start somewhere," she said moving towards the garden gate.

John, walking after her, trying to catch up, said, "It's closed, Cathy. The station is no longer in use."

"How far is the station from here? Is it walking distance?" she asked, ignoring his remark.

"We could walk, but I prefer to take the car. I want to do some shopping at the distillery anyway."

When they drove out of the main gate of Ballindalloch Castle, Cathy again noticed how familiar the surroundings seemed to her, as if she'd been here so much longer than twenty four hours. She was not born with a naturally gifted sense of direction, but intuitively could recognize where she had been or sense where to go. Even driving on the left side of the road didn't seem out of place anymore.

John drove his Ford Focus through the winding country roads. After only a few minutes, he took a sharp right, down a steep narrow hill into a valley. A few houses lining the road to their left marked the beginning of what looked like a small settlement, just before they passed a brightly painted red and white building on their right. The road leveled out and, a little further on, two old Victorian barracks appeared; one carrying the name Cragganmore, the other Ballindalloch.

"Let's get some refreshment first," John said smiling, and turned into a parking lot in the middle of some clean, white-plastered factory-like barns. An old iron gate wedged about ten feet high between two of the buildings carried the sign, *Cragganmore.*

"Stay here, I'll be back in a moment," he said, climbing out of the car.

"I'm coming too," she replied, "In case I need to book you for drinking and driving."

As she got out of the car, she noticed the sky was darkening. "The weather sure changes quickly here in the Highlands," she remarked, and ran into the distillery shop to shelter from the first heavy drops of rain.

The reception area displayed all sorts of whisky products. She sniffed the yeasty smell coming from the distillery. A tall gregarious man wearing a baseball cap bearing the name of the distillery greeted them. She noticed a round plastic nametag pinned on his brown shirt that read, "Brian".

"This is our cousin Catherine from the United States," John said, introducing Cathy, who felt slightly stirred by the blunt approving look the man gave her.

"Pleased to meet you. You'll be here for the Newtonmore booze-up then? You must have a lot of Scottish blood in you to come all the way from the States."

She only smiled, deciding it was not worth the effort to explain why she was in Scotland.

Tapping his badge with her forefinger, she said, "Pleased to meet you, Brian."

"Would you like to sample a whisky, Catherine?" Brian offered, making a wide gesture with his arm, indicating the large collection of attractive bottles and boxes behind him. "Let's call it a welcome drink."

"No thanks, a wee bit early for me," Cathy joked, imitating the Scottish accent, "and *he* is driving," she added, pointing to John.

Apparently John was a regular client, as without even exchanging a word, he was given a bottle. Cathy was first to leave the shop but still caught Brian whispering to John, "I love American women, they are so confident."

She smiled to herself and without turning said, "Come on, John, let's go. We have work to do."

John looked at her walking ahead of him and agreed with Brian. She had a determined way of walking and a great shape, he thought, running his eyes over her rear. "Looks like we're going to have a heavy one," he said, looking up into the grey murky sky. "We'd better hurry if you want to take a look at the old station."

CHAPTER 22

Saturday 2 November 1895 Ballindalloch Train Station, Banffshire, Scotland

Alexander was now taking long strides as he made his way from Lagmore, downhill towards the train station. He could smell the yeasty aroma coming from the nearby distillery. Slightly out of breath, he crossed the track and climbed onto the platform. Only a few other people were waiting. His cold fingers reluctantly plucked the train ticket out of the envelope Gordon had given him. He showed it to the stationmaster who stood waiting, a short chubby man wearing a dark blue uniform and a peaked hat.

"Are you going to Perth, son, a wee holiday at this time of year?" he asked, returning the ticket to Alex.

"Aye, that's right," Alex answered solemnly.

The stationmaster rubbed his head, pushing his hat to the back and gave him a wry smile, wondering what was wrong with the lad.

Alexander was chilled by the cold air. On his way from Lagmore he'd seen some of the hills in the distance were already capped with snow.

The sound of the approaching train almost made him jump. The rain started to fall like big icy tears from the sky, while the large red engine appeared in front of the platform pulling two wooden-framed passenger carriages and a guard wagon at the rear. The steam whistle blasted, smoke belching from its chimney. The smell of burning coal mixing with the rain, surrounded Alex like a cloak. The train let out another hiss and stopped abruptly, causing the wheels to squeal. Reluctantly, he entered the second passenger wagon. The stationmaster slammed the doors shut with a loud thud, leaving Alexander staring through the window.

He felt as if he was about to be transported to the gallows.

CHAPTER 23

Friday 5 August 2011, 11.45 am, Ballindalloch Train Station, Banffshire, Scotland

"Here, at the back." John beckoned Cathy to the rear of the old station building. She followed him onto what used to be the platform and was immediately captured by the feel of the open land in front of her. The atmosphere was that of an old-fashioned countryside, where nature was still allowed to find its own trails. The meadow stretching out in front of her carried bushes and trees and was not cultivated in any way. Some sheep were grazing on the grass and an old iron railway bridge could be seen in the distance.

The red wall of the building facing the landscape gave the name, BALLINDALLOCH, in large white letters. Even though the station was no longer used by the railroads, the station house was well maintained and recently painted. Only the old platform, now completely covered in grass and moss, betrayed the absence of activity.

Cathy jumped the four-foot drop from the platform onto where the track used to be. The rails had been taken away, but the line of the track was still visible. Birch trees, at least forty years old she guessed, were now covering the track where trains once had stopped. The whole scene mesmerized her.

"If you ignored the trees and the moss covering the platform," she said to John, "you could see exactly what it looked like on the day Alexander Stewart boarded the train for Glasgow."

"I think the train would have gone to Grantown and then on to, I don't know where, Perth maybe, and then to Glasgow," he replied. "It's starting to rain, Cathy. I think we'd better go now, before we get soaked."

For some reason, she was not ready to leave the old station, even though the rain was falling heavily now. She took the green rain cape she had bought during the excursion to Ellis Island out of her pocket, unfolded it and pulled it over her head.

John laughed as he took shelter against the wall of the station house. "You look a bit out of place," he said referring to the tourist slogan written across the back of the cape, "Ellis Island, Statue of Liberty".

"I'd say it's quite appropriate. Isn't this where Alexander was heading? Maybe he could have used it," Cathy said and then laughed.

John liked her smile more than her usually stern expression. It made her look more relaxed and approachable.

Taking one more look around her she asked, "I take it there wasn't an hourly train connection to Grantown from here?"

Smirking, John replied, "Once a week is more likely."

"So, how long would it take someone to get from Ballindalloch to Glasgow?"

"Let me think," he said. "Grantown-on-Spey to, say, Perth would take at least three hours by train in those days. Then, depending on how long he would need to wait for a connection to Glasgow, at least another four to five hours."

She climbed back onto the platform and checked the door of the station house to find it was locked. Shielding her eyes with her hand she peered through a dusty window. The empty rooms revealed nothing.

"Is the Stewart guy in there?" John jested.

Ignoring his remark, she turned to face the landscape again. "Which way would the castle be by foot from here?" she asked. A sign post holding a trail map between two wooden poles stood next to what used to be the train track. "Speyside Walk," Cathy said, reading the sign. "Is that how Alexander would have gotten here? Would that lead us back to the castle?"

"Yes," he said, "The castle isn't that far past the stone circle at Lagmore[9]."

"Stone circle? You have your own Stonehenge here?" she asked in surprise.

"Well, I wouldn't compare it to Stonehenge, but I believe it does date back to the same time and according to local myth it holds mysterious powers."

"Could I see it?"

"Whatever you say, officer." He chuckled. "Either way, I'll be glad to get into the car."

CHAPTER 24

Friday 5 August 2011, 12:15 pm, Lagmore Stone Circle, Ballindalloch

The rain was getting heavier and the windshield wipers screeched their way side to side as John and Cathy drove to Lagmore.

"So, do you have a girlfriend in Morningside?" Cathy asked nonchalantly without looking at John.

Such was the noise of the rain battering on the car, John had to raise his voice to answer. "Yes. I asked her to join me here this weekend, but she declined. To be honest, I don't blame her. Ghislaine is a Parisian, working at Edinburgh University."

"That's nice," Cathy muttered. *Lucky Ghislaine,* she mouthed, looking away from John.

"The area around here has a few relics apart from old Uncle Thomas," John chuckled, changing the subject. "The stone circle we're going to is around five thousand years old. And our church, Inveravon, which is also close to the castle, has four Pictish stones in one of its walls going back to the eighth or ninth century."

He pulled the car over in a shoulder parking. In typical Highland fashion, the heavy rain had changed to light drizzle by the time they got out of the car.

"Where are we? Where are the stones?" Cathy asked.

"Up there," he said pointing up the grassy hill to their left.

Without missing a beat, she climbed over the small old grey stone wall separating the hill and the parking spot. "Come on, John," she shouted.

It was a tough walk uphill as the grass was wet and muddy. The stones came into view ten minutes later. Walking slowly, they were now on the brow of the hill and the land flattened out. The landscape was bleak and she could hear the sound of a river in the distance as she walked toward the stones. There were five in total, grey stones with pointed heads, about seven feet high, three feet wide and a foot thick, forming what was clearly a circle. The stone furthest from her had fallen on its side.

She walked through the center of the circle and sat down on the fallen stone. Pulling the hood of the rain cape over her hair, she allowed the tranquility of the circle to slow down her thoughts. Utter silence, so still and quiet it felt heavy. No sound of birds, of whispering wind or rustling of leaves, nothing. She could see John standing at the outside of the circle looking in and yet she felt entirely alone.

I'll go to America, but I will be back, a voice sounded in her head. She didn't know where these thoughts came from, but she could hear them clearly in her mind. Hands under her chin, elbows resting on her knees, she was snapped out of her thoughts by John.

"Are you all right, Cathy? Can we go now?"

She looked up at a rather disheveled John and asked, "Alexander Stewart, did he ever come back to Ballindalloch?"

Perplexed, he replied, "I don't think so. Why do you ask?" He held out his hand to her, gesturing they should go.

"Oh, just a thought. Never mind, let's head back home."

Without noticing John's smile at her use of the word, "home", she headed back towards the car.

CHAPTER 25

Saturday 2 November 1895, Ballindalloch Castle, Banffshire, Scotland

The final blow to the relationship between Katherine and her father came when she returned from a short visit to Edinburgh.

Over dinner, in front of the family, her father announced the sudden departure of Alexander Stewart, after he had denied him Katherine's hand in marriage. Out of revenge, Gordon disclosed, Alexander Stewart stole some Macpherson family jewelry to fund a new life elsewhere and fled Ballindalloch.

Katherine simply knew that this was all damned lies and sensed all too well it was her father's way of getting rid of what he believed was a huge problem. It was at that moment she completely closed her heart towards him. A cold feeling gripped her by the throat when her father openly destroyed the last remaining bit of trust she could ever have in him. For a few moments, total silence fell over the dining room. Then, abruptly, Katherine stood up, knocking her chair over.

"You're lying and everyone here knows it!" she cried out, gesturing at all around the table. "Curse you, Father, curse you," she rasped, and ran out of the room in distress, leaving an ashen-faced Gordon behind.

The news that Alexander had gone also destroyed the last remaining affiliation between her brothers. James, Gordon's second-oldest son, had always felt sympathetic towards the Stewart lad and sided with his sister. He knew they were no marriage plans and was angry at the extremely harsh and unforgiving way his father dealt with the situation. He was sure his mother would not have agreed to Gordon's actions, had she still been there. James found it repugnant that his father would do something so degrading to bend fate his way.

The oldest brother, John, however supported his father, accepting that Alexander could no longer live at Ballindalloch. It wasn't clear if John was willing to believe Stewart had in fact stolen the jewelry out of revenge. What was important to John was that his sister and Alexander couldn't be together and that their father's decision had been correct. As the eldest son, his duty was to implore his brothers to respect their father's judgment.

Back in her bedroom, Katherine fumed as she strutted around with her fists clenched. Her rage was so great, the tears wouldn't come. Deep down, she could see how Alex had been forced away beyond his control. What she could not accept is that he would have left without as much as a single word. The least he could have done was leave her a letter.

It did make what had transpired over the past few days in Edinburgh more acceptable. With the help of a friend she had been granted a placement for the 1896 term, as one of the first women at the University.

She was very ready to leave Ballindalloch.

CHAPTER 26

Friday 5 August 2011, 1:00 pm, Ballindalloch Castle, Banffshire, Scotland

The grinding sound of wheels on gravel stones announced the arrival of John's car at the private entrance of the castle. Cathy noticed Wayne Stewart and his wife outside the main entrance, talking to some people who had apparently just arrived. Christie was busy unloading luggage from the trunk of his car.

"Thanks for showing me around, John, especially the stones. It really helped," Cathy said.

"Really?"

"Let's catch up later," she suggested, leaned over, and gave him a gentle kiss on his cheek.

She climbed out the car and started to walk towards the group standing outside the castle. As she got closer, she could clearly hear Wayne Stewart's voice. She smiled and thought, *American, no doubt about that, and East Coast for sure.* She watched him walk inside the castle together with the others that had just arrived. His wife spotted Cathy and walked over to her.

"Hi, I'm Eleanor Stewart," she said warmly, clasping Cathy's hand in hers. "You must be Catherine Stewart, or should I say Macpherson? Angus told us you were here."

Eleanor was a tall, slim, very attractive woman in her early fifties, clutching a red envelope-style Mulberry handbag under her arm.

"I'm Wayne's wife – or actually, he's my current husband," Eleanor joked.

"I'm currently married to a Stewart as well," Cathy responded, laughing.

"Wayne mentioned he was in contact with your husband by email. I guess that makes them cousins, of a sort." Eleanor laughed. "You must be intrigued by Wayne, wearing his kilt, many people are."

"Yeah, that's something you don't see every day. Fortunately, I got a crash course in the Macpherson-Stewart connection from Maggie during dinner last night. I was told that Alexander Stewart adopted a son, who I take it is the connection to your Wayne?"

"That's right, they fostered Michael and gave him the Stewart name," confirmed Eleanor.

"Listen to me," Cathy said, "I am getting as obsessed as my husband with genealogy."

"Is your husband here?"

"David will be here on Sunday."

"The two Stewarts will have a lot to discuss," Eleanor said, winking at Cathy. "It's a shame your husband's missing the games on Saturday. We were there before. It is really entertaining, you'll enjoy it. Mind you, I've heard the weather forecast for tomorrow isn't good. They're expecting a lot of rain."

"So how did Wayne find out about Ballindalloch?" Cathy enquired.

"He came here a few years ago to see where the man who changed his family's fortunes was born."

"Yes, but what led him to Ballindalloch in the first place?" Cathy pursued.

"Oh, he has some old letters that mentioned Ballindalloch."

The sound of the piper playing drowned out their conversation. Old Billy came hobbling out of the front door. Cathy expected him to collect the luggage of the new arrivals, but instead he approached the Stewart wives.

"There's a call for you, Mrs Stewart. You can take it in the study."

"Okay," they said simultaneously. Looking at each other, Cathy and Eleanor started to giggle, exchanging a spark of affection, leaving Billy feeling uncomfortable.

"It's your husband, I believe," he said, directing his gaze at Cathy.

Thanking Billy, Cathy excused herself from Eleanor and walked briskly into the castle. Finally, David had decided to call her!

The study door was open and Cathy walked inside, closed the door, and picked up the receiver that was lying on its side on top of an old oak writing desk.

"David, you took your time calling."

"Sorry, hun. I tried your cell a few times, but I kept getting a message that the number wasn't available. Is everything going well? How do you like Scotland? Are the Macphersons looking after you?" he asked, his questions rolling over each other.

"You know what," Cathy responded, "I don't even know where you are, David. Where are you?"

"I'm in Glasgow right now. I'll be heading up north tomorrow and will arrive quite late on Saturday night."

"Does that mean you'll be at the castle on Saturday?"

"No, I'll be in Grantown-on-Spey, that's about thirteen miles from where you are. I booked a hotel in Grantown as I don't exactly know what time I'll be there and didn't want to arrive late at the castle. I figured it was better to make my way over there on Sunday morning. Is everything okay Cat? Are you having some good downtime?"

She chuckled and said, "Like you, David, I'm quite busy, but you know what, I'll tell you all about it when you get here."

"I hope the guys from the PD aren't calling you, are they? They shouldn't, you're on vacation!"

"It's okay, David. I'll see you on Sunday, you take care," she said, and put the phone down.

David, back in Glasgow, stared at his iPhone, confused. *Why can't she just say no to these guys? Hicks should be covering for her.* He was wise enough not to call her back.

CHAPTER 27

Tuesday 5 November 1895, SS State of Nebraska, Atlantic Ocean

Alex sat brooding on the second-class port deck of the SS State of Nebraska. The cool sea breeze was blowing into his face, making his eyes water as he watched the ocean swell, clean and free of chop.

This was the third day of his estimated eight-day journey to New York. He had boarded the steamship in Glasgow on Sunday. Later that day, they'd docked at Molville in the northwest of Ireland, where many other passengers had boarded.

With bitter feelings, Alex mulled over the final confrontation with Gordon Macpherson. Staring out over the ocean, Alex now had to face the harsh truth of it all, but still could not find anything to justify what happened. How could the man on whose grounds he had lived for so many years have been so cold and calculating? What could have possessed him?

Alex thought about the loyal service his parents and his grandparents before them had shown the Ballindalloch family. He thought about his father giving all those years as gamekeeper – *my God! How he must feel now, my poor father.* Alex could understand that Gordon would want the best for his only daughter, but these were changing times, with the division between classes narrowing. Alex knew that the discussion in the study was only acted out by Gordon as if he was participating in some stage play, obviously abiding old values and beliefs.

Choking on his tears, his eyes filling up, and his throat starting to hurt again, Alex leaned over the port bow of the ship, feeling hot, dizzy, and miserable. He had been violently ill with nausea and felt his stomach heave again, but there was not much left to feed the fish. He had never been on a steamship or any vessel for that matter until now, and swore that next time he'd swim.

His back against the ship's rail, too exhausted to attempt to walk back to his cabin, he looked around the deck. The SS State of Nebraska was an old creaking ship and the crew worked extremely hard, he'd noticed, to maintain a level of acceptable standards. Alex shuddered to think what the conditions were like for the steerage passengers below. He'd heard the ship was carrying over one thousand passengers and crew.

On his first day aboard, Alex had learned the ship was sailing on her penultimate voyage. Sarcastically, he had wondered if Gordon had known that when he planned the passage, maybe hoping for Alexander to perish at sea.

His attention was drawn to a silhouette against the skyline on the first class deck above him. He distinguished a smartly clad man about the same age as him, his red hair towering up from the wind like dancing flames. Alex felt the hairs on his neck rise. The man was clearly watching him. *He must have seen me being sick,* Alex thought, deeply ashamed. With a curt movement he pushed his body away from the rail and walked quickly out of sight. He was embarrassed that someone from obviously good stock had seen him in such a degraded state. *I must have looked like a peasant to him,* he thought, looking down at the clothes he was wearing: his dark green woolen suit was stained, the normally shining brass buttons now dull; his white shirt seemed grey; and his brown shoes were scuffed. He dragged himself to his cabin and took off the clothes that now felt like rags, leaving only his undergarments.

During the night, lying in bed, he sweated and the dry sickness continued. His deteriorating physical condition made him apprehensive about his future, going into unknown territory, with little money and no friends or family.

When Alex opened his eyes the next morning, after a deep sleep, his stomach ache felt somewhat better. His throat, however, was still as dry as dust and his damp undershirt clung to his body as he climbed out of his bunk. He had no choice but to put on the same clothes from the evening before.

When he emerged on deck, he gratefully inhaled the morning air, a welcome change to the stale smell of the cabin. Alex reckoned it must be around nine o'clock in the morning. Mist surrounded the vessel and parts of the ship seemed to fade away in the haze. He peered over the rail of the ship. The dark waters looked mysterious and threatening.

From a tall white china container just beside the second class lounge, he drank some water, rinsed his mouth, and spat the water over the side. He hoped he could manage some breakfast later. He had eaten very little of the four meals offered each day by the crew. Judging from the loose fit of his trousers dangling on their suspenders, he must have lost some weight over the past three days.

Walking back to the lounge, he noticed a lady sitting on the edge of a deck chair. She was crying softly. He recognized her at once and recalled the conversation with her and her husband the previous day. They were a young Scottish couple from Airdrie in Lanarkshire who had introduced themselves as Mr and Mrs Gibson.

Mrs Gibson had mentioned her husband had been ill, but had not elaborated on his ailment. She had, in fact, emphasized how excited they were about starting a new life with her cousin's family in Boston and how she hoped it would help her husband recover. Based on letters from her cousin, she'd vividly described Boston to Alex. It was said to be smaller than New York, but equally vibrant, and offered many opportunities for work. She also told Alex it was apparently a very cultured city with excellent theatres. Many writers had in fact made Boston their home.

It was the first time since the start of his journey Alex had heard something inspirational. To discover Boston attracted writers made him wonder if perhaps it would be a good place for him to settle. When asked what were *his* reasons for leaving Scotland Alex spun a yarn about the sudden death of the lady of the house he used to work for, how he needed new employment, and had been given a contact in New York. The couple had been very considerate to Alex, taking pity on his unfortunate happenings and had given him their address in Boston, in case he ever needed help. Mrs Gibson had done most of the talking. Her husband had looked a little nervous, only occasionally smiling and nodding his head.

Wondering what could be the matter today with the friendly Mrs Gibson, Alex approached her hesitantly. He couldn't help but notice her bottle green velvet jacket and long black skirt looked disheveled and her jet-black hair had sprung loose in several places from under her wide brimmed hat.

"Pardon me for intruding, Mrs Gibson, but what is wrong?" he asked.

Clutching her soaked handkerchief, she looked up at him and muttered through her tears, her features distraught with grief, "I am sorry to behave like this, Mr Stewart, but my husband has gone."

She started to sob again and turned her head away. Without looking at him, she volunteered further, "He went for a stroll last night on the deck and never returned. The crew members are looking for him all over the ship, but they said…" With a desperate cry she burst into even more tears.

"Someone cannot simply vanish on a ship, Mrs Gibson," he tried. He gently squeezed her shoulder and slowly walked away, not knowing how to console her, trying to come to terms with what must have happened to Mr Gibson.

He had heard the stories during his first day on the ship of passengers disappearing during voyages. Mostly, these were the sick and vulnerable that feared they would not be allowed through the strict immigration process on Ellis Island and would therefore jeopardize the opportunities of other family members.

The tragic disappearance of Mr Gibson made the journey even more of a trial. The harsh fall weather was testing the ship's endurance, and that of its passengers and crew, as the ocean swell made the ship heave and groan. Sometimes Alex would see Mrs Gibson on deck, but they rarely spoke, as he had no words of comfort to offer. He also chose to have little conversation with anyone else, not knowing who to trust in these unfamiliar circumstances.

The deceit of Gordon Macpherson would take a long time to heal. For now, Alex would rather feel like a recluse in the middle of an ocean with one thousand souls, than to put his trust in anybody or anything.

CHAPTER 28

Tuesday 12 November 1895, Ellis Island, New York, USA

It was early morning when the ship approached New York's Ellis Island. The outside air was crisp and cold. Many passengers were gathering on the deck, their breath forming little clouds as they exhaled their warmth into the morning air.

The large ship had started to turn slowly so her port side was facing the island. Alexander had heard people in the dining room talking about how they dreaded the immigration procedure. Some referred to Ellis Island, as the island of dreams, others as the island of tears.

Even through the early morning mist, he could clearly see the outline of the immigration building with the shoreline behind it. "That'll be New Jersey," an elderly man standing next to Alex volunteered.

The huge buff-colored pine structure with its blue-tinted roof dominated the island. The square building had a picturesque tower on every corner, and from each tower a flag waved at the newcomers. It looked like a giant hotel from years gone by.

Small ferryboats were making their way towards the steamship, blasting their horns as they approached. One of the crew was shouting aloud, informing everyone that they were to disembark onto a ferry, in priority of class. Alexander smiled at the sailor's Glasgow accent.

One hour later, he found himself disembarking, down the gangway onto Ellis Island. He was given a paper identification on a string, displaying his full name and ship details, and was told to wear it around his neck at all times, keeping it fully visible. In his head, he was already writing a letter to Katherine to share his new experiences, just as they'd shared everything at Ballindalloch.

There were folks of all ages, some children crying and others uncomfortably silent. They all seemed to be swaying from side to side as they walked towards the entrance. He had the peculiar feeling of still being on the ship, with a sensation of the earth moving, just like the rhythm of waves underneath his feet. Everyone was directed towards a huge staircase leading them to the next level of the building.

They entered the registry room, a space of about two hundred feet by one hundred feet with an enormous vaulted ceiling. About a dozen narrow aisles divided by iron bars channeled new arrivals towards waiting officers.

Exhausted, and suddenly feeling how thirsty and hungry he was, Alex joined the throng. The memory of standing in that huge line of people, eager for a simple drink of water, would stay with him for the rest of his days. He felt to the core of his being that he was forced to create a new chapter in his life with no help from anyone else. He was totally and utterly on his own for the first time in his life.

He waited for what seemed like forever, the queue moving very slowly. The heat in the vast hall added to everyone's discomfort. The noise of people coughing, talking, and children demanding attention compounded the air of chaos. He was amazed at not only the number of people seeking immigration, but also at the vast variety of luggage. The worldly possessions the immigrants had dragged along were a sight for the observant eye. Chests, crates, cases, carpets, chairs, tables, tools, and belongings simply wrapped up in blankets. It was a surreal sight. Even some young children were dragging belongings that were clearly too big or heavy for them. He looked down at his own modest travel bag. He must look like he was visiting for a few days.

The realization started to stir again that he had no family or friends here – and he had the opportunity to do whatever he wanted. It was at that moment Alexander decided he would make his way to Boston and forget about the New York contact Gordon had given him. If he was going to do it alone, he may as well go all the way. He was excited about his change of plans, because Gordon would not know his whereabouts and Alex would be outside his control.

With a deep sigh, his thoughts went back to his departure from Ballindalloch Train Station, what was it, nine days ago. It seemed like nine weeks.

CHAPTER 29

Friday 5 August 2011, Glasgow, Scotland

Early on Friday morning, David Stewart was on the first flight out of London Heathrow. The Boeing aircraft was packed. He decided to rent a car in Glasgow and drive north to Speyside the following day. According to his calculations, it would be no more than a three-hour drive, and the route would take him past sights of interest such as Stirling and Perth. These two cities housed a lot of interesting attractions from Scotland's history. In fact Perth, known as the gateway to the Highlands, would be an interesting inclusion for his Scottish travel guide.

He spent most of Friday exploring Glasgow by public transport, leaving the car at his hotel. This was the third city in the world to have a subway, he discovered, its underground was opened in December 1896. Only London and Budapest had constructed subways earlier. He visited the Glasgow Transport Museum, where he took his time admiring the old steam engines on display. He wondered if his ancestor Alexander Stewart had boarded one of these before he traveled to the States.

From his hotel room, he finally managed to track down his wife at Ballindalloch Castle.

Their telephone call had worried him. It seemed Cathy was

busy. No doubt the guys at Raleigh PD were calling her about the Hooper case and that really annoyed him. It was always about work.

With a grim look on his face David had to remind himself that if it had it not been for the fact that Cathy was a cop, he would never have met her. His mind flashed back to the fateful day when he was attending a "Y2K" conference in Raleigh and witnessed a hit-and-run fatality. She had been one of the cops on duty responding to his call. He had been interviewed by the enthusiastic Cathy more times than he thought necessary. It all happened so fast, a whirlwind romance. It had been Cathy who had proposed to him the following year when they bought their house in Wake Forest.

CHAPTER 30

Tuesday 12 November 1895, Ellis Island, USA

"Alexander Stewart," boomed a gruff voice.

Alexander stepped forward into one of the aisles to an overweight immigration officer. The official was wearing a round skipped hat and sported a dark bushy moustache sitting above thick set lips and an unshaven chin. He was the fourth officer in a row of about ten, all sitting behind dark wooden desks. Alexander noticed that the buttons fastening the officer's jacket were under severe stress with the man's belly protruding over his lap.

Shuffling some documents, the official started asking a series of rehearsed questions; name, age, profession, reason for being here, relatives, place of residence, and how much currency he had. Not once did he look up at Alex while posing all these questions, concentrating only on writing the answers on the official-looking document.

"Can you read and write?" the officer asked, finally looking up.

"Of course," Alexander replied, appalled by the question.

The officer smiled. "Don't be smart, son. Read this to me then." He handed over a paper with a few lines of text.

Alex recited the words back perfectly. The paunchy officer was clearly perspiring. The heat accumulating in the giant hall and the rancid aroma of body odors made it altogether unpleasant. When the official asked for his papers, Alexander produced the document he'd found in Gordon's envelope.

The officer skimmed over it quickly. Alex saw him write down "Scotland" on his own document. Then he handed another paper to Alexander. It read, "United States of America, Declaration of Intention."

This was for Alexander to now declare under oath his personal description – height, eye, and hair color and other distinguishable marks – and pledge his allegiance to the United States of America. He felt too confused and overwhelmed to realize the significance of that moment.

He was asked again to give the details where he would be staying. Like the first time, Alexander gave the address in Boston provided by the Gibsons. He would probably never see Mrs Gibson again, but it satisfied the official.

Finally, after what seemed an eternity, Alex was asked to sign the document. The officer then took an ink stamp from a drawer and quickly stamped two different documents, signed them both, handed one to Alexander, and said, "Welcome to the United States, Mr Stewart. Either you make your way to the ferry for New York Harbor or you can go queue for accommodation here until you find a permanent residence. Maximum stay here is five days free of charge." He then faced the waiting queue and bawled, "John and Martha Williams and family."

Alex shrugged his shoulders, feeling very anxious, and walked towards a huge sign that read; "Ferry - New York Harbor".

His attention was drawn to a family with five or six children crying and shouting not ten yards away. He overheard one of the children, a skinny pale boy about ten years old, being denied entry – he was to be admitted to a hospital on Ellis Island. It made him think of Mr Gibson and for a moment he looked behind him at all the people in the hall to see if he could find Mrs Gibson, but saw no sign of her. Maybe it would have been polite to tell her that he gave the officials her address in Boston as his destination.

He was constantly being asked by uniformed officers to keep moving along through the iron-railed passageways packed with men, women, children, and their belongings.

Before he knew it he was caught up in the mere act of keeping pace with all that was happening. He boarded a small ferry boat which seemed so overcrowded that he was convinced it would sink. Twenty minutes later, he found himself on the shoreline of New York Harbor.

As he set foot on American soil and took the first steps in his American life, his mind flashed back to the promise he had made at the Lagmore Stone Circle.

I'll be back Katie, he thought, *I'll be back.*

CHAPTER 31

Tuesday 12 November 1895, New York Grand Central Station, USA

Alexander's feet were now on *terra firma*. He could see a clock in the distance. It was just before one o'clock in the afternoon. The autumn breeze made him shiver. It must have been almost four hours ago that he'd stepped onto Ellis Island. He tucked the collar of his jacket around his neck and turned around to stare out to the ocean. On the horizon, he could see two steamships heading towards the island. To his right, he could just make out the silhouette of the Statue of Liberty through the haze.

Carrying his light travel bag, he followed the direction of the crowd. A pang of regret shot through him when he looked at the lucky few that were being greeted by loved ones or friends. However, many, like him, were trying to orientate themselves in their new environment and find their way alone.

He decided to take one of the free streetcars, to the train station. Surely, from there, he would find a locomotive to Boston. Slowly walking with the crowd, he checked if his bag still contained the dollars Gordon had given him. He hoped it would be enough to keep him in Boston until he found work. He had no comprehension how far away Boston was. All he knew was that it was north of New York. Leaving the harbor, like many other arrivals, he headed for the streetcar terminus some fifty yards ahead.

A picture painted on the front of a wooden stand made him stop. The drawing of a smiling couple was a promotion for somewhere called Coney Island. For five cents, a trip by trolley car was offered to go there for a day out. *If five cents is the cost of a car ride, I wonder what two hundred dollars could buy me?* he thought. Directly underneath the sketch, an old man in a long black woolen coat was standing at a wheelbarrow cart cooking food in a copper saucepan. The aroma reminded Alex of just how hungry he was.

"You want a frankfurter, sonny?" the man asked.

Might as well, Alex thought, and said, "Yes, please," handing the old man a one-dollar bill from his envelope, hoping that would cover it.

"I don't suppose you have anything smaller, it's only a dime. You immigrants are all the same," the man muttered under his breath in a Germanic accent, clearly annoyed that he always had to bring a bag of coins every day. Alex was given his frankfurter – a long piece of rolled meat of pork and beef wrapped in doughy white bread.

He continued walking towards the streetcars. He ate greedily, savoring the smooth textured meat. With all the people noise around him and focusing on his food, he failed to notice that someone was shouting at him.

"Hey, you! You, stuffing your mouth. Better watch you don't be sick again. You deaf as well?"

Finally, he looked up and there, popping out of the window of one of the streetcars, was the same shock of red hair that he had seen on the first-class deck of the ship.

"Come on, I'll keep you a seat beside me," the young man shouted.

Without thinking, Alexander responded with a wave, as if he knew the lad. To board the streetcar, he squeezed himself past the chaotic sea of people, desperately holding onto his travel bag. He found the red-haired lad without any problem and sat down on the wooden bench beside him, his bag on his lap.

"I'm Sean, Sean Devane. Who might you be? And where are you going?" he asked, sticking out his right hand.

They shook hands vigorously. Alexander knew the accent. Ballindalloch Castle often received visitors from different parts of Ireland and Alex recognized this Sean was from the south.

"I'm Alexander Stewart. I was going to stay here in New York, but after talking to a few people on the ship I decided I'd rather go to Boston."

A whistle sounded and the streetcar jerked forward.

"A damn good decision," Sean said, smiling, "I'm on my way to Boston as well. You could do with a bath there, Alexander," He wrinkled his nose.

"And you could do with some manners, Sean."

After this brief episode of measuring each other up, they exploded into laughter while the packed streetcar nosed its way forward. The screeching noise from the steel tracks and wheels was deafening.

"Is this streetcar going to the train station?" asked Alexander.

"Yes, they all do from the harbor. With some good fortune, we'll catch the train for Boston. It's at three o'clock every day."

"You have done your homework," said Alexander, surprised that he knew this.

"This will be my third journey to Boston and I'm staying for good this time." He went on to explain that his father moved to Boston after his wife, Sean's mother, was killed in an accident many years ago. He, along with his sisters were looked after by an aunt and uncle in Dublin. Meanwhile, their father had worked as a laborer at the Boston Gas Company. "He eventually climbed his way up the ladder to foreman," Sean added proudly. "My father sent money home to Dublin to help fund the upkeep of my sisters and older brother, who lives in a church institution. About five years ago, my father started his own construction business, initially doing work for the railroads. Now he's also into commercial buildings. So I'm a spoiled little rich boy now and here to work in my father's business."

"What about your sisters?" Alex asked. "Will they also move to Boston?"

"They're happy enough in Dublin. One is married and the other gets wed next year."

Alexander guessed Sean was a bit older than himself – maybe twenty-two or twenty-three; a stocky lad, much shorter than Alex, with pale skin and freckles on his face, and of course his thick wiry red hair that made him stand out in a crowd.

"What part of Scotland are you from? You sound quite an educated person," said Sean.

"I'm from Banffshire, the son of a gamekeeper on a Highland estate." Alex spun the same yarn as he told the Gibsons about the lady of the house dying and how he needed to find work. Sean listened, but did not react in any way.

When everyone started to collect their belongings, as the streetcar was entering the vicinity of Central Station, Sean stood up and said, "You'll need a ticket for the train. Let me treat you so we can travel together. Mind you, it might be difficult to get one at this short notice."

"No thank you," replied Alex. "I'll make my own way."

"Alexander, I don't mean to patronize you in any way, but

I'm traveling first-class and it will cost you a lot of money. I enjoy your company and it *is* a six-hour journey, you know. And besides, I can help you find wherever you're heading for in Boston. I know the town very well. Come on, please, Mr Alexander from Scotland."

As they were stepping out of the car, Alexander said, "All right, but one condition must apply, Sean. I will pay you back every penny."

Sean laughed out loud. "Consider it accepted! Let's go, then."

Alexander was amazed as they walked into the giant railway station. It smelled of oil, smoke, people, and food. A bedlam of noise overwhelmed him. Hundreds of people were milling around. There were large shops that Alexander had never imagined before and so many different sounds, not only of people, but of locomotives and whistles.

"I'll go and negotiate with the ticket office," Sean said, leaving his bulky suitcase with Alex.

While he stood waiting on Sean, Alex was taken aback by the many colored people in and around the busy station. It made him realize that he was indeed from a very sheltered background and there was still a lot to learn in the world.

Ten minutes later, Sean returned and said, "You have your ticket, Alexander. Come on, it's platform one, we still have thirty minutes."

CHAPTER 32

Tuesday 12 November 1895, "The Ghost Train", USA

Approaching the platform, Alexander gasped and stopped abruptly. The huge black Pullman engine stood proudly on the track with all the passenger cars lined up behind it. Alex looked at the rolling stock in awe. The carriages were all painted white with gold trim. He couldn't even count how many there were; they just stretched on and on. People crowded the platform and for a fleeting moment he wondered if Mrs Gibson would be boarding this train as well.

Sean interrupted his thoughts. "The train sometimes hits a speed of forty-five miles an hour, would you believe that? It is known as "The Ghost Train," because of its white carriages standing out in the night."

Alex nodded his head slightly. He could imagine it must be a spectacular sight for anyone watching the train pass in the darkness.

A railroad attendant dressed in tropical white overalls was standing by the entrance of their first-class wagon. The name of the rail company, Air Line[10], was written in gold on his left breast pocket. Sean showed him the tickets. As they boarded, the attendant gave Alex a look, as if wondering how someone dressed so poorly was traveling first-class. Another Airline attendant dragged Sean's luggage away to the storage wagon. Alex kept a firm grip on his own travel bag.

The interior of the car was the epitome of affluence to Alex. There were velvet carpets, silk draperies, white silk curtains, chairs upholstered in old gold plush, and large plate mirrors. There were also two card tables and two writing desks. Gas wall lights lined either side of the cabin. Their carriage was already occupied with wealthy-looking men, some hidden behind their newspapers. He just shook his head and smiled as he thought of the basic train he'd boarded at Ballindalloch.

"This is so luxurious, Sean," he said, sitting down and stretching his long legs out in front of him.

"It is," Sean agreed. "And the dining car opens when we're about thirty minutes into the journey. Hope you're as hungry as I am."

At exactly three o'clock, the doors closed and a whistle sounded. Giant hissing clouds of steam obscured the platform and the heavy train slowly pulled into motion on its way to Boston.

Settling into the journey, Alex and Sean started to share their experiences aboard the SS State of Nebraska. Sean had also heard the stories about the missing Mr Gibson.

As Alexander peered out the window, not really absorbing what he was looking at, his mind went back to his train journey from Perth to Glasgow. It seemed a lifetime ago. He thought of Katherine riding her horse, her laughing and teasing him. He thought about the castle, his father. *I should have stayed,* he thought. *James Macpherson would have sided with me.*

"Would you care to tell me what really happened in Scotland, Alexander?" Sean probed, snapping him back to reality.

Without answering the question, Alex said, "You can call me Alex. Alexander takes too long."

Sean smiled, understanding his newfound travel companion was not ready to reveal his past to him just yet. Alex intrigued him. His proud stature and choice of words showed he was not just any working-class lad. Coming from a similar background, Sean knew what to look for.

They were both distracted by a gentleman behind them, who asked the attendant in a loud voice what Scotch they had on board. The waiter promptly offered a Johnnie Walker or a Glenlivet.

Sean nudged Alex and said, "The bugger didn't ask for an Irish."

The sound and rhythm of the constant turning of the wheels on the metal track had almost made Alex drift into sleep, when an attendant, again dressed in white overalls, announced the dining car was now open.

The dining car was as opulent as the passenger wagon. The compartment had exactly the same decoration, except for the tables that supplied enough room to seat four people comfortably. Cotton napkins, silver cutlery, a cruet set, and a personal lamp adorned each table. From the menu, Alex and Sean ordered exactly the same: vegetable soup to start, followed by salmon, boiled potatoes and greens, and a bottle of dry white wine.

As they started their meal, Sean tried again. "You didn't answer me earlier. Why are you here, Alex? What happened in Scotland?"

Alex looked at Sean and although they had only met a few hours ago, he decided to tell his story to the man who had just bought him the train ticket.

"I know what I see, Alexander, what brought you to the United States?" Sean urged.

The dining car was filling up. Alex dropped his voice and started to tell Sean everything that transpired in Ballindalloch.

Sean listened intently, genuinely upset for Alex as his story unfolded. Occasionally they drew the attention of other diners, especially when Sean boomed at one point, "You must hate that bastard Gordon," and slammed his fist on the table, making the cutlery jump.

The train made its way through the scenic flatlands and beautiful dense forests of Connecticut. The early evening darkness prevented Alex appreciating the views.

He was lulled to sleep by the drone and rhythm of the train, helped by the comfort of his seat and didn't wake up until five past nine in the evening, when the Pullman arrived at Boston Sumner Street Terminal. As passengers were standing up, preparing to alight and collect their luggage, Sean pulled out a silver card holder and handed Alex a card.

"Take this, it's my father's calling card and our home address is on the back. Our house is just off Boston Common, near Tremont Street."

Alex looked at the card and then, smiling at Sean, said, "You're a good person, Sean. Thank you for listening and everything you've done. I'll find your house and pay you back for the ticket plus interest. But first I need to look for lodgings for the night. Do you have any suggestions?"

"You know what," his new Irish friend laughed, putting an arm around his shoulder, "I know a great place just off Boston Common, near Tremont Street, and it's cheap."

Nobody greeted Sean as they left the station onto Dewey Square. Perhaps his family hadn't expected him yet, not knowing when his ship had arrived or which train he would be on. The Air Line porter wheeled Sean's luggage, which was about ten times the size of Alexander's modest bag, outside the station building. He called a horse and carriage and loaded Sean's case on top.

The square was busy with people and streetcars and the cold evening air mingled with an unpleasant smell, a far cry from the crisp Highland air in Scotland.

"Phew, what a smell!" said Alex, curling up his nose.

Sean laughed, "The stink is coming from the Charles River. It's polluted like hell. Don't go swimming in the river, Alex."

Tall buildings lit up the streets and their coachman struggled to get them out of the square congested with vehicles and pedestrians. About twenty minutes later, they passed Boylston Street in the center of Boston Common.

"This is the main park in Boston Alex. Huge uh!"

Alex didn't comment, his mind trailing back to the grounds of Ballindalloch.

Although the evening darkness had fallen, the park was well lit with street lights. A huge church spire in the distance dominated the landscape.

"My goodness, look at this! What are they doing here?" Alex asked.

All down the far side of Tremont, huge excavation work was being undertaken. Machinery was scattered everywhere. A huge open ditch that must have been thirty feet wide and thirty to forty feet deep spanned the full length of the road.

"They're building a subway. It should be open in a couple of years. I know they plan to have stations all over the city and I think Park Street will be one of the first," Sean said.

Both of them were now extremely tired and the dialogue became less and less by the time the carriage came to a stop.

"Here we are …" said Sean.

Alex looked out of the carriage window and saw a wrought iron railing lining marble steps, leading to a large red door.

Sean jumped out of the carriage and pulled on the door chain. His bones aching, Alex followed him while the coachman offloaded the luggage.

A few moments later, an old frail gentleman in a black evening suit and a white shirt with a red tie stared at Sean with watery eyes and said in an Irish accent, "Welcome, Mr Sean, come in lad. Who might this be?" He looked at the rather untidy Alex. Sean still looked miraculously crisp and clean, in comparison.

In a jovial gesture, as if to protect his friend from scrutiny, Sean, having to stretch, put his arm around Alex's shoulder and said, "Let me introduce Alexander Stewart from the Scottish Highlands to you, Breen. Alexander, meet Breen, our butler. He can be a bit of a snob sometimes," he whispered into Alex's ear.

"I heard that, sir," Breen responded without looking at the young men.

Alex noticed dandruff drifts on the shoulders of the old butler's jacket.

As they entered the warm, beautifully tiled hall, a rotund, short, bald man in his fifties, sanguine complexion with an untidy beard and bushy eyebrows, came rushing out and greeted Sean with open arms. "Sean me boy, come here to your father!"

They hugged affectionately, slapping each other on the back. After what seemed a long time, Sean's father finally looked at Alex and said, "And who might you be?"

"Apparently an Alexander Stewart from the Scottish Highlands, sir," Breen said in a dry tone, standing behind the two young men.

Alex stepped forward and put out his hand, "Alexander Stewart, sir, um, from Scotland."

"I can hear that," Sean's father said, shaking his hand vigorously. "I am Sean's maker, Michael Devane."

"Father, we met on the journey. We traveled together from New York," said Sean.

"You're probably one of those Protestant boys, for Queen and country, Presbyterian no doubt, I can tell," Michael Devane teased.

Sean tried to interrupt, but Alex smiled and said, "Yes, you're right, Mr Devane, I am Presbyterian, and proud of it by the way."

With that, the ice was broken.

"Father, we are tired, hungry, and in desperate need of a bath and sleep," Sean said, changing the conversation.

Breen served up traditional Irish stew with soda bread together with hot tea. Alex and Sean enjoyed every morsel as Michael Devane watched them eat and posed the occasional question about their journey from Scotland and Ireland. He also enquired about his daughters. Sean gave him some letters from them.

Alexander was now in Boston, a roof over his head, and money in his pocket, but his heart still in Ballindalloch.

CHAPTER 33

Friday 5 August 2011, 1:15 pm, Ballindalloch Castle, Banffshire, Scotland

The sound of the piper and guests arriving filled the warm, damp summer air surrounding Ballindalloch Castle. On her own in the library, Cathy took a few moments to gather her thoughts after the phone call from David. She felt unsettled about not telling David about the things that had happened since her arrival. It was not as if she was hiding anything. She was still digesting her impressions from the visit that morning to Lagmore Stone Circle and the old Ballindalloch Station, she told herself.

Taking a deep breath and loosening up her shoulder joints, she headed for the main hall. John had told her the guest buffet lunch was being served around one o'clock, in a special marquee erected on the lawn, close to the tea room. While she walked towards the large tent, her thoughts kept returning to Gordon Macpherson and Alexander Stewart. But what exactly did happen?

"Hello, Catherine," Uncle Thomas said in a friendly way.

"Oh hi, Uncle T. You're looking suave today."

Thomas laughed at her affectionately for shortening his name in typical American fashion. "Well, thank you, Catherine."

"That's not a Macpherson tartan you're wearing, is it?" she asked, looking at his kilt.

"Well caught, lass, this is the Black Watch tartan."

"The Black Watch? What's that?"

"It's a kind of nickname for the Royal Highlanders, an army regiment. The dark green and black tartan is the reason for the name. I was an officer for many years, Catherine."

She smiled and realized she was not surprised at this handsome gentleman being in the military.

To her delight, Uncle Thomas offered her an arm, which she graciously accepted. She loved the decorum of being escorted towards the marquee by the sophisticated Mr Thomas Macpherson.

A huge buffet covered the line of tables placed side by side in the center of the tent, draped with beautiful off-white linens. Steam was rising from hot plates as people traipsed down the buffet line and a mix of aromas filled the air. People were mingling and chatting, the noisy ambiance much helped by traditional Scottish music in the background. Some of the men were wearing kilts, mostly Macpherson tartans, and some were wearing casual dress. Most of the women were dressed in smart-casual making Cathy feel slightly under-dressed and very American in her totally casual outfit.

To her right, she saw Eleanor and Wayne talking to some people. Wayne was wearing his formal Stewart Scottish apparel. He was a tall, rather plump man in his fifties, going bald. Eleanor caught Cathy's eye and waved.

"Would you dare try a wee bit of haggis, dear?" Thomas asked, drawing her attention to the food.

She'd heard of haggis, but was a bit doubtful about its ingredients. "With that look on your face, Uncle Thomas, I don't think I can trust you."

"You eat and enjoy whatever you like, my dear. Excuse me, I need to go have a word with these two gentlemen," he said, pointing to a group of people standing close by.

Cathy really didn't feel particularly hungry. Her life as a cop, with in-between meals and snacks, had left her with unhealthy and irregular eating habits. Looking at all the food on offer, she spied the deserts at the far end of the table. *Decisions, decisions,* she thought, and picked up a piece of delicious-looking chocolate cake. Still standing, she tasted the cake, smiling as it melted in her mouth.

"I see you've discovered our famous chocolate cake," Angus said, approaching her.

"I'll come back next year… just for the cake," she managed to say with her mouth full. She swallowed and added, "David should mention this in his travel guide."

"Let's have a seat over here," Angus indicated, pleased at Cathy's referral to the guide. She followed him to an empty table that could seat eight, picking up a glass of white wine on the way.

"Did John show you the gardens this morning?" Angus asked once they were seated.

"Yes he did and even more, Angus. We went out in his car and visited the Cragganmore Distillery."

"Ah! The rogue took you to his favorite shop."

She smiled and said, "Yes, but we also went to see the old train station and the Lagmore Stonehenge."

"What took you to the stones?" he asked, looking serious.

"I'm not sure. It just seemed like a place I wanted to check out."

"I don't like Lagmore," Angus said, slowly leaning back in his chair.

"Why don't you like the circle?" Cathy asked.

After a short pause, Angus answered, "Well … it brings back the unpleasant memory of a conversation with my father many years ago."

Cathy remained silent sensing she was about to hear something significant. Angus seemed to hesitate for a moment but then continued.

"We'd been having a father-and-son afternoon out hunting. We took a break and were sitting on the fallen stone at the circle to clean our shotguns. There, right out of the blue, my father told me something about a family matter that disturbed me a lot. Looking past her now staring into the distance he added, "Something needs to be done, you know, before my boy John has to carry the burden."

"What needs to be done, Angus? What are you talking about?"

Snapping out of his mood he answered, "Sorry my dear, I should not have troubled you with this."

Cathy probed, "Angus, does this family matter have anything to do with the Gordon Macpherson discussion at dinner last night?"

It took Angus a little while to decide what he was going to tell her.

"Can we step outside for a moment?" he said, lowering his voice. "This is not the right place for such a discussion."

Strolling in the direction of the river, he began. "You see, Catherine, this is a bit hard to explain, but as Laird of Ballindalloch, I am in possession of information that nobody else has. You could, in fact, sort of compare this, on another scale of course, to secrets being passed on from president to president in your country. I know for a fact, and don't ask me how, that Gordon Macpherson did not drown in the Spey. The thing is though, I have nightmares in which Gordon tells me, excuse me dear…"

He lit a cigarette with shaking hands. "I know this is going to sound strange," he said, taking a long drag from his cigarette, "but in my dreams I am haunted by Gordon's spirit. I am worried my son John will suffer the same fate."

"But why would your dreams be passed onto John?"

He shrugged his shoulders and said unconvincingly, "Maybe I worry too much. I really don't know why I mentioned this to you."

"Angus, you said you knew for sure that Gordon didn't drown in the Spey. How do you know that?"

He just stared at her and threw his cigarette stub to the ground.

"Or am I treading on some presidential secret here?"

"I'd better get back to my guests, dear. We can talk some more later."

As she watched him walk back towards the marquee, Cathy's usual policewoman composure eluded her. For the first time, a strong feeling of destiny about being a Macpherson overcame her.

CHAPTER 34

November 1895, Boston, USA

With Christmas approaching, the next few weeks were to be a special time in Alex's life. Michael Devane had warmed to him. In fact, Devane had told him he was welcome to live with his family as long as he wanted. Sean and Alex bonded like brothers and staying there was altogether easy.

The Devane house was grand. The foyer was a large square space with a tiled floor. The hall had a tall chest of drawers on one side and a mahogany table on the other. A grandfather clock stood proudly in one corner. It chimed on the hour and on the half hour. A crystal chandelier adorned the center of the ceiling. To the left of the hall was the drawing room and to the right a sitting and dining room with a large kitchen at the back of the house. A door off the kitchen opened onto to a long walled garden. A lush green lawn covered the full length of the garden with perfect herbaceous borders. Two out-houses were adjacent to the rear of the house, one for storage, the other a washroom. The second level of the house contained four bedrooms, a study, and a bathroom. Alex occupied one of the guest rooms.

Breen, the butler, was a very efficient supervisor of the household. Although he was there usually every day, he did not always stay overnight. A cook by the name of Helen Slater, a cheery and weathered woman with a very strong Bostonian accent, came by each day and prepared the meals and a young cleaning lady would come to the house on Tuesdays and Fridays. Alex liked her. She had an unusual name he found hard to pronounce at first, Greetje Pugh. She was pretty, tall and slim with honey-blonde hair, blue eyes, and red cheeks. Perhaps because they were a similar age, they got on so well. Alex would often spin Greetje stories about Ballindalloch, the people, and the Scottish customs to make her laugh. She had a Dutch mother who told her tales about growing up in a town called Leiden in Holland. He would tease her by saying that one day she would make a grand voyage to Leiden, and on the way, make a stop in Scotland. He would try to pronounce her name "Greetje", with the Dutch throaty sounding "G", which reminded him a little of Gaelic. This made her squeal with laughter.

Alex had curiously inquired if she was attached. Greetje smiled and said she was well acquainted with a fellow who was a friend of their family. She added at the end to confuse Alex, "Maar ik wil best een kusje," leaving him to wonder what exactly she had said. She warned him not to ask any Dutchman in Boston for a translation, as it could get him into trouble. Alex laughed as she walked away with a cheeky look in her eyes.

Sean directed Alexander to the nearest Protestant church, a stone's throw away from the house. Park Street Church was on the corner of Park and Tremont, across from the Common. It had the church spire Alex had noticed when he'd first arrived. It was a major landmark and clearly visible when approaching Boston Common from any direction. By American standards the church was old, founded in 1809. Although it was not a Presbyterian church, Alex joined their flock as the location was ideal.

Alex and Sean often went on long walks when they returned from their own church on Sundays. Sean showed off his knowledge of the town and took Alex to some of the historical buildings and monuments. This, as well as reading the books Mr Devane owned on Boston and Massachusetts, ensured Alex quickly began to appreciate the history and international culture of the city. But every now and then when he heard a bird caw, it reminded him how much he missed the sights, sounds, and smells of nature that were in abundance at Ballindalloch.

Both Sean and his father worked Monday to Saturday. In the first week, Alex rose early each morning so that he could at least have a chat with Sean before he set off to work. He would then spend a few hours looking for employment, not really knowing what he wanted to do.

It did make him knowledgeable on the streets of downtown Boston. He was amazed at the number of theatres, especially on Washington Street. Here, on the narrowest part of the street, he saw the offices of at least seven Boston newspapers all cluttered together.

One morning, Alex decided to spend some of his dollars on snuff for Mr Devane as a thank-you. He had noticed Mr Devane was partial to bringing out his silver snuffbox after dinner and thought it would be a nice way of showing his appreciation to give him an ounce of good quality snuff. He also treated himself to some new clothes.

It took Alex a week to find a part-time job, off-loading cargo ships in Boston Harbor. It was a physically demanding job with unsociable hours. He would hardly see Sean or Michael

Devane, with his early-morning shifts or late hours in the night. However, he could earn anything from $10 to $12 a week.

Most days, in the solitude of his bedroom, Alex would write letters to Katherine, keeping her up to date on all his news, asking her to write back on what was happening in Scotland. In some of his writings, he even suggested that she join him in Boston. He never mailed any of the letters though. The guilt of the way he left Katherine was weighing so heavily, he didn't know quite how to approach it. Would he dare cause more unrest within the Macpherson household or leave well alone. Writing the letters was a way to sooth his longing for life as it used to be. He kept all the letters in the dresser of his room, little bundles tied by cord in date sequence.

He did send letters to his father, asking about his health, work, and what it was like at Ballindalloch now he had gone.

Two months later, Alex and the Devanes were sitting round the dining table having supper. As usual, Mr Devane was discussing his work; how he was negotiating some potential contracts, worrying about deadlines and how difficult it was to find honest labor. Sean said very little about his day-to-day work. He was being groomed on the commercial aspects of the company, but would rather talk about the social goings-on in Boston.

"So Alex, how long are you going to be working with the scally's at the harbor?" Michael Devane asked, slurping his tea. "You're a well-educated young man and I'm sure your father has much higher expectations of you."

Alex smiled and said, "To be honest, sir, my heart is in writing. Not books, but for the people, to write about what is going on in the world. To write in a way people will understand and then have the knowledge. I'd like to be a journalist, but

I don't think it would be possible here. I did try and build up the courage to check out the newspapers, but why would they employ a young Scotsman who's only been here a few weeks?"

"You're right, lad. They're a bunch of crooks in the press, anyway, and they only employ family and friends. Cronyism it's called, you know."

The conversation soon changed when Mr Devane asked, "Do you write to your father and Katherine?"

Alex turned to Sean whose face went a little red with embarrassment. "You told him didn't you?" challenged Alex, staring at Sean.

Mr Devane jumped in to save his son's skin, "Leave Sean alone, Alex. Yes, he did, and I think if you are staying in my house I should know about what is going on in your life. If you have any letters, give them to Breen and he will see to them. They can be mailed along with my business correspondence. It's no wonder you're an angry boy, Alex, but you will get over it, believe me. You will work it out and if I can help, or Sean, just you let us know."

Mr Devane asked more questions about Alex's father and what happened to his mother, but did not pry about Katherine. Alex spoke about his parents and his upbringing at Ballindalloch. It all became too much for him when he started explaining the events that led to his sudden departure. Alex appreciated Mr Devane's art of listening, as he did not pass judgment on what Alex or his father should have or should not have done.

Michael Devane was a good man. He would leave the house early in the morning, dressed as though he were going to build roads himself. In old trousers and boots, black woolen jacket, and leather cap, he hardly looked like the picture of wealth. He transformed in the evenings, in a smart suit, shirt and tie, and shiny shoes, when he was entertaining potential clients. On occasions, Mr Devane would go out alone. Alex and Sean thought that perhaps he had a female acquaintance, but, of course, that was never spoken of. It was customary for gentlemen like Michael Devane to seek their pleasures discreetly.

Contrary to his father, Sean would go to work smartly dressed every day. He confided in Alex that he had no long-term interest in the construction business. With the invention of the automobile and innovative industrial machinery Sean was more excited about the oil industry, as he believed oil would be the more lucrative commodity in the coming years.

All in all, Alex's relationship with the Devanes continued to grow, although he had a constant guilt complex about living in the household as they never asked anything of him and had refused his offer to pay for his board His relationship with the outside world remained somewhat distant. He hated his job and rarely talked much with any of his fellow harbor workers. His irregular working hours also reduced the time spent with Sean. Six days a week were dominated by work and Sunday was the proverbial day of rest, when Sean and his father would sometimes host some friends for lunch after church. Although Alex was invited, he often declined, feeling he should give the Devanes some time on their own with their friends.

In church, Alex often thought of Gordon Macpherson standing in Inveravon parish, singing hymns and praying to God. *He should pray for forgiveness,* he thought. Alone in bed at night, he continued to reflect on the injustice done to him, his father, and Katherine.

One day, he would say to himself to stay strong, *One day, I'll go back and make things right.*

CHAPTER 35

Friday 5 August 2011, 2:30pm, Ballindalloch Castle, Banffshire, Scotland

Exhausted by all the new information Cathy walked back to the castle and went straight to her bedroom. So many things had happened that it was hard to believe she had only arrived yesterday afternoon. Her body still wasn't in sync with the new time regime either. She decided it justified a nap, undressed and slipped between the cool linen sheets of her four-poster bed.

Sleep overcame her immediately.

Cathy found herself standing at the center of the stone circle. At the edge, she saw John carrying a travel bag. He was wearing shabby old-fashioned looking trousers and a heavy jacket. That can't be John, she thought, Bankers don't dress like that. It must be someone else. A bunch of roses fell into her cupped hands as if she were expecting them. She slowly turned around, dreading it might be Cameron. Instead, a familiar-looking man in his fifties, short and chubby, was facing her. Remember who you are, Catherine, he seemed to say. Then the flowers were snatched from her by David. He threw them into the water. They watched them floating away in a noisy running river. Cathy started to cry, tears clouding her eyes. A phone rang in the distance, the old-fashioned British tone, ring ring, ring ring... It continued, getting louder. She heard Old Billy call out. She tried to answer, but found her voice was unable to produce any sound. There was a gurgling noise and John's head popped up out of the water like an emerging submarine, holding her battered flowers. "I have them, I have them," he said, struggling to catch his breath.

It's too late, I don't want them anymore, they're dead. Give them to Gordon if you find him, he's not that far away, she thought.

She wanted to go back to Lagmore, but the stone circle had gone.

Cathy sat up in bed, startled and sweating. She rubbed her hands over her face, trying to come back to reality and realized she had been crying. What a relief to be awake. Her dream had been so vivid.

Disorientated, she wondered what time it was and picked up her watch, blinking rapidly to focus. 4:20 pm – *my God!* She had been sleeping for almost two hours.

She stood in the shower for a long time, reflecting on her dream, waiting for the warm water to do its magical trick of calming and re-energizing her body.

Fuck it, I need to find out what Angus was holding back this afternoon. Let's do it to them before they do it to us," she said out loud, quoting the start of an old American cop TV program. *Was it Hill Street Blues?* Cathy wondered, as she left the room to look for Wayne Stewart.

CHAPTER 36

February 1896, Boston, USA

"The Boston Globe," Michael Devane said out loud over supper. Looking at Alex, he repeated, "The Boston Globe for you lad. I had a drink yesterday with Peter Reagan and he needs some help on Foreign News, something like that. Journalist job, apprentice, and you told me you were a good writer. So, go and meet Peter in the morning around nine at the Globe Building on Newspaper Row on Washington Street and tell him Mike sent you. Don't you let me down now, Alex."

So, this is cronyism, Alex thought smiling.

The next morning, Alex put on his best clothes, polished his shoes, and made his way to the Globe. The wind of the Charles River was beginning to have an edge as he walked down the narrow, twisting section of Washington Street. He now realized why the area was called "Newspaper Row". There must have been seven or eight newspaper companies all crammed together: *The Herald, The Evening Telegraph, The Chronicle, The Globe* and many others.

He met Peter Reagan and a Frank Murray at the offices of the Globe. Both gentlemen were of Irish stock and they spoke highly of Mr Devane. They asked Alex a lot of questions about why he wanted to be a journalist. Alex answered as sincerely as he could. The thought of thousands of people from all walks of life reading his words excited him, he told them. He particularly mentioned his aspirations of becoming a foreign correspondent, as the world was now much "smaller", with the advances being made in communication. Peter and Frank smiled when he said that although he had not yet used a telephone, he was certain that the day would come when people could automatically speak to anyone, anywhere in the world.

He was hired by the Boston Globe as an apprentice journalist, focusing on European news. They agreed he would have a three-month trial and his prime focus would be on a new international athletic event being held in Athens, Greece, in April – Games of the I Olympiad. Fourteen nations planned to participate, including the USA, and it was forecast to be the largest sporting event ever held.

He would need communication training, using the telegraph as well as the telephone. The typewriter was also new to him, although he remembered being curious about one of these devices. He'd seen a typewriter in Gordon's study at the castle. He even recalled the name on the machine, "Remington".

Mr Devane certainly had some influence within the Globe. He found the job diverse and challenging and enjoyed being able to travel around Boston reporting on a wide variety of topics as he learned his trade. However, foreign news, especially from Europe, was his preferred work.

In March 1896, Alex moved out of the Devane residence and rented a modest one-bedroom furnished apartment in Boylston Street, in the Back Bay area. Breen helped him move what few belongings he possessed. On his last evening before moving out, Alex gave Sean an envelope containing enough dollars for a first-class one-way ticket from New York, plus some interest.

"These were once precious dollars to me, Sean, and they've given me more than money could ever buy."

Sean and he embraced and said nothing else, knowing their unspoken bond was very much alive.

The move gave Alex the sense of independence that he had craved. He thrived on his work and constantly impressed Peter Reagan and his fellow colleagues.

During the quiet moments of his busy life he still thought about Katherine, who was probably being groomed for one of the Grant sons.

One evening, returning home from work, there was an envelope pushed under the door, along with a note from Sean: "This has arrived from Scotland. Hope it is from Katherine." Alex recognized the handwriting on the envelope immediately and tore it open impatiently.

26th January, 1896

My dearest Son,

I hope this letter finds you well and healthy.

The events here at Ballindalloch have not been good. After your sudden departure, I have to tell you that Gordon Macpherson has disappeared. There has been no trace of him since you left our shores. The police have concluded he drowned while fishing in the Spey, which I find hard to believe, as his body has not been found. I fear something bad has happened, but cannot feel any grief. There are other rumors, my son, which I cannot yet write about.

Even with this situation, I find I can no longer work for the Macphersons. The Stewart name has been tarnished in

*the community and I cannot bear the shame that Gordon
Macpherson has lashed upon us.*

*It is also not good news about the lovely girl Katherine. She
has become a recluse and is rarely outside of the castle walls.
I hope one day the girl will find herself again.*

*Alexander, I plan to come and live in the USA, hopefully with
you for a little while until I find my own space. I have a ticket
for a sailing at the end of March on SS Furnessia from Glasgow
to New York. The ship's estimated arrival date is Friday 10th
April. Maybe you can arrange to meet me in New York or
arrange some transport to Boston? I tried to get a sailing
directly to Boston but it was too expensive.*

*I have your address and with God's mercy will see you soon
and tell you more about Ballindalloch.*

Your loving father,

Robert Stewart

After the initial elation of having heard from his father coming
to America, Alex started to feel upset. The thought of Katie
being miserable relentlessly revived his embarrassment over
forsaking his responsibilities towards her. He contemplated on
going back to Scotland and face his fate. With Gordon now
gone it might be possible to start with a clean slate. What if
Gordon should suddenly re-appear? Also with his father coming
to America, Alex could not possibly return to Scotland now.

To give himself peace of mind he decided to wait for
detailed information on what had been going on at Ballindalloch
before making any decisions. Perhaps later he could even sail
to Scotland with his father. By now he would be able to buy
them both a second class ticket.

CHAPTER 37

Friday 5 August 2011, 5.00 pm, Ballindalloch Castle, Banffshire, Scotland

With her disturbing dream still embedded in her mind and determined to find out more about the Alexander Stewart story, Cathy briskly made her way downstairs to look for Wayne Stewart. Eleanor had mentioned letters. Cathy was sure they would supply more information on why Alexander Stewart left Ballindalloch and maybe what happened to Gordon Macpherson, if Stewart indeed had anything to do with it.

In the hall she bumped into Mr Christie.

"Whoa, missus, you're in a hurry, being chased by a ghost?" he asked, amused.

Cathy stopped abruptly and looked him in the eye. She was now in police mode. "Have you seen Wayne Stewart, Mr Christie?"

"Why do you want Mr Stewart?"

Taken aback by his tone, Cathy was beginning to wonder if Christie's past was also connected to the military. "I just need to ask Mr Stewart some questions, so if you know where he is, tell me."

"Well, if it's that important to you, I think I seen Mr and Mrs Stewart walk towards the walled garden."

Cathy turned on her heels and made her way to the garden, where she found Wayne and Eleanor admiring the roses.

"Hi, Catherine," exclaimed a smiling Eleanor, as Cathy walked towards them. "You look flushed, is everything okay?"

"Well, to be honest, I'm getting wrapped up in some weird stories and happenings here. That's why, if you don't mind, I need to ask you guys some questions."

Wayne stepped forward, his hand extended in greeting. "Hi, I'm Wayne, pleased to meet you at last, Cathy. Eleanor has told me all about you. How can we help?"

Accepting his hand, Cathy said, "Well, I would love to know a bit more about Alexander Stewart."

"Alexander… So you've heard what they say about him around here? "

Eleanor was getting anxious about how serious Cathy looked.

"Yes, what I would like to know is why he left Scotland and moved to Boston, Wayne?"

"Are you standing-in for your husband's research?" Wayne enquired. A smile in his eyes betrayed his amusement over Cathy's eager tone. For a fleeting moment, Cathy wondered if David had mentioned her discomfort with genealogy to Wayne.

A bit flustered she answered, "Well I'm intrigued and think David might be in for a surprise."

"Okay… Let me start by saying Alexander must have been a good man. He is the reason I am a Stewart. He and his wife Sarah adopted my great–great-grandfather from an orphanage for black children. Can you imagine that, a white couple in 1899 adopting a black child."

Hearing the affection in his response, Cathy decided to tread carefully. "What did you mean by your comment about the stories they tell about him around here?"

He gave a deep sigh and looked at his wife. "Okay, let's sit down and I'll tell you what I know. I was planning to speak to your husband anyway. I think he should know this, too. It's a shame he's not here."

As they all sat down on one of the benches beside the west wall of the garden, Wayne started his story.

"Four years ago, I started researching my family tree and it led me here to Alexander Stewart's birthplace, and Angus invited me to visit. The first time I came to Ballindalloch, three years ago, I discovered the story was still very much alive about Alexander being a possible murderer and accused of stealing family jewelry in order to finance his emigration to the US."

"Still very much alive?" Cathy echoed. "What do you mean? You heard about this before?"

"Yes," Wayne replied. "I have letters, letters from Alexander to the daughter of Gordon Macpherson – the same Gordon that disappeared in the Spey. I didn't tell Angus or anyone else this. My sole reason for coming here was to see where Alexander Stewart came from. It wasn't my intention to stir up old tales and spirits. But his story was so extraordinary that I wanted to come here and experience for myself the land he was chased away from."

"So he didn't steal any precious jewels and flee to America?" Cathy asked.

"Oh no. It was Gordon who was the crook. He blackmailed Alexander into leaving. Now when I came here first, it was obvious Angus wasn't ready to discuss any of this. He even told me the old tale that Alexander killed Gordon, which is a ridiculous accusation. You must have seen the castle website. They *need* to keep the ghost of Gordon alive, so to speak."

He grimaced at the memory of the conversation he had with Angus three years earlier. "We're not sure your ancestor was altogether free of misdemeanors, you know," Angus had told Wayne when he'd addressed the issue of his forefather's sudden departure.

"And then there was also this weird thing Thomas told me. You have met Thomas Macpherson, lovely old guy?"

Cathy nodded her head.

Wayne continued. "He suggested I ignore all the tales. He said they didn't make any sense. But when I asked him to elaborate, he said some things were best left buried. He seemed annoyed with himself, having to say that. My bet is Thomas knows more than he's showing. In fact, I think this whole family knows more. Gordon vanished, just like that?" Wayne clicked the fingers of his right hand.

"These letters you have," Cathy said, choosing her words carefully, "they are *from* Alexander to the daughter, Katherine. How come you have them, if they were mailed to Scotland?"

Wayne looked at Cathy and kept her gaze, "Alexander never mailed any of them. He just wrote them, lots of them. They read like a diary. Every letter starts with 'Dearest Katherine'. Each letter covers a time frame of a few weeks and has its own envelope addressed to Katherine at the castle. It was the letters that led me to Ballindalloch. Can you understand why I simply had to come here?" he said, with a look of melancholy in his eyes. "I was drawn here by Alexander's story. For me, it's not Gordon's spirit that won't rest, but Alexander's."

"Just think," Cathy said. "It was the letters to a Katherine Macpherson that brought you here and now you're talking to one. Spooky, isn't it?" She laughed, trying to make it sound like a joke. Somehow her words only created an uneasy silence.

"So what was she like, this Katherine?" Cathy asked.

"She was Gordon's daughter. From what I've read in the letters she must have been a spirited lady."

"How many letters do you have from Alexander?"

"I would guess two dozen."

"Were Katherine and Alexander lovers?" she asked, raising her eyebrows.

"I'm not sure. What is certain is that Gordon chased him away, accusing him of theft."

Maybe Alexander did murder Gordon; some kind of quarrel? Cathy thought. "Is there anything else from Alexander's letters that you think would be important?" she asked.

"Well, for what it's worth, there was one letter to Alexander from his father, Robert Stewart. He was the gamekeeper at Ballindalloch for many years. In the letter, Robert said he was coming to the US to live with Alexander. But in one of the letters Alexander wrote to Katherine, he explained how his father died at sea on his way to New York."

Cathy shrugged her shoulders like a cat shaking water from its fur.

"Okay," she said, rubbing her hands together as if she felt cold, "Thank you for all the information, Wayne, you've been very helpful."

Frowning, Cathy turned around and made her way to the castle. On her walk back, Cathy kept mulling the new information over in her mind.

She wished she had those letters. Another thought crossed her mind. Why did Alexander's father plan to go to the US to join his son? Was there also a reason for him to leave Ballindalloch? Blackmailed, Wayne had said. Had Gordon also blackmailed Alexander's father? What could be so horrendous that would force Gordon to chase the Stewarts away? It must have been Alexander and Katherine being lovers? That would not be acceptable to Gordon.

What could Gordon have blackmailed them with, the stolen jewelry accusation? How Alexander must have hated Gordon for all that he did. Maybe he *did* kill Gordon, after all, simply out of revenge, and made it look like an accident, hid his body in some old Scottish cave or something. He wouldn't mention that in his letters to this Katherine of course.

With all these thoughts swirling around in her head, she arrived back at the castle and went looking for Maggie. Maybe she could tell some more tales about what transpired within the family Macpherson a hundred years ago. As for Angus, Cathy now knew for sure he wouldn't volunteer any more information.

CHAPTER 38

April, 1896, Boston, USA

A few weeks after the arrival of Robert Stewart's letter to his son, news broke of a lost liner at sea, the SS Furnessia. A hundred and twenty passengers and crew were feared to have drowned, in a storm in the Atlantic. Through his contacts at the *Globe*, Alex frantically tried to find out more details about the ship and the passenger list, but at this early time that proved difficult.

In the office the following day, his colleague Kenny Harris approached Alex and handed him a list of names from the doomed ship. Underlined was "Stewart, Robert, M, age 41. Profession: Gamekeeper. Country of birth: Scotland."

He just stared at the list as Kenny patted him on the back and left him alone. He felt numb. His throat tightened and his anger and pain went like an arrow to the pit of his stomach. He crumpled the paper in his hands and broke down in tears.

Alex grieved for his father. He visited the Devanes on a regular basis, and they would listen to him describing his childhood memories, talking about his parents and his life at Ballindalloch. Alex's hatred of Gordon Macpherson increased and he hoped he was dead. The guilt returned and he thought that if he had stayed in Scotland, his father would still be alive. It also made him ponder about going back, but with the Olympiad Games approaching and his backlog of work, he didn't want to leave now.

In the Athens games, Boston had high hopes for their ex-Boston University School of Law student, Tom Burke, who would represent the USA in the sprint races. He didn't let the Bostonians down, winning gold at the 100-metre and 400-metre sprints.

Alex wanted to write on an unusual incident in Athens involving Stamata Revithi, a mother of a 17-month-old boy. Women were not allowed to compete in Athens and Stamata ran the marathon on her own the day after the men's race. She was refused entry into the Parathinaiko Stadium. The editor of the *Globe* refused to sanction the report as he thought it was "not appropriate." Alex could not help thinking how livid Katherine would have been at this story. Again he thought of actually sending a letter to her. However he couldn't decide. With Gordon gone, John, the oldest Macpherson son, would probably have taken over the reins at Ballindalloch. Alex remembered him as a serious, humorless young man full of his own importance. Any letter to Katherine would surely be intercepted and get her into trouble.

During May, Alex was seconded to cover one of the worst natural fires in history, in which almost three thousand acres of land were destroyed in Cape Cod. This proved to be very emotional and sensitive, as many people had lost their livelihoods. Alex was praised by the editor and his colleagues for his articulate articles during that month. His writings encouraged the *Globe* to appeal for donations from its readers to help those who had suffered.

In the summer of 1896, the north-east of the USA was suffering a prolonged heat wave. This was making people short-tempered and working in the office became uncomfortable.

One evening, Alex was attending an open-air dance at Park Street Church. The church organized this event every second Friday, but this was the first time he had been bold enough to go along. The dances were usually in the large hall at the rear of the church. Due to the warm weather and high humidity, this time it was being held on adjacent parkland.

He looked around the crowded and noisy park. People of all ages were there, from young children to elderly couples. A pianist was warming up on a stage and Alex gave him a wave. He was the regular organist from the church.

At one point, he saw a woman who had just walked into the park. She looked very familiar and he watched her glancing to her left then to her right, as if expecting to meet someone.

"Excuse me," Alex interrupted, "Mrs Gibson?"

For a moment, the woman looked at him with a serious and questioning expression. When she recognized him, a smile broke through like rays of sunlight.

"Alexander Stewart!" she exclaimed. "What a wonderful surprise."

Shyly circling the hat he had just taken off upon greeting her, he answered her smile.

Amazing how a journey bonds people like kin, he thought. It felt like he was looking at a family member he had not seen for a long time. She was wearing a grey skirt that hid her long legs and a black jacket with a frilly white blouse. Her hair was tied back, showing off her fine features. She was obviously delighted to see him. Ignoring the dancing, they sat at a table for nearly two hours, exchanging their experiences since arriving in the USA. Alex, his grief over his father abated, managed to inform Mrs Gibson about his sad loss.

She told him she was still living with her cousin. She had found work as a seamstress and also helped at an orphanage for black children, teaching English and arithmetic.

At one point in their conversation, Mrs Gibson waved to a female friend to join them, but she declined. Time passed quickly and eventually she said, "I need to go, my friend is waiting on me."

"Would it be possible for us to meet up again?" Alex asked. He caught himself holding her hand a little longer than intended.

"Yes, I'd like that," she said.

"I will write to you and propose an afternoon tea," he suggested. "I still have your address."

As Mrs Gibson walked towards her friend, he called after her, "By the way, what's your first name?"

She turned and gave another one of her sunray smiles. "Sarah," she called out, and then she was gone.

CHAPTER 39

1896 – 1900, Boston, USA

The next few months were busy at the *Globe*, with the run up to the Presidential Election. Massachusetts was a Republican stronghold. However, Alex did not have any conviction for McKinley or the Democrat, Bryan.

Alex and Sarah Gibson were meeting on a regular basis now and becoming close. At the start of the fall, they were spending almost every weekend together, frequenting theatre shows and supper restaurants. They even spent a long weekend at Cape Cod, booking separate rooms of course, at a small hotel by the harbor in Hyannis Port.

During April of 1898, Alex was assigned by the *Globe* to cover the Spanish-American War. The USA began with a blockade of Cuban ports and the *USS Nashville* captured a Spanish merchant ship. Alex reveled in these situations and he was fast becoming *Boston Globe*'s rising star as a war correspondent.

Later that month, Alexander and Sarah attended the wedding of Sean Devane to an Irish woman, Colleen Doherty. In fact, Alex was honored by being Sean's best man. As expected, it was a grand affair held in Young's Hotel in Court Avenue, downtown. At the end of the evening, Alex proposed to Sarah and, to his delight, she accepted without hesitation.

Alex and Sarah married on Wednesday 19 July 1898. It was a quiet wedding, attended by only a few friends; Michael and Sean Devane and his wife, a few colleagues from the *Globe*, and acquaintances from the church. Sarah's guests were her cousin and his family, a couple who'd befriended Sarah when she first arrived in Boston and fellow parishioners from her church.

ˮA few days later the following acknowledgement appeared in the *Boston Globe*.

MARRIED

STEWART – GILLESPIE – On Wednesday July 19 at the First Presbyterian Church, Boston, by the Rev. Dr. George S. Mutt, assisted by the Rev. Dr. John Hall, Sarah Gillespie, formerly Gibson, to Alexander Stewart.

Sarah moved in with Alexander, although Back Bay was quite a distance from the orphanage and her friends. She also joined Park Street Church.

During their first year of marriage they both continued to work. No children were conceived. Sarah showed Alex the orphanage where she taught children on a regular basis. She adored the orphans, especially Michael, a six-year-old boy. He was shy and not as imposing as the other kids. She recognized he was a pensive boy. When asked any questions, he had a habit of rubbing his chin before answering. His spoken English was very good for a boy of his age. However, like the other children, his writing abilities were poor.

Sarah knew that Alex was uncomfortable with these visits, as it was a black-only orphanage in a poor area of town. Not many white people would be seen walking in those streets, let alone a white woman on her own.

"Please come with me more often, Alex," she asked him once. "Not because I'm afraid on my own, but so you can get to know Michael more. I'm sure there's a scholar hidden inside him and in some way he reminds me of you. He's a survivor," she said, flashing her smile.

Alex didn't comment. Instead, he just looked at his wife admiringly. She lived her passion and in that respect she reminded him of Katherine.

Sarah waited a few months for Alex to be in the right mood to listen to a special request. It was 11 October 1899, on a Wednesday evening. Alex had come home from work that night looking exceptionally pleased. He gave his wife a hug and declared they were going out to celebrate his promotion to deputy chief journalist of Foreign News.

With the United Kingdom at war against the Boers in the Transvaal and Orange Free State, a lot of challenging work was waiting for Alex. It might even get him a trip to Africa as a war correspondent.

That evening, at an intimate Italian diner just off Washington Street, while celebrating this new achievement in his career, Sarah with some trepidation told him they should try and foster Michael. At first, Alex would not even contemplate such a thought.

"Can you imagine how people would react?" he whispered to his wife, not wanting to attract the attention of the customers at the table behind her. "It's not that I'm against helping Michael out, please understand that. You know I'm very fond of him myself, but to invite him into our home would be inviting in a whole lot of division, Sarah, believe me. In my own way, I've been there before. Classes and races don't mix. It causes nothing but trouble."

Sarah, knowing the bigger part of what had chased Alex out of Scotland, could understand his doubts based on his own experience, but felt it should not affect Michael.

"Somebody needs to be the first to make a difference, Alex," Sarah argued. "He's a bright wee boy and we can help him make something of his life. Besides I want, in fact I *need* a child, Alex. What am I to do when you're travelling for the newspaper?"

Conflicting feelings rose in his throat. Had it not been for his privileged education with the Macpherson family, he would never have come as far as he had now. He knew that. The humiliating memory of not being found good enough, in spite of having had the same upbringing, had left deep scars. Fostering Michael would mean fighting a lot of prejudice, one way or the other, both for them and for Michael. Was he allowed to decide for the boy? Alex wondered. Who was he to determine if Michael would be able to handle the controversy of living with a family of a different skin color? However by the end of the meal, Sarah knew she had won Alex over.

It would be difficult to get legal custody of Michael. The orphanage was funded by the local All Saints Catholic church. Alex planned to ask Mr Devane to use his influence with the church, as he was a large donor to their funds. A week later, Alex found himself entangled in deep discussion with Michael Devane.

"You're sticking both your hands in a bees' nest, son!" Devane exclaimed, throwing his arms in the air desperately. "You'll do more harm than good for the boy. How will he survive the glares and stares of everyone around your family? And think what it will do to your position in society! You could lose your job over this if you don't watch it. I admire your boldness, but I have to stop you from making this mistake!"

Devane had plenty objections. But once Alex had made his decision, he could be a truly stubborn and determined Scotsman. He also knew how much Sarah wanted to raise this boy. As for himself, he realized it was like passing on the lucky hand that had once been bestowed on him. Only *he* wouldn't give it the ending Gordon had. Finally, after a few weeks, Michael Devane reluctantly agreed to speak to the priest, Father Murphy. After that, the process to foster Michael only took one month.

Alex and Sarah met with Father Murphy on a few occasions to discuss their plans and talk about how best to go about this adoption in the interest of the child. Father Murphy disclosed that Michael had no known surname, so he would be given the name Stewart.

In December, a few weeks before Christmas, Alex, Sarah, and Father Murphy signed a document handing over the responsibility of Michael to the Stewarts. How legal this was, Alex really didn't care, as laws didn't seem to be upheld anyway where it concerned segregation. He just wanted to get on with their lives and face the challenges the new century was undoubtedly going to bring.

CHAPTER 40

Friday 5 August, 2011, 6:00 pm Ballindalloch Castle, Banffshire, Scotland

As Cathy arrived back at the castle, a large group of people were already gathered in the library for pre-dinner drinks. She was looking around, hoping to find Maggie, when John tapped her on the shoulder.

"How's the cop tonight?" he asked, with a big adoring smile.

"John, have you seen your Aunt Maggie? I need to talk to her," Cathy said ignoring his question.

"Maggie? People rarely ask to talk to her, she always talks to them," he joked.

"Well, if you see her, tell her I need some time with her? Will you do that for me, John?" she asked urgently.

Before he could even try to respond, she started to walk away in search of Maggie. She stopped, turned and said, "Do you know a quiet place where I can hook up to the internet?"

John, puzzled by Cathy's behavior, walked towards her and said quietly, "There's a connection in the library, but if you want some privacy, you can use the laptop in my bedroom. If you trust me, I can show you," he said with a playful grin.

Immediately taking him up on the offer, she looped arms with him and directed him away from the crowded hall.

"What's going on, Cathy? You're acting kind of funny. Have you found out anything new?"

"John, you need to trust me. I need to check out a few things," she answered.

"You mean about Gordon Macpherson, don't you? I didn't mention it this morning, but I have heard my parents argue over the years about Gordon. My mother often ended up in tears."

"Did you ever overhear details of these arguments, John?"

"Let's wait till we have some more privacy," John offered, as he opened his bedroom door.

They stepped into a warm, spacious room. A double bed was placed in the middle of the wall on the right. The room had matching antique wooden furniture: a tall-boy, a wardrobe, and a writing table with a laptop. A brown leather sofa completed the picture. The tall windows, draped with maroon curtains, let in a lot of light. The evening sunshine gave an extra warm glow to the wine colored wall-to-wall carpet with its pattern of intermittent crests.

"John?" asked Cathy seriously, as she pulled a chair away from the writing desk to sit on. "What else do you know?"

"Not much. Among ourselves we really don't discuss the Gordon story that often, or we're wise enough to keep our mouths shut."

"But you want to solve what disturbs your father don't you?" she coaxed. "Tell me what you know."

He sat casually down on his bed, observed the attractive American woman for a few moments and tried to articulate his feelings, "My dad suspects Gordon must have been murdered. If that's true, just imagine – a Laird and chief of the clan murdered, and nobody brought to account. The story goes that Alexander Stewart was having some sort of affair with Gordon's daughter, Katherine."

Cathy remained stone-faced, silently urging John to continue.

"Now, this guy," John said, "was the gamekeeper's son. In those days it would have been totally unacceptable for a Laird's daughter to have a friendship like that. So, some of the Macphersons believe a quarrel took place and that Alexander killed Gordon, hid the body and stole some family jewelry to fund his escape to the States. Mind you, my father keeps promising that he has more to tell me about this family tragedy, when it's my turn to become Laird of Ballindalloch."

"Does that make sense, Cathy?" John was becoming more anxious sharing his fears. " I really think I would have disliked Katherine and Alexander for all the trouble they caused."

Cathy just nodded her head, wondering what Angus was keeping secret. He sure as hell wouldn't come clean with her if his own son didn't even know.

John, enthralled in his own story, said, "I've heard stories of Gordon's ghost haunting the castle. I've never seen any ghost. I don't believe in that stuff. All I do know is my dad's health is declining through this. He's tormented by the mystery. That's the word, tormented."

Suddenly he jumped up, walked over to his desk, opened the top drawer, and turned to Cathy. "There's something I wanted to show you. Take a look at this." He handed her a small black-and-white crumpled picture.

It was a photograph of a young woman in her twenties, tall and slender, dark hair tied in a bun, her skirt caught by a breeze revealing the outline of her shapely legs. She was holding the hand of a young girl of eight or nine, who had obviously been told to smile at the camera. The young girl also had dark hair tied back. Their pale complexions and facial features matched. The woman and girl were standing on rocks at the edge of a river. Even though the picture was small, Cathy could see the white tops of the water. It resembled her walk by the Spey the previous day.

"It's amazing, isn't it, Cathy?"

Cathy peered at the woman again, and then looked at John. "Jeez, that could me in that picture."

"She's your double. Spooky, isn't it?"

Cathy looked at the back of the picture which read:

ALEX. LEDINGHAM[11] PHOTO ARTIST

GRANTOWN-ON-SPEY

1904

She handed it back to John. "Who's the young girl?"

"Katherine's niece, I believe."

"Do you have any more old pictures?"

"My father has more, but they're from a later period. He keeps them in the study, that's where I got this one. And before you ask, no, there aren't any of Gordon. Somebody must have destroyed all the photographs from that time."

After a short pause, Cathy suggested, "Maybe you better head for dinner, John. Your father will be wondering where you are."

"Are you not joining us?"

"I'm not sure. I need some more time. I'd still like to find Maggie."

"I'll let my father know I was delayed because I had a woman in my bedroom," John grinned, winking.

She returned a vacant smile, her mind wandering back to the picture.

"I'll leave the door unlocked for you," John said, "so you can use the laptop whenever you want. The password is *godfather123*, all lower case. If Maggie's already in the dining room, I'll tell her you want to talk to her."

On that note they each went their separate ways, leaving John wondering what Cathy was up to.

CHAPTER 41

1900, Boston, USA

It was a difficult few months for Alex and Sarah. Michael took his time settling into their family home and routine. When he and Sarah would go out walking, he was very sensitive to the glaring looks of their white neighbors. He could not bring himself to call his adoptive mother "Mommy" either. The transition felt too awkward after having called her 'Miss Sarah' from the time they first met at the orphanage. Sarah stopped working, but continued to visit the orphans. This pleased Michael, as he enjoyed seeing his friends there. Sometimes he would even cry when they had to leave, making Sarah wonder if it had been a selfish act taking the boy into their home.

During March 1900, Alex picked up a story from Germany on women protesting over the German ban on females participating in university entrance exams. It made him think of Katherine and, like so often before, he still felt a dark shadow over how they were torn apart, even though he dearly loved Sarah.

Two months later, Alex was assigned to the second Olympiad Games, held in Paris. He clearly remembered the first games in 1896. It made him realize how quickly time had passed.

Many of Sarah's days were spent teaching Michael English language skills and basic arithmetic, so that he could meet the criteria necessary to enter a school when the new term started later that year. Gradually, he settled into the routine of a safe and secure family environment. Many of the neighbors, with their inbred racism, snubbed the Stewarts. Alex and Sarah remained vigilant and accompanied Michael at all times wherever he went, to protect him from any possible harm.

One evening, though, when Michael was playing alone outside their home, he was cornered by a gang of young white boys. He was beaten up severely until Sarah, hearing the commotion, intervened and managed to get Michael inside the house. Alex reported the incident, but the police officer involved did nothing. He only commented that Alex should know better than to bring trouble into a respectable neighborhood.

The following evening, the small Stewart family sat down for supper. Michael was sporting a bruised eye and struggling to chew his food with his swollen jaw, when a stone was thrown through the window, shattering the glass into pieces. Some fragments actually landed on the table and in their food. Nobody was physically injured, but the fact that the offenders were apparently watching them made it all very threatening. Wrapped around the large stone was a handwritten note:

Don't think this will be your last beating nigger, we know where you live. Go back to the trash you came from.

Alex read the note and ripped it up before Sarah or Michael could see it, telling them it was only some comment about his going to the police.

Even though he knew it was against all odds, the incident didn't stop Alex from exploring the possibility of Michael attending a local regular public school. Some forty years earlier, the Boston Negroes had won their legal case that any child, irrespective of color or creed, should be permitted to attend any public school close to their homes. This ruling, however, was totally ignored. Only four years before, in 1896, a Supreme Court case in Louisiana, Plessy versus Ferguson[12], had ruled in favor of the doctrine of "separate, but equal", yet the white-only schools continued to be funded way above the budget for black-only schools. Using his native stubbornness, Alex tried to make a point by getting Michael admitted, but was met with constant excuses as to why the boy could not be accepted. Michael himself said he would prefer to continue being taught at the orphanage or at home. This constant balancing of bowing to discriminative rulings and wanting their son to lead the life he was entitled to often drove Alex and Sarah to the brink of despair.

Later that year, Michael was accepted at a black-only school on Fydell Street, a good forty-minute walk from home. He quickly made friends at school and Alex and Sarah tried to socialize with his friends' parents, but were often met with racist barriers. Given the abuse the Stewarts had themselves experienced, Alex could well understand why.

One early Sunday evening, Alex and Michael visited Michael Devane. As they were walking hand in hand through the Common, Alex noticed that as usual people were staring at them. He was not perturbed, now being used to this kind of behavior. Michael didn't even seem to notice, although Alex knew all too well that his son was hiding his true thoughts and feelings.

Their time at the Devane household was brief, as Alex sensed that Michael Devane and Breen were uncomfortable, even though they tried not to show it. After only fifteen minutes, he conjured up some excuse and left.

That evening, lying in bed, his eyes wide open and staring at the ceiling, Alex reflected on his time in Boston. He knew he was successfully evolving in his work at the *Globe*. Sarah was a fine wife and they both loved Michael. He was proud of their new home in suburban Boston and they had money in the bank. As for the resistance encountered over their black son, they would continue to learn how to handle that with every incident that came their way. He simply had to believe that. Just before falling asleep, he had one final thought; his promise at Lagmore Circle that one day he'd return.

Sarah Stewart gave birth to a healthy son, Robert Gibson Stewart, on Wednesday 19 September 1900. A few months after fostering Michael, she'd found out that she was pregnant. It was overwhelming at first, with Michael there and so much adjusting to do already. But seeing Michael and his baby brother together made Sarah and Alex feel giddy with happiness.

"These boys will have a special childhood together," Alex answered Michael Devane, when he questioned Alex if he had any regrets now about having adopted Michael. "They will have to overcome more than many other children, but it will make them more resilient as well, Mr. Devane."

With that, Michael Devane had the decency to admire Alex for his daring commitment and invited the young Stewart family for Christmas dinner that year.

Sean and Colleen Devane were also at the meal with their one-year-old daughter, Mary, having traveled all the way from Beaumont, Jefferson County, where they were now settled. During the fall of 1899, Sean had seen his wish come true.

His father bankrolled him to move to Texas and invest in the petroleum business with two other speculators. They established The Texas Fuel Company. Colleen and their daughter had joined Sean in Beaumont during July. During the meal Sean Devane presented Alex with a $1000 Bond in his new company.

"Is worthless now Alex, but that will change, I am certain," Sean had predicted.

The birth of a natural son, named after his father, ratified that Alex would never return to his country of birth. His son Robert was born an American, and this was now their home. In fact, even Alex now referred to himself as being a Scottish American.

A few weeks after the New Year of 1901, Alex and Sarah decided that they should plan a christening for both their boys. At the end of a church service on a bitterly cold Sunday, Alex approached Reverend JR Tomlin of Park Street Church.

"I enjoyed your sermon today, Mr Tomlin," Alex opened. "Could I have a few minutes of your time, please?"

Mr Tomlin, still clutching his Bible answered, "Thank you, Alex. Yes, that would be fine. I wanted a quick word in your ear anyway."

The Reverend was a small square man in his early sixties. His thick silvery-grey hair almost reached to his shoulders and his tiny reading glasses dangled precariously on the tip of his dominant nose. They walked into the cozy rectory just off the main body of the church.

"Sit down, Alex," Tomlin said, as he sat on the edge of his desk, and pointed to a straight-backed chair in the corner of the room. "Now, what can I do for you?"

"You said you wanted to speak to me, what about?" Alex asked, ignoring Tomlin's remark.

Clearing his throat, the minister said, "Yes. It's of a rather delicate nature and I hope you will not be upset, Alex, but I have received some concerns from members of the congregation."

"Concerns," Alex echoed, "about what?"

"About the boy attending church," Tomlin said, now looking at the floor.

It took Alex a few seconds to formulate his answer, knowing full well what the minister was referring to. "The *boy* has a name, Mr Tomlin. It's Michael. Michael Stewart," Alex finally produced, his voice cloaked in suppressed anger. "So what concerns do these people have? Has Michael been misbehaving in church? Has he not been appropriately dressed? Or is it that God has given him a different skin color from you and me? Is that a crime, Mr Tomlin?"

Tomlin raised his head. "You are making this difficult for me, son. There are other churches in Boston that would be much better for Michael. I would also ask you not to use that tone of voice."

Abruptly, Alex stood up and stepped closer to the minister. "Mr Tomlin," he said, back in control of his emotions. "How dare you suggest that Sarah and I should attend one church and my boy another? How Christian is that, sir?" He was now almost mocking the sheer irony of the meeting. "My reason for approaching you today is that I wanted to ask you about arranging my boys to be baptized, but I can now see that Park Street does not meet our Christian needs and beliefs."

Walking out of the room, he turned one more time to the shamed clergyman and said, "I hope you sleep well tonight, because you have failed in your duty today."

It wouldn't be the last time Alex was confronted with blatant discrimination because of his fostered son. The following week in the *Globe* offices, Alex was summoned to the editor's office. A dour man, Harold Welbeck had been the editor for the past three years now and had built a well-respected name in the industry. He was also renowned for his ability not to beat around the bush.

"Alex, come in," Welbeck said. "I just want to get something off my chest."

"Mr Welbeck, I got your message, how can I help?" a curious Alex asked.

"You're a great journalist, Alex, and I really hope you have a bright career ahead of you. I'm told you have taken a black youngster into your home. Is that correct?"

"Yes, but…" Alex started to reply.

Welbeck interrupted, "You're a damn fool. Don't bring any trouble into the *Globe*, Alex, and don't try to poison any of your colleagues with your do-good attitude. The minute I start to see your work deteriorate, you're out."

"Is that you finished?" Alex asked.

"Yes, you can go."

Alex left the office without another word, having now learned to control his emotions. He couldn't help thinking about Michael Devane's warning that he could lose his job over this. But rather than feeling defeated by this threat, he was determined to use this experience to make him stronger and be an even bigger asset to his employer. It also made him think of Scotland and his fight against a different type of discrimination. Maybe it was about time to share this with Michael, so his son did not have to feel so darned alone.

Later that week Alex was assigned to report on the Buffalo Pan-American Exposition, where, before his eyes, the president of the United States, William McKinley, was shot by a deranged anarchist while shaking hands with ordinary citizens in the Temple of Music. It jolted Alex into the understanding that nobody, no matter who they were, was safe from harm when they stuck their heads out one way or the other. This strengthened his resolution to raise his sons to fend for themselves even more.

It also made him think of his own mortality and about his father, who died so tragically after having had the courage to break the Macpherson-Stewart tradition. He wondered if they'd ever found Gordon Macpherson.

CHAPTER 42

Friday 5 August, 2011, 7:00 pm Ballindalloch Castle, Banffshire, Scotland

In her search for Maggie, Cathy found herself in a tourist wing of the castle. The walls of the hallway stretched out before her, long and narrow. Both sides were cluttered by pictures and paintings of people from the past. She'd never been in this part of the castle and was glancing at the framed photos and portraits. To her left, she saw a thick oak door, with a small window at eye level with metal bars and a plaque, no doubt for the tourists. The plaque, no more than six inches square read;

THE DUNGEON[13]

It is believed that there may be a lower dungeon in this room, which was filled in after the flood of 1829. However, superstition prevents any investigation – excavation might disturb the spirits below! – let alone involving the agitation of the spirits you see laid out above! Certainly the ring-vaulted ceiling could have acted as an anchoring point for a pulley to any bottle dungeon below. Nowadays, life in the dungeon would not be so bad housing as it does as the Castle cellar – you could die happy inebriated!

In the sixteenth century, the Laird would have drunk of the best cognacs and drambuies while the Highlanders enjoyed the fiery product of their various illicit stills. This has now turned into Speyside's most famous drink – whisky.

Cragganmore is the local distillery from which the Castle takes its own whisky. Sir George Macpherson-Grant of Ballindalloch together with the distiller John Smith started producing whisky at Cragganmore in 1869. Why not sample a Ballindalloch miniature?

Intrigued, Cathy peered through the window. The dungeon was quite small, no more than twelve feet square. It was dark, but she could see an old wooden barrel on its side with "Cragganmore Whisky" stenciled on the outside. A pulley hung above the barrel, the ropes dangling as if they had been recently used. The floor was grey stone slabs, each section at least two feet square. She nearly jumped out of her skin as someone suddenly tapped her on the shoulder.

"You were looking for me, dear?" It was Maggie. "John told me you wanted to talk to me. I must say, it was a good excuse to leave the dinner," the old lady said, grinning.

"Dinner was that exciting, eh?" Cathy joked.

"Let's go and sit over there." Maggie pointed towards a small semi-circle shaped turret, displaying antique crockery. Four equally old dining-room chairs lined the walls. A sign was attached to each of them reading "DO NOT TOUCH".

Maggie ignored the instruction, sat down casually on one of the chairs, and gestured Cathy do the same.

"Maggie, what I wanted to ask you was, do you remember how you told me before dinner last night about Gordon Macpherson?"

The old lady removed her glasses. "Aye and you were spooked by him. Have you felt him since?"

Ignoring her question, Cathy continued. "Tell me, do you have any more thoughts about what could have happened to Gordon?"

Absentmindedly, Maggie plucked a thread from the cushion of the antique chair and said, "Let's make one thing clear. I don't think anybody really knows what happened, but since you're asking me, I'd say Gordon Macpherson couldn't have been a very happy man. His wife died very young, you know, and his only daughter stirred up the whole family by having a relationship with the gamekeeper's boy."

Cathy nodded her head. "And why has Angus never pursued this, or the lairds before him?"

"I don't really know. Angus never talks about it," Maggie replied. "It's a skeleton in our family closet that we've all learned to live with. Mind you, I've often wondered why Scotland Yard didn't search for Gordon – or Alexander Stewart, for that matter."

"Well," Cathy said, grabbing Maggie's attention again. "Maybe previous lairds did try to get the police to re-open the case?"

"I'm not sure about that, Catherine. I do remember a story about Angus's father being confronted by auld Colin MacFarlane at a New Year party many years ago. It must have been the early seventies, because Angus's grandfather, James, was still alive." Maggie grinned, "Aye we use to call Angus 'Junior' then, so not to confuse him with his father who had the same name. Angus hated that. Anyway, where was I… Oh yes. Colin was a gardener here at the castle for years. He got a wee bit inebriated, you know, with the whisky. Apparently, in front of a lot of people, he asked the laird, what had the Macphersons done to auld Gordon? He started singing a wee song,

Don't go fishing in the Spey,
As you will dread and fear,
Especially with a Macpherson
They'll make you disappear.

Or words to that effect."

"So what happened to Mr MacFarlane?" Cathy asked.

"He retired after that. Anyway, at least our Angus had the brains to promote Gordon's ghost on that inter thing. The tourists like castle ghosts, especially the Americans, don't they?" Maggie held Cathy's hands and said, "If I were you, I'd leave Angus alone and go talk to Uncle Thomas. That one knows more than he lets on."

"Maggie, thank you so much."

"Right, lass, I better go then," Maggie said as she stood up. Just before leaving the porcelain room, she turned around and with a canny look in her eyes, said, "You know what, you were brought here for a reason."

With a sigh, Cathy got up from the chair and started walking in the direction of her bedroom. On her way, she heard the noise drifting out of the dining room.

Probably Angus impressing his guests at dinner, she thought. Following an instant hunch, she diverted her route to Angus's study and found the door closed. After glancing both ways, she turned the doorknob and pushed. The door opened and without hesitation she slid herself quickly inside the room. Earlier that day, while talking to David on the phone, she had noticed a flipchart. She knew she needed her routines to clear her mind and walked over to the chart, ripped off the top page that was covered in what she assumed was Angus's writing, and threw it in the corner of the room. She grabbed some pens, took the frame and paper under her arm, and promptly headed for her bedroom, feeling the familiar rush of adrenaline now she was back in control.

In her bedroom, she placed the flipchart defiantly in the center of the room, and started to write on it with focused determination, as if she were in one of the project rooms of the Raleigh Police Department. After a while, she stepped back to take a look.

OBSERVATIONS

Gordon's Ghost ! Angus tormented! –

Drowning / murder (motive?)

What is Angus hiding?

(President to President)

What is with Lagmore?

Did AS ever return?

When did AS leave from Glasgow?

When did AS book ticket?

Where did AS get the cash?

How did AS pay?

When did GMcP disappear?

Was a theft reported and when?

Where is missing body?

AS and KMcP lovers: GMcP motive

Why did RS leave Ballindalloch? – fall out with Gordon? Shame?

Wayne's letters: has he told everything?

<u>*ACTIONS*</u>

WEB:

Ships Passenger lists

Old Police Reports

Newspaper clippings

GMcP disappearance – BIG NEWS!

Theft at Ball'doch

Check out local Museum?

TALK TO UNCLE T

Will Angus say more?

At first, she couldn't bring herself to name the ghost of Gordon Macpherson with the list of facts. "What idiot," she murmured to herself, "would include a ghost as evidence?" Rubbing her head, she recalled part of her dream: "Give the roses to Gordon, he's not that far away!"

Three minutes later, she tapped on John's door, expecting the room to be empty, but John's smiling face greeted her. "I hoped you'd do this!"

"I thought you'd be at the dinner. I need your laptop. My God, John, how much have you been drinking? You smell like

Cragganmore distillery."

Cathy went straight to the computer, opened the web browser, and searched for "Ships Passenger Lists Scotland / New York". Turning on her seat, she asked John, who was lying on top of his bed looking at her. "The year Gordon disappeared, it was 1895, right?"

"Yes," was all he gave her in response, producing a big yawn at the same time.

"Good. And, Scottish emigrants would board their ships in Glasgow, right?"

Without waiting for his answer, she swiveled back in her chair and typed "Ships Passenger Lists Glasgow / New York 1895".

It took her a while, distracted by the noise of John snoring behind her, but she found what she was looking for.

STEWART, Alexander, Year of birth: 1875, Sex: Male, Ethnicity: Scotland

Date and Port of Departure: 3rd November, 1895, Glasgow

Ship of Travel: SS State of Nebraska, Manifest No: 0133

Date of Arrival in New York: 12th November, 1895

Cathy grabbed some paper from John's desk and noted the details. Rolling the mouse back to Google, she searched for "Gordon Macpherson, Ballindalloch 1895". Two old archived newspaper clippings were displayed.

Speyside Advertiser: Thursday 7th November, 1895

LAIRD OF BALLINDALLOCH MISSING

It was reported yesterday that Gordon Macpherson, the Laird of Ballindalloch and Chief of the Macpherson Clan, has not been seen since Sunday 3rd November.

Chief Constable Ewan Wallace of Grantown-on-Spey Police Force made a formal statement yesterday. "The Macpherson family, a few days ago, reported the disappearance of Laird Gordon Macpherson. Our investigation to date has been inconclusive, but at this stage in the proceedings we suspect a tragic fishing accident has befallen the laird. We do not suspect any foul play. A full search of the Spey and surrounding lands of the Ballindalloch Estate is being carried out with the help of loyal public servants."

Mr Macpherson is 55 years old and has been the Laird for 17 years. His wife, Lady Elizabeth Macpherson, passed away earlier this year.

We hope and pray to God that he will be found safe and well.

Cathy went to the second article;

Speyside Advertiser, Thursday 14th November, 1895

DEATH OF THE LAIRD MACPHERSON OF BALLINDALLOCH

It is with regret that we report the tragic death of Laird Gordon Macpherson of Ballindalloch and Clan Chief of the Macphersons. It seems Mr MacPherson was salmon fishing on his beloved Spey River on Sunday 3rd November, when tragedy struck. The police have reported there has been enough evidence to substantiate his death despite no body being found as yet. Many of Mr Macpherson's belongings, such as his fishing rod, waders, and lunchbox, were found either in the river or on the riverbank itself. This is a sad blow to our community as he was a generous contributor to the welfare of our people.

Our thoughts go to his family at this difficult time.

A memorial service will be held this coming Sunday at his local church at Inveravon.

Cathy sat back in the chair. She didn't need to write anything. Sunday 3 November 1895. Alexander was already on the ship when Gordon disappeared. On Google again, Cathy looked for "Theft at Ballindalloch 1895". None of the hits were anything close to what she was looking for. Finally, she checked for a museum in the area and found one in Burnfield Avenue, Grantown-on-Spey, thirteen miles from the castle. Sure enough it had a website, and she noted the phone number. It also mentioned the curator was a Mr John Durie, living at the same address. The opening hours were shown as 10:00 – 16:30 Monday to Saturday, May to September.

She'd seen enough. She shut down the computer and looked at John, who was still snoring. Shaking her head she wrote a note and placed it beside him.

Thanks for a wonderful time!

Cat

Laughing, she closed the door gently and headed back to her own bedroom.

CHAPTER 43

1911, Boston, USA

During March of 1911, using one of his contacts at Reuters in London, Alex requested some help to find a photographer in Inverness, Elgin, or Grantown-on-Spey. He wanted to commission photographs of his beloved Ballindalloch and share them with his family in Boston, to give them some idea of where he came from. Michael was now eighteen-years-old and Robert eleven. Michael would be leaving for Scotland in the summer, as he'd been accepted at Glasgow University, to study science. Despite huge efforts, Alex had failed to find any university in the US that would accept his son.

While waiting for news on a photographer, Alex's thoughts often wandered to his past, especially when he wrote an article on an event being organized by a German woman, Clara Zetkin: International Woman's Day. He was convinced that Katherine would somehow be involved in promoting this. His article was published in the *Globe* and caused some concerns with the Boston authorities that it might incite protests.

A week later a cable arrived from his contact in Reuters, recommending Alex Ledingham of High Street, Grantown-on-Spey in Morayshire.

Finding someone who could fulfill a longstanding desire affected Alex more than he had anticipated. Almost immediately he sent a letter to Mr Ledingham, detailing the locations he would like to have photographed. He did not tell Sarah, as he wanted this to be a big surprise. Many months later, the photographs arrived at the *Globe* offices. Alex took his time, carefully going through the small bundle of black and white photos, each mounted in a cardboard frame. He didn't even hear his colleague Kenny knocking his office door, to remind him of an appointment, mesmerized as he was by these images of his past.

There were two photos of the castle, taken from different angles. It was strange to see automobiles parked near the main entrance, but other than that, Ballindalloch Castle was exactly as he remembered it. The "Stewart Lodge", his real ancestral home, looked much smaller than he recalled and the fascia had changed. A path now led through a small fenced garden and the shrubs his father had tended for years were gone. Lagmore Stone Circle was photographed on what must have been a bright clear day, the stones looking robust in the sunlight.

Mr Ledingham had made sure a train was arriving when he took the photo of Ballindalloch Station. Some people were standing on the platform. Using a magnifying glass, Alex looked to see if he could identify any of them, but they were all unknown to him. He also had asked for a photo of the old run-down farmer cottage. A picture of the woodland was included, but a note explained that the old building was now completely demolished.

It was surprising how all evidence of something that had played such a significant role in his life, had been wiped out without hardly a trace after only fifteen years. It made Alex wonder if perhaps it had all been a dream. He felt so much part of American life now that it was sometimes hard to remember what it had been like to live in the Scottish Highlands.

Alex, at the age of thirty-six, was now recognized as one of Boston's most reputable journalists. Although he was employed by the *Boston Globe*, he was often sub-contracted as a freelance journalist, not only for American based newspapers but also for British publications as a foreign correspondent.

There was a lot of unrest in Europe. Italy and Turkey were on the brink of war. Alex picked up a story from his contact in *The Times* of London, that the British First Lord of the Admiralty, Winston Churchill, had sent a controversial memorandum to the Premier Asquith. He advised that British troops should be used to aid France, if Germany attacked France through Belgium. Alex developed this storyline in conjunction with the advances being made in industry and technology. He used the first non-stop crossing in a monoplane from London to Paris by Pierre Prier, in April of 1911, as an example. "Monoplanes could well be used in warfare," he wrote, "and have a significant impact on battle strategy."

In April 1912, Alex experienced perhaps the most traumatic task of his career so far: covering one of the deadliest peacetime maritime disasters in history. RMS Titanic, a liner of which her builders had boasted it was unsinkable, went down, causing more than two thousand souls to perish. The ship sank on her maiden voyage in the icy waters four hundred miles south of the Grand Banks of Newfoundland. It was headline news around the world. Alex spent many hours reporting on the tragedy and its aftermath. Over seven hundred survivors were brought to New York. Alex met and interviewed many of them. His reports on the happenings received the full attention of the *Globe* readers, causing a sharp increase in circulation. The horror of what these survivors witnessed impacted Alex greatly.

He was particularly sympathetic to survivors from Aberdeen in Scotland, a Mrs Elizabeth Inglis Watt and her twelve-year-old daughter, Robertha. Sarah and Alex befriended Mrs Watt when she and her daughter settled in Boston, some weeks later.

With all these happenings, the Stewarts' destiny became more and more bound to the United States.

Alex's work at the *Globe* was challenging. The sub-contract work added additional pressures as he often spent time away from home visiting other major cities in America. He was also a dedicated father to his boys. Alex and Sarah missed Michael, who was now in Scotland, sent him letters every other week, and planned a short telephone call every month. However, this was not always practical as Michael had to rely on the university telephone being available.

Sarah was a wonderful mother and wife. Alex was very proud of her in the way she had conducted herself through the many dramas they had faced over the years.

Alex, although he still had occasional thoughts of Katherine, had made peace with himself.

CHAPTER 44

Saturday, 6 August, 2011, 7:00 am Banffshire, Scotland

Cathy woke early in the morning, hearing the rain battering on her bedroom window. Her watch told her it was only just after 7 am. *I hope for Angus's sake the weather clears for the Highland Games,* she thought. She showered, dressed in casual clothes, and made her way downstairs. As usual, Old Billy was already in the hall, brushing the steps of the main doorway.

"Good morning, Billy. Can you get me a cab?" she asked, picking up an umbrella from the stand beside the main door.

"A *cab*?" he retorted, as if he'd never heard of such a thing.

"Yes Billy, a cab, a taxi. I need to go to Grantown."

"What, at this time? Nothing will be open. Why do you want to go to Grantown? Maybe I could help?"

"How much will a taxi cost, Billy?" she asked, checking her wallet for British currency.

Fifteen minutes later, she was on her way to Grantown-on-Spey.

I must speak with Catherine, thought Angus as he wiped the remains of egg yolk from his mouth. *She's far too inquisitive for my taste and I really would like her to attend the games.*

I've even announced her in the program, so she'd better show up. Placing his napkin next to his empty breakfast plate, Angus excused himself to Jean, who was engrossed in the morning newspaper, and walked to Catherine's room.

He knocked on her door twice. No response. He pressed his ear against the door for any sound. All seemed quiet. Knocking on the door more firmly, he called out, "Catherine, are you awake, my dear?" There was still no answer.

Taking a deep breath, he made the most ungentlemanly decision to open the door and peek in. The room was empty. He noticed the bed had been slept in at least, with the duvet hanging over the side. Surprised, he walked into the room and closed the door. Almost immediately he saw the flip chart. *That's mine!* he thought and was drawn towards it. His eyes darted over the words.

"Jesus Christ Almighty," he bellowed out loud. He felt the blood rush to his face and his heart beat getting faster. "That woman is too damn smart for her own good!" he cried out in the empty room his voice echoing around him.

A grinding sound announced a bus arriving on the gravel driveway. He stepped towards the window and drew one of the curtains aside. The heavy rain made it difficult to see what was going on. Casting another glance at the flipchart, Angus felt utter panic rise in his throat.

What do I do now? he thought, caught up in the sudden dilemma? *I need to be with my guests, the bus will be leaving soon, but I also need to talk to Catherine. Where could she be? Cannot have this... this is not right. I cannot have this girl find out everything. What a mess! What was I thinking inviting her here?*

Feeling totally helpless, Angus decided he had no choice but to join his guests. *I'll go to John's room first,* he thought, annoyed that his eldest son had not appeared at breakfast either. After a short knock on John's door he walked straight into the room, only to find his son fully dressed on the bed snoring heavily.

You'll be spitting feathers all day, my boy, he thought angrily, and started to shake John's shoulder. As he did, he noticed a hand written note lying by John's side which read;

Thanks for a wonderful time!

Cat

Feeling faint, Angus staggered back towards the door and headed for the dining room to join his visitors.

On the way, he met Wayne Stewart who slapped Angus on the shoulder and said, "Good morning chief, how are you doin', everything okay? Don't worry about the weather, eh?"

Cathy arrived at the museum in Grantown-on-Spey, a sleepy little town with grey buildings dominating the centre of the community. A couple of houses close by carried "For Sale" signs stuck on a post in their front gardens. *Jeez, I sure wouldn't want to live here,* she thought.

Few people were around at this early hour. The museum was just off the main square at the north end of town. For the first time in what seemed ages, Cathy felt she was back in relative civilization. She asked the taxi driver to wait and stepped out of the cab into the torrential rain.

The museum was a small two-level detached building and the windows on the ground floor had closed shutters. She pushed the doorbell. The noise it made seemed very loud, as there was no sound other than the rain splashing on the concrete. Not receiving any response, she rang again, this time holding it for a few seconds longer.

Above her, to the left a window opened, and a pale-faced grey-haired head popped out, looking disheveled and annoyed. He looked down at Cathy. "We d-do not open until t-ten," he stammered. Cathy looked up at the man in his mid-sixties.

"Raleigh Police open up," she said, feeling for her badge, which wasn't there. "I need to talk to a John Durie. Hurry up, I'm getting soaked here!"

Mr Durie was stunned. All he took in was the word "police" and with such an accent! Sighing, he closed the window. The taxi driver stopped reading his newspaper, rolled down the car window, and asked, "You really a police officer? What's going on?"

"Sir, if I were you, I would close your window and wait," Cathy suggested, to which he promptly obeyed, muttering something about loud Americans.

Finally, the grey haired man opened the door. He was tall and skinny, his skin almost the same color as his tousled hair. He was wearing a dark housecoat and slippers.

"You really from the p-police? I don't know you," he said.

Before he could start his next sentence, Cathy brushed past him and walked in. The morning daylight streaming from the open door disturbed the dingy hallway.

She turned to face the man. "I take it you are Mr Durie?"

"Aye, and you are?"

"I am Cathy Stewart and I'm here on police business. I want to tap into your local knowledge about the Macphersons of Ballindalloch."

He sighed, "Well, I think it is very r-rude of you," he answered, "B-but you b-better come up." He showed her to his lounge in the upstairs apartment.

"I want to know what happened in 1895," she said directly, sitting down on an old dark brown leather sofa.

"Eh, 1895? Y-your digging up old skeletons, I take it?"

"You know what I'm talking about then?"

"Of course, I am a l-local historian. It w-was one of the most significant events ever in these parts, a laird being k-killed."

It took Cathy a while to outline her reasons for her visit, without disclosing everything she knew. John Durie just sat there listening, occasionally rubbing his stubbly chin with his hand or simply nodding his head.

"My dear," Durie said, realizing Cathy wasn't as dangerous as she had looked at first sight, "as c-curator of the museum, I am one of the experts in l-local history. B-but I am not sure I can help you. We do have some old files on the Macpherson family. Next to the Grants they are one of our most p-prestigious families. You need to give me some t-time to go to our archives. If you will wait here p-please."

Durie left the room after he glanced at her doubtfully. For a moment, he thought about calling the local police but decided against it.

While Cathy was waiting, she walked over to the window and stared down on the square. The blue cab was sitting there and across the street she saw the local police station.

When she heard the sound of slippers shuffling on the hallway floor, she sat back down. Coming in to the lounge, Mr Durie was holding an old brown manila folder, bulging with papers. "M-Maybe this will be of interest to you," he said placing the slew of documents on the coffee table directly in front of her.

She picked up the file and leafed through it until something grabbed her attention. She pulled out a clipping from a newspaper, brown with age, with a note attached, detailing the source of the article: *Speyside Advertiser*, Tuesday 5 November 1895.

THEFT REPORTED AT BALLINDALLOCH CASTLE

It was reported to the police office in Grantown-on-Spey, on Saturday 2nd November, that precious family jewelry has been stolen from the Macpherson home at Ballindalloch Castle.

The Laird, Mr Gordon Macpherson, personally provided the police with the details: gold necklace with three rubies in a pendant, a diamond ring set in gold, and pearl drop gold earrings. These pieces have been in the family for three generations. Laird Macpherson has promised a generous reward for their return. The police enquiry uncovered that the son of the Ballindalloch gamekeeper, Alexander Stewart, has absconded from his home around the time the jewelry was reported as stolen. The police have at their disposal some witnesses that have seen Mr Stewart board a train at Ballindalloch Station on Saturday 2nd November and others testifying he was sighted later that day at Grantown-on-Spey train station, where he boarded a locomotive bound for Perth.

Alexander's father, Mr Robert Stewart, when questioned by our correspondent on Monday, denied all knowledge of the theft and said it would most certainly be out of character for his son to commit such a crime. Mr Simpson, the castle butler, also passed a personal opinion that the theft would be uncharacteristic of Alexander Stewart.

The police are looking for help in this matter and if anyone has any information, they should visit the local police office in Grantown-on-Spey.

Cathy noted that the date of the newspaper was two days after Alexander boarded the ship bound for New York. She started to flick through the second set of papers from the local police files. One stood out:

GRANTOWN-ON-SPEY POLICE CONSTABULARY:

DATE: 5 November 1895

Name and Rank: Robbie Grant, Sergeant

Incident Type: Missing person

Name and known residence of citizens involved:

1) Gordon Macpherson, Ballindalloch Castle.

2)

3)

Comments:

Laird Macpherson of the Ballindalloch Estate has been reported missing by the eldest son Mr John Macpherson at 11:00 am, on the Monday morning of the 4th November 1895.

An interview at Ballindalloch Castle, with the family butler, Mr Simpson, disclosed that he had seen the Laird walking towards the Spey from the castle, dressed in his familiar fishing apparel, carrying his rod. This was mid-afternoon of Sunday 3rd November.

Upon the search for the missing person on the day of Monday 4th November, the investigation advanced to the Spey River in the grounds of Ballindalloch. At approximately 1:15 pm a sandwich box was found on the river's edge close to where the Spey and the Avon meet. Also trapped in some rocks, some 7 ft. from the water's edge in the river, was a fisherman's wader.

At approximately 1:40 pm, some 500 yards downstream from the first discovery, a fishing rod and reel were found on the river bank, the fly still attached to the line. Also a hat, typical for such fishing, was found.

At approximately 2:45 pm the son of the missing citizen, Mr John Macpherson, identified these objects found as belonging to his father Gordon Macpherson.

The disappearance of the Laird occurred one day after he reported a theft from the castle. Any connection between both incidents at this moment in time should be considered as pure speculation.

Cathy dug in her handbag to retrieve her notebook and copy some details from the clippings. She recognized two other articles in the file from her earlier internet research. She looked up to notice John Durie was still there staring at her.

"W-was that any help at all?" he asked. "What is this all about and w-why so urgent? Is there trouble at Ballindalloch?"

"I'm not sure," Cathy said, without looking at him. She was still thinking about the theft and the disappearance.

"Drowning in the Spey must be rare?" she asked, now looking at the old curator.

"On the c-contrary my dear, we have had m-many accidents

in the Spey over the years. Why only yesterday!" he said, stretching over to pick up a newspaper from the table. He started flicking through the pages and then handed the *Daily Mail*, dated 5 August, to Cathy, tapping the page.

Spey angler is swept to his death[14]

A wealthy tourist was swept to his death while salmon fishing on the River Spey yesterday.

A massive air, land and sea search was launched when the man was seen to be caught in the river flow in the Advie Bridge area of Strathspey.

The angler, who, according to locals, was staying in a nearby lodge, was discovered five hours later by a rescuer searching the river in a canoe four miles from where he was last seen.

Trevor Sandford, of Carrick Glen said, "We had our swift-water rescue team out and a body was found".

One local said, "He was up with a group, fishing in a posh lodge. He was swept away while on the river."

The victim was believed to be with a party from an Estate in Strathspey.

The River Spey runs for eight miles through the estate and offers one of the best sources of salmon fishing in Scotland.

Frowning, Cathy handed the newspaper back to Durie. "Would you happen to know if over the years you have had people disappear in the Spey? You know, their bodies never found, assumed drowned." Cathy asked.

"You m-mean like G-Gordon Macpherson? It would b-be unusual. I would have to research that Miss, um Stewart you said?"

"Macpherson actually."

After apologizing for disturbing his Saturday, Cathy walked out of the museum, leaving a rather bemused John Durie behind.

The rain was still pouring down when Cathy climbed into the back seat of the taxi. "Take me back to the castle," Cathy instructed the driver.

In the car, leaning her head back, she closed her eyes and thought about how shocked David would be when she told him about Alexander Stewart. *Put that in your family tree*, she thought. The reported theft was still a mystery, but Alexander could not be in any way responsible for Gordon's disappearance. The tourist drowning in the Spey was a surprise, but his body was found easily. What happened to Gordon? And why would Alexander change his life so dramatically? Run away? Yes. But to the US? No. In 1895, he could have just made his way south to London and lose himself. And, where did he get the money? Also he would have had to book his passage tickets way in advance. *It's time to follow Maggie's advice,* Cathy thought, *and have a chat with Uncle T.*

CHAPTER 45

December 1915, Boston, USA

Fifty-one year-old James Macpherson walked into the small *Boston Globe* office where Alex sat behind a wooden desk cluttered with papers. A black candlestick telephone sat to his right. The room was dingy and dark, and despite it being nearly twenty years since Alex had seen him last, he immediately recognized James. The Macpherson face and eyes surged him back to his past and Alex almost lost his composure. Both men didn't think twice about it and hugged, slapping each other on the back.

James stepped back and looking at Alex, said, "Well, you're looking as though you are doing just fine." James's Scottish accent had not deserted him.

Alex, wiping his misting eyes said, "Good to see you! What happened to the locks?"making fun of James's bald head. "Sit down James, sit down," Alex enthusiastically gestured him to a brown leather chair as if afraid his long-lost "brother" would leave him as suddenly as he had come in.

"Thanks for the letter. I must admit it took me by surprise," said Alex. "So, you're in Boston on business, how long will you be staying?"

James was smartly dressed in a black suit and white shirt with a red tie and was holding a heavy overcoat and hat. He sat down, "A few days," he said, after a brief pause. "Is this where all the inspirational writing is done?"

Alex jumped ahead to what was really on his mind. "Sorry for being bold here, James. It's probably not good etiquette, but I need to know, how is Katherine?"

James just shrugged his shoulders and stared at Alex, "I really don't know, Alex. I left the castle years ago. Moved to North Carolina to start up my own business and my own life, I might add. I have to say, the move has served me well. I am doing fine."

"Sorry." Alex rubbed his hand through his thick dark hair. "How is North Carolina? You married, have kids? Oh, how rude of me! James, do you want a coffee?"

"No thanks, Alex, I already had coffee," James said. "I live in Raleigh with my wife and two sons. I'm in the cotton business and have some investments in brick manufacturing. That's one of the reasons I'm in Boston. Now tell me, Alex, how are you doing?"

"I'm good. I'm also married and have two great sons. I'll be leaving shortly to go to Europe, Turkey, to be precise. I'm a war correspondent for the *Globe* and the London *Times*."

"You must be a brave man, Alex. Europe is a mess, a real hell hole. Talking about being brave, that was a controversial article you wrote about race segregation. Found its way into a magazine in Raleigh, that's how I got to know you were in Boston."

"Well, you know all about racism in North Carolina, I bet."

James went a little red in the face and said defensively, "I employ quite a few blacks, Alex."

"Yeah? And how much do you pay them? I bet they have separate washrooms. My boy had to go to Glasgow University as no American school would accept him…" Alex started.

James interrupted. "Alex, I didn't come here to listen to you pontificate equal rights for blacks."

"I'm sorry, James," Alex said waving a hand. "So you don't know anything about Katherine?"

"I haven't spoken one word to my brothers or Katherine for nearly eighteen years."

"Why did you leave Ballindalloch?"

"Let's just say I had a disagreement with John. He became the laird after my father died."

"Whatever happened to Gordon?"

James flinched at this question and rubbed his mouth. "How much do you know?"

"Not a lot. My father sent me a letter and told me your father had disappeared shortly after I left the castle. Drowned in the Spey, he told me, but my father never believed that and neither do I. Did they ever find him?"

"Well, I left in ninety-six and they still hadn't found him. And, your father was right. I know for a fact he didn't drown."

"So he is dead? You know that for sure?"

"Aye, he certainly isn't roaming the streets of Grantown, or Boston for that matter."

"How do you know?"

James put up a hand as if to stop the conversation and said, "I just know. Leave it be."

"He set me up, you know, with that bloody bogus theft." Alex raised his voice. "And he killed my father!"

"Aye, your father was a fine man, but you should have left our Katherine alone, Alex. You should have known better. Don't blame Gordon for your father's death."

Alex sighed and simply said, "We loved each other, James. I was only twenty years old."

"You loved her that much you ran away from her and the baby she was carrying."

The small office fell totally silent. Alex stared at James with wide open eyes.

The look of utter surprise was obvious and James whispered softly, "Jesus Christ, you really didn't know, did you?"

"Baby, what baby? No, you're right there, James, I never knew she was pregnant. Do you honestly think I would have left her if I had known that?"

James didn't answer his question.

"You have a daughter, Alex. She'll be nineteen years' old now. Almost the same age as you when you ran away."

Alex fell back in his chair, eyes wide open and covered his nose and mouth with both hands trying to come to terms with the news. Finally, after a long pause, he spoke again. It was almost as if someone else was saying the words. "What's her name?"

"Alexandra. Poor Katherine, can you imagine what her life must have been like, having a bastard child? At least my parents were spared that shame, Alex."

"My God!" was all Alex could say.

James stood up and started to put on his overcoat.

After a moment of hesitation, he made one more comment, almost an afterthought. "One last thing I should mention. Before I left Scotland, there were some Macphersons that believed you murdered our father because he forbade you to marry our Katherine, and that's why you stole the jewelry to finance your escape. Aye, those rumors spread around the shire, but I knew that it was all baloney."

Alex was flabbergasted. He thought of the one letter he ever received from his father saying that Gordon had disappeared and that there was more to tell when he arrived in America. He flinched at the thought that these were the rumors his father had been facing on his own.

As James started lo leave the office, Alex, still seated behind his desk asked, "What happened to Gordon, James?"

James turned and softly said, "You mind your back in Turkey, Alex," and then he was gone.

Over the next few days, Alex made some decisions. He did not tell Sarah about Alexandra, just that James was in Boston on business and they had done some reminiscing about their days in Ballindalloch.

After his assignment in Turkey, Alex's plan was to travel to Scotland and meet up with his son, Michael. He could now sail into Leith Port at Edinburgh first and contact Katherine from there. If she agreed to see him, he could make his way to Ballindalloch or she could come to Edinburgh with Alexandra.

He hoped he was not being too naïve.

CHAPTER 46

Saturday 6 August, 2011, Scottish Highlands

Early on Saturday morning, David drove north in his Avis rental, a Honda CRV, on the M8 and M90 highways to the city of Stirling. He visited Stirling Castle, where the infant son of Mary Queen of Scots was crowned James VI of Scotland in 1567. His next stop was on the outskirts of Stirling, Bannockburn, scene of the great battle where the Scots, led by Robert the Bruce, defeated the English in 1314. He sat at the foot of a huge statue of the Bruce overlooking the site of the battle, and wondered if the Stewarts had been involved in this piece of history. He also saw the Wallace Monument standing tall and proud outside the city, overlooking the scene of Scotland's victory over the English, led by William Wallace, at the Battle of Stirling Bridge in 1297.

Early in the afternoon, he continued north, driving to Perth, to visit Scone Abbey, home of the Stone of Destiny where Kings of Scots were crowned.

On leaving Perth, he continued on the A95 in the general direction of Inverness. The weather was initially kind, dry, and sunny, and the scenery was magnificent as he drove through the Cairngorm National Park, the biggest in the United Kingdom.

With mountains on both sides of the road, he felt his ears pop as the car gained altitude. A few mountain tops showed the first signs of snow for the year. The weather changed quickly, with little warning. Mist covered the mountain tops, the sky blackened, and then the heavens opened. He found himself driving through an incredible and frightening thunder storm, while he passed the exit for Newtonmore. He had to pull over in a side-parking lane, as the windshield wipers couldn't deal with the lashing rain.

He was going to arrive much later than planned at his hotel in Grantown-on-Spey. He started to search his papers for the hotel phone number and the leaflet for the Highland Games fell on his lap. *Poor Cat*, he thought, *I hope she packed her raincoat.*

CHAPTER 47

1916, Boston, USA

Alexander Stewart died on Wednesday 5 January 1916 at forty-one years of age, leaving his wife Sarah and two sons, aged twenty-three and sixteen.

He had been contracted by *The Times* newspaper of London as a war correspondent with the Royal Engineers at Gallipoli Peninsula in Turkey. This was a major campaign by the British and French operations during World War I to capture the Ottoman capital of Istanbul. Alex, working with British, Australian, and New Zealand forces perished along with over 28,000 soldiers.

He was buried at Helles Memorial Cemetery in Turkey, Grave No. 328.

On a Sunday morning in August of 1916, his widow, Sarah, told her sons Michael and Robert about their father's story of the events in Ballindalloch that had forced him to leave. She also explained their father's affection for Katherine Macpherson.

On many occasions, Alexander had told stories about Ballindalloch to his boys. However, he had never mentioned anything about what Gordon Macpherson had done. He had confided in Sarah, though. She knew the full story about the bogus theft, Alex's father drowning at sea, and Gordon's disappearance.

"Did he tell you all this?" asked Michael, "Even about his love for Katherine?"

Sarah Stewart smiled at both her sons. "Not exactly. I found a collection of letters your father had written to Katherine, but he never mailed them. Every letter was in an envelope addressed to the castle."

"And you never said anything to him?" asked Robert, her youngest son.

"No. He was a good man, a fine husband and father, and I loved him. I would never do anything to spoil that. The letters were written when he was a young man and they eventually stopped."

The following day, early in the morning, Sarah Stewart picked up the phone, asked to book a long-distance call, and gave the details of the address she was trying to contact. Some hours later, the telephone rang and Sarah quickly picked up.

"This is your call Mrs Stewart. Hold on, connecting you now."

"Hello, hello, this is Ballindalloch Castle," a male voice answered. The quality of the connection was poor, faint, with a slight echo.

"May I speak to Katherine Macpherson, please," Sarah shouted into the phone piece.

"Katherine, did you say Katherine?" the Scottish voice asked.

Sarah repeated, "Katherine, yes, Katherine."

"She no longer lives here. She left years ago, went to America, she did."

"America, where in America?"

"I couldn't tell you, Mrs Stewart, you would have to ask the laird. She went to Canada first, that I do know, but later she moved to America. Thank you kindly for calling, Madam."

Sarah heard a click and then a strong sound as if wind was blowing through a tunnel. She frowned. She had wanted to inform Katherine Macpherson that Alexander had passed away. She was sure she would have wanted to know.

CHAPTER 48

All sorts of thoughts about Alexander Stewart and Gordon Macpherson were bouncing around in Cathy's mind when her taxi turned into the Ballindalloch Castle driveway.

A coach was coming from the opposite direction. As the two vehicles passed, she peered out of the rain-swept window and saw Angus staring back at her from one of the first windows of the bus. He had the most amazed look on his face. The car and bus were moving at a snail pace. She rolled down the window and shouted, "Enjoy the games, Angus! Hope the weather picks up for you!" and waved enthusiastically.

The way he glared back confirmed her suspicion that the weather was not his only concern of the day.

While paying the taxi driver, Cathy heard a familiar voice behind her.

"Back already, are you? Well, you've missed the bus to the games. Suppose you'll want the taxi to take you to Newtonmore now?"

Cathy turned around to find the doorman glaring at her,

hostile. Billy clearly didn't like people to behave out of accordance with usual routine.

"No thank you Billy. I will be staying in this afternoon. This is not my kind of weather." The rain had almost stopped, but the sky was still grey and heavy, and seemed very low.

Not commenting any further, Billy walked into the hall, making sure he increased his distance from her. "Silly, willful woman," he murmured as he walked away.

On a hunch, Cathy walked to the library, hoping to find Uncle Thomas there. He was sitting at the reading table, nurturing a cup of tea while leafing through a newspaper.

"Hi, Uncle T!" she said casually. "Not going to the games?"

"Good morning, Catherine," he replied, looking up from his paper. "I'm too old, lass, but why aren't you there?"

"Well, actually," she said, sitting down beside him, and looking at him seriously, "I've been playing a game of my own. It's called, Who Stole the Jewelry and Why. Do you want to play?"

Thomas carefully placed his tea cup on its saucer and looked back at her. "I knew it," he said. "You're the type of girl who will just not let go, aren't you? John told me you were on the prowl."

"Can I tell you what I found out, Uncle T?"

"Maybe you don't need to, girl. It might be time for me to tell you what I know, but not here."

"You're right." She grinned, "Don't take this the wrong way, but how about my bedroom?"

"Aye, if only I was forty years younger," he replied, smiling, but the joke quickly faded in the tension of the moment. Billy looked up from his post at the door to watch Thomas and Cathy walk up the stairs towards the guest wing and just shook his head. *Something doesn't feel right about that woman,* he thought to himself.

In her bedroom, she cleared some clothes from the chair of her writing table. When she looked up, she saw Thomas's attention had already been drawn to the flipchart.

"This reminds me of old times, lass," he said, looking at her notes. "In my days with the Black Watch, this was exactly how we used to work. Write everything down, facts and figures, make sure we had it right, and then devise an action plan to send the troops on their way."

Taking some more time to observe her chart, he said, without looking at her, "You've come a long way, Catherine. I think it's time I filled in the blanks."

"Would you mind verifying a few things first?" she asked. "I've been to the museum at Grantown."

"Ah! You've met my old pal J-John D-Durie then," Uncle Thomas said, mimicking the local historian.

Cathy laughed, "Yes, Mr Durie was very helpful and I can now actually add some more information to the flipchart."

She started to integrate her new findings of that morning to her notes, explaining along the way how she had reached certain conclusions.

He listened intently and said, "I think you should know, there is more here than meets the eye." Taking a pause for effect, he turned towards her and said, "I have actually seen Gordon Macpherson."

"Well, that's great," she replied, "But a ghost is no evidence."

Smiling thinly, Thomas put a strong hand on her shoulder. "I don't mean his apparition, Catherine," he said. "I'm talking about his bones."

Her jaw dropped. "Where…?" was all she could muster.

"How about a dungeon," he said, looking at her with sad eyes. "Isn't that the most appropriate place for a skeleton?"

She frowned for a moment, not sure if he was ridiculing or helping her.

"But that's been closed off!" she said. "I read the plaque on the door myself. You tell all your tourists that it was sealed off early in the nineteenth century. So unless the dungeon was secretly re-opened…?"

"It wasn't."

For a moment, she held her breath, trying to balance the odds. Looking at Thomas, she said, "Pardon me if I sound ignorant, but how did you manage to find the bones in a dungeon that was sealed up?"

"I'll tell you that in a minute, love. By the way, it's not just poor Gordon's bones I found, also some jewelry."

"The jewelry Alexander was accused of stealing?"

"That's right, I know of no other." His face muscles were now taut as he stared at Cathy.

She walked towards the window, trying to recover her composure. This new information was so startling that she struggled to think clearly about what to ask next.

Her back to Thomas, looking out of the window she said, "Uncle T, I think you should tell me the whole story."

"Before I tell you, Catherine, I want you to know I am very happy it is you who has discovered our family skeleton, so to speak, and are about to hear the truth. The thought of passing away without having confessed my secret to somebody troubled me deeply. I can't think of a better person than you to tell my story to."

She sat down on her bed, her elbows on her knees cupping her head in her hands, not knowing what to say, trying to hide her excitement. She felt it too, as if it were some mission she had to perform, something urging her to pay good attention to what she was about to hear. She felt *responsible* in some peculiar way.

Thomas sat down at the desk and cleared his throat. He seemed apprehensive.

"Nineteen-forty," he began. "Second World War, the Germans were bombing Britain. All the children across the country were being educated on how to best protect themselves in the event of a bomb raid. I remember we were shown how to use old doors propped against a wall as make-shift protection. In fact, all the doors of the main rooms in the castle were removed for this purpose."

She looked at him in surprise. Although she had vowed not to interrupt his story, she couldn't help herself and exclaimed, "You mean the Germans came all the way to Scotland? I thought they only bombed London. No disrespect meant, Uncle T, but what's in Ballindalloch they'd want to drop bombs on?"

Thomas smiled at her naïve comment. "It wasn't all about London and Churchill, Catherine. Coventry got a terrible bashing and here in Scotland the Germans pulverized Clydebank. Their main target was the shipyards. More than five hundred civilians died over a few days of bombing. Belfast suffered greatly as well. Up here, in Banffshire, their target was Boyndie Airfield, near the town of Banff. It's about fifty miles from Ballindalloch. The RAF had squadrons at Boyndie called the Banff Strike Wing. I had a cousin who worked there, Archie Macpherson. They flew Mosquito planes from Boyndie, attacking German shipping in Norwegian waters or their ground positions in Norway. Sometimes a rogue German pilot would wander further inland looking for easy pickings, like transport heading for the airfield, so everyone had to be vigilant."

Cathy felt embarrassed at her lack of knowledge on World

War II, except for the D-day landings, but Thomas was too enthralled by his own story to notice her discomfort.

"I was only ten years old, then. One day, it was July, maybe August, summertime for sure, I was in the old scullery at the back of the castle that hadn't been used for many years. Like most wee boys, I liked to explore and was rummaging around there."

"The siren from Grantown sounded to warn us that German planes had been spotted. I still remember that sound. In a panic, I started to look for a loose door for shelter that I could put against a wall. There was none. My father had the doors in the main living area removed, but not the old scullery. Why would he? But there was an old dusty wooden panel, twice my height that still had old pots and pans hanging on it. I tossed off the pans and tried to take it off the wall. You know, lass, when you're scared it's amazing what you're capable of. I managed to pull the panel away from the wall with just enough space to shelter. Crouching behind the wooden frame, to my huge surprise, I found that there was a large hole in the wall. I peered inside.

It was dark and I could only see some seven or eight feet inside. It appeared to be a tunnel of some kind. The back of the wooden unit had an old fashioned brass grip, like a handle, which I thought was strange. Driven by my curiosity, I forgot about my fear and went to the kitchen to get a lamp.

I remember the tunnel being just about my height and when I lit the lantern, it looked like a miniature mine-shaft without the tracks. It must have been four feet high, if that. I thought about going for my father to tell him what I'd found, but the siren was still sounding, and again wee boys are adventurous. I was no exception, so I went in. I crawled, holding the lantern in front of me." Thomas mimicked with one arm stretched out in front of him how he'd held the lamp.

"I could feel the dry earth crumble underneath me and there was a thick layer of dust. I drew a trail over the bottom of the tunnel like a snail. The air was rancid. Even as a ten-year-old, I remember being conscious of crawling carefully so as not to disturb the edges of the tunnel. I was moving very slowly, still not sure if I should continue, but something pulled me towards the darkness.

The tunnel had a slight gradient. I had the feeling that I was sliding down a small slope. I'll tell you, I must have been at least twenty yards inside before I spotted the first sign that something was in front of me. I moved a little closer and about ten yards away the light fell across what looked like a dressed skeleton, lying face down in the tunnel with one arm extended and a leather pouch clutched in its bony fingers. Just behind, a large boulder was covering the legs and blocking the rest of the tunnel.

My heart was beating like a drum, Catherine. I needed to get out of there, fast. But that leather pouch beckoned me. I was hoping I'd find secret treasure in it, like old smugglers coins or something. Anyway, I nudged myself forward and snatched the pouch and started to make my way out. Have you ever tried crawling backwards on your knees, lass? It's not easy. It seemed an eternity before I reached the old scullery again. Funny thing is, when I reached the scullery and stood up, the only thing I thought about was my mother scolding me for my dirty knees and clothes. I knelt down on the stone floor of the scullery and scattered the contents of the pouch. I was disappointed when all I found was girl's jewelry."

"What happened next?" Cathy asked. She poured Thomas a glass of water from her night-stand, mostly because she needed to do something to quell her own rising excitement. Thomas gratefully accepted the glass, his hands shaking with the emotion of recalling his traumatic childhood memory.

"It's okay, Uncle T. Tell me the rest of the story." She was hardly able to contain her eagerness to hear more.

Thomas swallowed hard and continued. "I waited until my father came home that evening. I didn't want to show my mother the dirty clothes and also, I thought my story might scare her. I decided my father should know first. He was the laird, after all. When I showed him the tunnel and the pouch and told him what I'd seen inside, he quickly ushered me away. After that, I wasn't allowed anywhere near the kitchen quarters or the old scullery. My father told me I was never ever to mention to anybody what I'd found. It was a few weeks later when I summoned up the courage to check out the tunnel again. But the entrance was bricked up.

Many years later, I learned that the tunnel probably dated back to the seventeenth century, from the times they stored illegal barrels of whisky. They'd roll the barrels with their feet to an area at the end of the tunnel.

Aye, even the Macphersons would be trying to hide their whisky from the taxman."

"And your father of course never reported this to the police."

Thomas looked at Cathy wide-eyed, "Just imagine, Catherine, what this would have done to the reputation of the Macphersons! Gordon had offered a reward to recover stolen jewelry and had openly accused Alexander Stewart of being the thief. Cathy, there *was* no stolen jewelry. The whole debacle had nothing to do with Alexander. That skeleton was Gordon clutching his own crime."

"What happened to the jewelry?" Cathy asked cautiously.

"I don't know. I never saw it again. I did confront my father, years later. I must have been about twenty or twenty-one and I asked him if the body was removed before the entrance

to the tunnel had been sealed. I also asked about the jewelry."
He sighed. "My father stared me in the eyes and simply said
that everything had been put right. His tone of voice was such
that I never asked him again.

You know, Catherine, Angus is tormented by all of this. I
hope my telling you this today, though, might just let Gordon
rest in peace."

"You've never told anyone this?"

"Well, I did speak to Angus about it. That was years ago
when he became laird. His father would have told him. He
made it clear, though, that this was never to be exposed to the
outside world and never to be spoken of again"

President to president, Cathy thought, and nodded
her head.

"You know what, Catherine? You can't imagine the relief
to get this off my chest after all these years. Everything I've
told you is true as God is my maker. One last thing, though.
Over the years, I still have in my mind very vividly what I
saw in that tunnel. Let me tell you what I think. In retrospect,
after all my years and experience in the military, I'd say from
the way the body was positioned, Gordon must have been on
his way *out*, rather than on his way *in*." Thomas ran his hands
over the top of his head and then added, "Why would that be?
I never quite figured that one out. Was he retrieving the jewelry
for some reason? Anyway, I always hoped the poor bugger
died instantly."

Cathy looked at him and said, "Maybe so, Uncle T. It
must have been so hard for you all these years, attending clan
gatherings, dinners, and so on, with them always talking about
the mystery, and you not able to say anything. Tell me, do you
really think having told me the story will appease the ghost
of Gordon?"

"No," he replied honestly, "More than anything, it's the guilt that must have haunted the lairds of Ballindalloch, not the ghost."

"So then it's about time Angus started to really dig up some old skeletons," she said seriously.

"Oh, forget it!" he exclaimed. "The day Angus agrees to uncover his secret will be the day the world comes to an end, his world for sure. Angus will never ever give permission to excavate the old tunnel. Think about it Catherine, he is the *laird*. Can you imagine if he were the one to disclose the fact that Gordon's bones were actually in the castle all this time, with all previous lairds knowing and never saying a word? It would be a sore disgrace. Not only towards the Macpherson family, but to the whole community – they've always looked upon their lairds as 'role models', as you Americans always put it," he said, scratching the air with the first two fingers of both hands. "I've never really discussed it with Angus, but my fair guess is that all the lairds from 1895 till now must have known what really happened to Gordon. You know, Cathy, it's really intriguing that you should be the one to unearth this."

She arched her eyebrows. "Tell me."

"Well, you're not just any old Macpherson are you? I think Fate has finally shown its hand, an inevitable course of events spanning a hundred and fifteen years."

"What do mean?"

"Do you know, you look like the very reincarnation of Gordon's daughter? I saw it the first time I set eyes on you in the library. I'm sure fate sent you here to make things right."

"You mean Katherine, don't you?"

"Yes, I noticed you put down her name on the chart," said Thomas.

"Well, John showed me a picture of Katherine and her niece standing by the Spey, and I must say the likeness is scary."

She walked back towards the window, ran her hands through her hair, and stared out at the rain storm. *Remember who you are Catherine.* The words from her dream were ringing in her ears over and over again. She heard Thomas's voice behind her, but it sounded like a distant echo. Her heart rate was increasing and her breathing heavy. All of a sudden she turned, her eyes dancing, and asked with a sense of urgency, "I know it was a long time ago Uncle T, but this tunnel, you said it was maybe thirty yards long at least, right? Starting from the scullery wall, where would it lead?"

As she was speaking, she walked over to the flipchart, tore off her notes, picked up a black marker, and sketched a makeshift plan of the outside wall that held the dungeon. "Where's the tunnel?" she asked.

"Underneath the dungeon, I told you, the old dungeon. In fact, I know where your thoughts are heading," he volunteered, now getting excited as well. "I've wondered that often myself. My guess is that the tunnel ends somewhere between the second and third window left of the scullery, about five or six feet below ground level."

"Are you one hundred percent sure Gordon's bones are still there?" she asked anxiously.

"Yes, they must be. Why brick up the tunnel unless you have something to hide? Besides, nobody in their right mind would go back into that tunnel to retrieve a skeleton, unless they wanted to give it a proper burial, and *that* is exactly what they didn't want," Thomas replied, a little worried about the frantic manner in which Cathy was asking her questions. She didn't seem to look at him anymore, as if something else possessed her.

Without ceremony, she took Thomas's arm and dragged him to the window.

"Look, *look*, Uncle T. See the digger? Do you happen to know where the keys are?"

They both peered out the window at the bright yellow machine standing out like a beacon in the rain.

She repeated, "Do you know where the keys for the digger are, Uncle T?"

"Aye, they'll be hanging behind the main doors. All the workmen leave their keys there. I hope you're not thinking what I think you're thinking," he said nervously.

Cathy grinned eerily. "Think again, Uncle T. Do you want to wait until Angus gives permission to dig up Gordon?"

For a moment Thomas was taken aback. "You wouldn't dare," he said.

"Oh yes, I would! You up for it?"

"We can't, lass. Angus would have our guts for garters."

She smiled thinly, took his hand in hers, and said, "Do you want to end this once and for all? Angus will never let you. We have to act now."

In a desperate attempt to keep his wits together, Thomas took a step back. "Lass, I can't permit you to do that! Telling you my story is one thing, but you can't dig the bloody skeleton up!" In a panic, Thomas was now shouting at her.

"Give me one good reason why not!" Cathy yelled back. "If I don't, nobody else will and this fucking tragedy will live forever. This is our only chance, Uncle T. Will you help me?"

He stared at her in horror and, not believing his own ears, heard himself say, "I'd better say yes before I change my mind."

CHAPTER 49

Saturday, 6 August, 2011, 6:00 pm Grantown-on-Spey, Morayshire, Scotland

David Stewart walked into the hotel lobby pulling his black Samsonite suitcase behind him. He had just arrived in Grantown-on-Spey, some twenty miles south of Inverness and the famous Loch Ness. His arrival was later than planned, after being delayed by the thunder storm.

He walked to the vacant reception desk and waited. A wall-mounted television was on, just above the desk, the volume low.

A sudden commotion behind him made him turn around and look towards the glass conservatory that also served as an entrance to the building. A tour bus had parked in front of the hotel. Hordes of passengers were pouring out like ants. They instantly cluttered the lobby with bodies and luggage of all shapes, sizes, and colors.

"Your timing was perfect," a voice commented, making David turn back towards the desk. A short, blond-haired girl in her twenties had miraculously appeared .

"Stewart, one night only," David said.

The receptionist, her nametag on the lapel of her blouse displaying the name, "Dora", asked if he would be having dinner at the hotel. He declined.

"What about breakfast?" she asked next, "We can do seven-thirty, eight, eight-thirty, or nine."

David was getting a little annoyed he had to decide on the spot when to get up in the morning and settled for 8:00 to get it over with. An Italian man interrupted David's check-in procedure by cutting in to complain about the size of his room.

"It looks like a cupboard," he cried out to Dora.

"Well, I'm sorry about that, sir, we have no other rooms available. We are fully booked."

"*Mamma mia*," the Italian exclaimed. "I've been in all hotels in the world, but never one as terrible as this one."

"Now, now, sir," Dora commented. "I think you must be exaggerating. You can't have been in all hotels in the world."

Defeated, the man turned around and left the lobby, after which Dora returned her attention to David as if nothing had happened.

He was given a bulky old-fashioned key to Room 1, with "Macallan" printed on the heavy brass key holder.

"I won't lose this key easily," he jested to Dora, but she did not respond, already occupied by the busload of tourists. Feeling invisible, he made the short walk to his room on the ground floor overlooking the main driveway.

He tried to call Cathy to let her know he'd arrived safely and to arrange a time to meet up in the morning. He was also keen to find out if she had enjoyed the Macpherson gathering at Newtonmore.

"Darn," he muttered as he stared at his phone. No connection. He tried calling the castle using the hotel phone in his room. Nobody picked up. He reckoned they would be at dinner.

After a quick shower, he pulled on some clean jeans, a casual shirt and sweater, walking boots, and returned to the hotel lobby. The foyer was almost empty now. He asked Dora about the cell phone signal and she said it could be very poor, depending on the service provider. He walked out of the hotel, down the driveway, and turned left on High Street, which would take him to the town center.

He had read that Grantown-on-Spey was a small town with just over two thousand inhabitants, founded in 1765 as a planned settlement by Sir James Grant. The streets were very quiet now with just a few people around and little traffic on the road. He walked slowly, glancing in the windows of many shops that were already closed. He was amused to see an old bottle of Macphersons Gin from 1921.

He crossed the street when a small bookshop called The Bookmark[15], caught his eye. On display in the window were many historical books about Scotland and his attention was drawn to a book on all forty-six whisky distilleries in Speyside.

Seeing the lights on and a woman moving around inside, David realized the shop might still be open. When he tried the door handle it gave way and he stepped inside. A tiny lady, light brown hair, was behind a counter to his left, busy reviewing some documents. She looked up at David.

"Good evening Sir," casting him a pleasant lingering smile. "It's good of you to distract me during this dreary job of stock taking. I am actually closed, but thought I might as well leave the door open hoping someone would come in. If you're looking for anything specific just ask."

"I guess I'm interested in the book on the Speyside distilleries, the one in the window," he replied. "And any local historical books would be great too. I'm in the process of writing a travel guide on the Speyside whisky trail."

"Ah, you are a travel writer, always welcome here. Maybe I have one of your books here."

"Well, this is my first assignment in Scotland. I have only been professionally writing for the past ten years. It was a hobby that got out of hand. Before that, I was in the IT industry selling solutions."

The lady walked around the counter towards David.

"What part of America are you from?"

"I live near Raleigh in North Carolina. However, I was born and raised in Charlotte."

While reaching out for some books she commented that although she had been to the USA on a few occasions, she had never been to David's neck of the woods.

"Have a look at this," she said handing David a slim oblong shaped book. David looked at the cover; *Old Grantown to Aviemore, Upper Strathspey* by *Ann Glen*[16].

He flicked through the pages and saw it was a book of old photographs of the area from late Victorian era. He duly purchased the book for £7.99 and the book on the Speyside distilleries for £12.99, but the lady settled for £20 even.

She discussed Scottish history in general with David. He was very impressed as she was obviously well read on the subject. She even mentioned a few books during their chat, retrieved them, and had the knowledge of what page and paragraph to look for to confirm some of her discussion points.

Before leaving a good half hour later, David made a mental note to definitely return to this bookshop and enjoy its encyclopedic owner.

When he walked another fifty yards into the town square he noticed a sign for the local museum. *That would make a nice place to visit with Cathy.* A little further up the street, he saw a hotel called The Garth [17], a charming black-and-white square building with long narrow windows. It had a beer garden just off the main road. He decided to try a local malt whisky and sat down in the evening sunshine.

He started making mental notes on what else to include in the travel guide other than the whisky-related content. *Grantown-on-Spey*, he thought, *The book shop with its wealth of information for the dedicated tourist; and potentially the museum, depending on his visit, would make good inclusions in the guide.* He didn't note any of his ideas down, knowing from experience that the really interesting items would stay with him and present themselves again once he sat down to write.

"Finally, the rain has stopped, it was one terrible storm. Can I get you anything, sir?" asked a slim blond lady with an English accent.

"Yes, that was quite a storm," he replied. "I drove right through it. I think I deserve a Cragganmore single malt."

"A Cragganmore it will be, sir, will the 12-year-old be okay?" she asked.

"That will be just perfect, make it a large one, please Ma'am."

Cragganmore was going to be one of the distilleries he would select for the trail. He had a short list of others that he decided could be of special interest, but he planned to get some local opinions first.

David checked his cell phone and to his delight saw he had a signal. He tried Cathy's number, but found no connection at her end. After he savored his whisky, he ordered a burger with fries and another whisky for the road.

Walking back to his hotel, he wondered if Cathy had discovered anything interesting about the Stewarts. *She can be such an inquisitive woman*, he thought.

CHAPTER 50

Saturday, 6 August, 2011, 3:00 pm Ballindalloch Castle, Banffshire, Scotland

As they rushed downstairs towards the exit, Thomas tugged on Cathy's arm. "Hold on. Do you know how to operate these machines?"

"That'll be a piece of cake, Uncle T." She smiled apologetically, knowing very well the risk she was taking. She did feel apprehensive about her own plan, but also knew when to grab an opportunity. With everyone at the games, including Angus, she might never get another chance like this. And she had to, she simply had to. There was no stopping her now.

Billy, sitting close to the door, looked at the odd couple approaching him like two children that had stolen the cookie jar.

"It's not a good day for a walk if that's what you're thinking," offered Billy.

Thomas went behind one of the main doors and pulled all the keys off their hooks, hoping one of them would be the key for the excavator.

"Mr Thomas, Mr Thomas what are you doing?" Billy shouted in amazement.

"Billy, believe me, I'm going through a life changing experience," Thomas replied, leaving Billy baffled as he followed Cathy into the August rain.

CHAPTER 51

Sunday, 3 November, 1895, River Spey, Ballindalloch, Banffshire, Scotland

Gordon Macpherson felt the cold water of the Spey running fast against his waders. He swung his fishing rod over his right shoulder and cast the fly into the river sixty feet in front of him like an overseer whipping his slaves. Angrily, he pulled the line back into the reel before allowing it to veer downstream. He hardly noticed his movements, guiding the rod without thinking. Since childhood, fishing had been Gordon's most effective way to put weary thoughts behind him.

However, on this particular Sunday afternoon his spirit could not be soothed by the stilling practice of salmon fishing. His thoughts kept darting over the events of the past week. Had he been wrong to expel Alexander from his grounds and enforce his departure by staging a jewelry theft? Could he have convinced his willful daughter differently of the need to carry on family traditions? Times were so confusing for Gordon. People didn't seem to recognize anymore that God had meant for every person on this earth to have their own role and place in life. How was he to run his estate when the thin line between rulers and the ruled was evaporating?

He had never meant to do his Katherine and the boy Alexander any harm, but had found no other way to control their unruly behavior than by using deceit. And now he had lost them all. His beloved wife who had always supported him through all that he did. His spirited daughter, who had cursed him in front of all the family, had left for Edinburgh without even consulting him. His loyal and honorable gamekeeper, who had told Gordon curtly, that he was questioning how he could possibly stay at Ballindalloch after what his laird had done to his son.

Nothing was as it should be anymore and Gordon Macpherson felt desperate. Distracted by his tormented thoughts, he failed to notice the unexpectedly strong tug at the fishing rod. As if to serve as a metaphor for the control over his life that Gordon felt slipping away, the sudden pull of an apparently large fish loosened his grip on the rod. Almost on purpose, Gordon let it slide from his hands and watched the expensive rod disappear downstream.

What's the use anyway, he thought. *What's the use of it all when I cannot enjoy anymore.* He suddenly felt stupid, standing in the Spey up to his thighs in freezing cold water. His legs were stiff with previously unnoticed cold as he tried to wade back towards the white cobblestones.

CHAPTER 52

Saturday, 6 August, 2011, 3:00 pm Ballindalloch Castle, Banffshire, Scotland

Cathy ran directly to the JCB machine, the rain splashing into her face. Thomas had given her the keys he took from the hallway and was walking a few paces behind her. The rain was coming down in torrents and the sound of distant thunder rumbled as she reached the excavator. The water was bouncing off the gravel driveway and puddles were forming everywhere. She stared at the machine: a mid–sized digger about ten feet high with caterpillar tracks. The bright yellow of the machine body glared back at her, as if daring her to enter. The manufacturer's logo was on the side facing her, white with a black background, "JCB", and underneath the number "8085". The boom projected from the front of the digger and a huge bucket with dozer teeth hung from the end waiting to be filled.

She was now completely soaked, her hair lank and tangled, her white blouse and jeans clinging to her body. Rubbing the rain water from her face and still clutching the bunch of keys, she pulled on the cabin door. It opened, and she could hear Thomas shouting behind her, "Go Catherine!"

She climbed inside, mounted the seat with the door open, and glanced around her. She squinted out of the windshield through the pouring rain. The boom of the machine seemed to be staring back at her. The inside of the cabin smelled of newness, like the freshness of the interior of a brand new car. Looking around the controls frantically, she was immediately confused at the complex apparatus.

"Shit," she cried out loud, as she stared at the floor of the cabin. Four foot pedals were spread out in front of her feet. Beside the two middle pedals, a pair of black levers projected. To her left was a grey joystick with a red button on top, to her right was another with two buttons. An electronic device was attached to the edge of the windshield like a stand-alone GPS. It held a tiny screen with a mini keypad. A control panel sat beneath the right window with an array of choices.

She finally spotted what she assumed was the ignition and tried one of the keys. It didn't fit and she threw the key on the floor. The inside of the windshield was now covered in condensation and the noise of the relentless rain was deafening as it continued battering the roof of the cabin. Wiping her face, she tried another key. No success. She let out a scream of frustration and threw away the key. Quickly, she made a third attempt and again, no luck. She looked at the two remaining keys in the palm of her hand. Selecting one attached to a key ring displaying a plastic whisky bottle, she shouted, "Come on, you fucker." The key turned.

There was no reaction from the JCB. *"Oh shit, maybe the battery is flat,"* she thought. Quivering and looking around her in panic, she caught sight of a green button on the electronic panel. Leaving the key in the ignition, she pushed a green button on the keypad. A bright blue screen lit up: "Please enter the four digit security code."

Cathy, her eyes blinking more rapidly gawping at the screen, was now desperate. Rubbing her forehead she thought,

new machine, factory fucking settings, just like a cell phone!
She punched in "0000".

"Incorrect, two more attempts remaining."

Thomas shouted through the noise of the pelting rain, "what kind of 'cake' is this supposed to be, lass? I thought you said it was going to be easy!"

She ignored him, fearing he might change his mind on their plan. She was now addicted to the chase and simply had to do this. More rumbling of thunder filled the air, this time noisier as the storm drew closer. She jumped out of the cabin into the rainstorm. She gaped at the machine's logo, "JCB 8085". Shivering, her wet clothes cold against her skin, she climbed back inside and entered "8085" into the console.

"Welcome. Select program or manual"

"Yes!" she shouted and without hesitation selected "manual".

Billy appeared, holding a bright orange umbrella over his head. The cabin door was still open and he pushed his head inside.

"Okay, Miss America, I've called the police in Grantown," he bawled, "You should get out now..."

She pretended the old man didn't exist and turned the key. The 2.2 litre diesel engine roared into life. The noise of the engine drowned the sound of the rain and diesel fumes filled the air. Billy fell back on the gravel in shock and sat there in the rain, staring up in disbelief, his umbrella toppled to his side. Thomas laughed nervously and tried to help him to his feet, but the old doorman brushed him away.

Looking up at Thomas, he shouted, "It's not so funny now, the police are coming."

Cathy didn't flinch and pushed on the right of the two centre pedals. She yelped as the machine lurched to the right, the caterpillar tracks destroying a huge patch of the lawn. She pulled on the right black lever in front of her and the machine moved slowly forward in a jerking movement. The digger's tracks ploughed up even more lawn before she managed to guide the JCB back onto the gravel driveway. The door of the cabin had now closed with the movement of the machine. A soaked Thomas was shouting, "Follow me, lass, follow me," as he walked briskly around the corner of the castle to show her the intended target. In the left side mirror Cathy could see the reflection of Billy climbing to his feet.

The blower had now automatically switched on, clearing the condensation on the windscreen. Cathy found the controls for the windshield wipers. A flash of lightening illuminated the castle followed by a deep rumble of thunder. The machine was moving slowly forward, crunching the gravel beneath it, and the boom gently rocked with the motion of the digger. Her confidence growing, Cathy's next challenge was to turn the digger to her left. She pushed on the foot pedal left of centre, but used too much pressure. The machine turned sharply and Cathy let out a yelp, as the boom decimated a six-foot ancient statue of a lion. In horror, she watched its head roll along the drive then smash into the castle wall. Thomas caught her attention by waving and bawling, "Here, lass, over here!"

Once in position, she took her foot from the pedal. The machine stopped about thirty feet from the castle wall.

Thomas opened the door of the cabin and popped his head in. "Well done."

They both glanced behind them as Billy appeared yet again, shouting, "You're done for. The police are coming to get you."

"Back off, Thomas," Cathy said sharply, and started playing with both grey joy sticks to her right and left. Nothing happened. Instead a message appeared on the electronic screen: "Set stabilizers".

With a look of defeat on her face, she thought, *I'll just ram the fucking thing into the wall.* Thomas was standing by the castle wall pointing to a small square-shaped window with a metal bar running horizontally in the center.

"Here, Catherine, here."

Cathy assumed this window must be the modern-day dungeon. She knew she had to get beneath ground level. She looked at the control panel to her right with its many buttons. She pushed on the red key and they all lit up. She had a closer look and observed that two of the keys had a sign that looked like old fashioned scales; one with an "R" the other with an "L". She pushed on both simultaneously and the colours changed. She hoped this was the correct move.

Taking the grey joystick, she pushed the button on top with her thumb and in parallel moved the lever forward. The boom reacted and lifted away from Cathy and the cabin. The machine remained stable. With a similar stick to her left, she did the same and the boom moved downwards, digging into the gravel and soil. She gasped as lightening again flashed in the sky and a clap of thunder rumbled above, the rain continuously battering down in torrents.

She rolled the JCB forward towards the castle wall. Thomas was waving his arms. His excitement was at fever pitch as he watched the JCB's bucket slowly sink in to the earth as the machine drew closer. He stepped to the side. He watched the bucket slam into the castle wall and part of the mortar gave way. A thick cloud of dust mushroomed, mixing with the rain. The diesel engine roared as Cathy struggled to get the machine in reverse gear. The bucket lifted from the soil and swung to the right, smashing one of the castle windows, showering glass everywhere. Finally, the digger started to reverse. Some fifteen feet back, it stopped.

Thomas could see Cathy's outline, her head constantly turning side to side. The machine lurched forward for a second attempt. The bucket went much deeper into the earth. *Slam*, more brick collapsed, and a huge hole opened in the castle wall. This time it was more difficult for Cathy to get the JCB to reverse out of the gaping hole, but she managed. The smell of burning diesel almost made Thomas choke.

The sound of a police siren could be heard in the distance and Billy shouted, "They're here, Mr Thomas! You better get her to stop."

They both turned around as the machine roared and watched Cathy drive the JCB forward for its third assault.

CHAPTER 53

Sunday, 3 November, 1895, Ballindalloch, Banffshire, Scotland

Gordon could not remember the pull of the Spey being this strong before. Or was he simply weaker? For a moment, the thought ran through his head that he wouldn't mind being taken by the current, just like his fishing rod.

"Don't be ridiculous, Gordon Macpherson," he mumbled to himself. "You have responsibilities here." Pushing his legs against the current, he waded back towards the river bank. He heard the water gurgle as it streamed past him. It almost made him lose his balance when an unexpected high stone caught his left foot as he moved forward. It was as if the stones were teasing him, making him feel what it was like to be unstable. Anger surfaced. He was enraged by the stupidity of the situation he had created.

Another stone caught his foot. Combined with the strong current, it made him stumble forward, almost falling head down into the Spey, making him lose his hat. He tried to grab it from the water, but the current was quicker and he watched the hat being swept downstream.

This must cease, he thought. *What has become of me?* Fuelled by his wrath, he dragged himself against the current until he felt the water level lessen and he could walk on to the cobblestones lining the river bank. Shivering, he stripped off his fishing trousers and without thinking twice threw them over his shoulder into the Spey.

"You can have that too, you trickster," he muttered angrily at the river.

Suddenly, all was so clear to him. He had used deceit to support what he felt was right, but it had turned against him. He saw that now and knew he needed to turn back the clock. *I'll go to the police*, he thought, *and tell them I've made a terrible mistake. That someone has put the jewelry somewhere I didn't expect, and that it's all based on a misunderstanding. I'll talk to Katherine and explain to her what I did and why. I'll even apologize if need be, to restore the harmony on Ballindalloch, just as it always was when Elizabeth was still here by my side. Everyone will surely understand and forgive me.*

Not feeling the cold anymore, he walked alongside the Spey as fast as he could, following the path that ran from his favorite fishing spot to the castle. Instead of opening the two gates that separated the cattle's meadow from the castle and the river, he climbed over them. He had to smile at himself.

"You haven't done that for a while, have you now, old chap?" he said out loud.

Hastily, he walked towards the back door of the main kitchen that led into the old scullery. Still having his wits together, he carefully checked no-one was there to catch him, just as he had done the first time when he went in to hide the precious artifacts. No need to let the whole castle know what he had done.

As for Alexander, well, Gordon had always been doubtful whether the boy wanted to become a gamekeeper.

"Besides, the lad will have learned, like me," Gordon muttered, "and will surely leave Katherine alone now. "

He barged into the scullery and went straight for the panel that hid the old whisky store room. Using the handle of an old iron pan that hung against the panel, he prized open the wooden frame, exposing the darkness of the low tunnel. He cursed silently under his breath. Unlike the first time, he had not come prepared. Without a lamp, it would be impossible to see anything inside the tunnel and he did not want to leave the panel open in case anyone came into the scullery unexpectedly. He glanced around and noticed an old-fashioned brass lantern hanging beside the coal-cellar door. He snatched it from its hook and looked inside. A used candle was still firmly stuck on the base. *I'll have to make do with this,* Gordon thought, wishing it had been an oil lantern. Shrugging his shoulders he decided to enter. *I know that tunnel like my back pocket,* he thought. *It's about twenty paces in on the right, just behind the big bulge where a stone is protruding out of the roof.*

He pulled out his silver Vesta case, took out a matchstick, and lit up the lantern. He clumsily lowered himself into the tunnel and closed the panel behind him. Engulfed in almost total darkness, he sank to his knees and started to crawl forward, holding the lamp in his left hand. Every now and again, he would reach out his right hand to touch the roof of the tunnel to look for the marking stone. His nostrils twitched, irritated by the pungent earthy smell. He took short sharp breaths, cherishing what little air was being offered.

After what he thought should be twenty paces, he stopped and reached out with both hands to search for the boulder. Despite the sparse candlelight, he found it almost immediately.

"Good guesser you are, eh, " he muttered, using the reassurance of his own voice to dim the solitude of his situation.

He placed the lantern on the dry soil floor and leaning one hand against the stone in the roof, began to search the rough surface.

His hand did not find what he was looking for. Leaning a little harder against the boulder with his shoulders, he started to scan the earth with his feet. Maybe the jewelry was a bit further out. It took him some time to find his pouch. Clutching his prize, he pressed his body against the large boulder for support while he tried to squeeze his body around in the narrow tunnel. Unbelievably, he felt the stone shift. *This can't be real.* His final thought, as the weight of the tunnel roof collapsed on him, were of Elizabeth and the children playing on the lawn of Ballindalloch on a bright summer day.

CHAPTER 54

Saturday, 6 August, 2011, 5:45 pm Ballindalloch Castle, Banffshire, Scotland

"She did what? A hole, where?"

Angus had returned from the Highland Games to find his front lawn littered with police cars. Christie, who had been summoned by a panic-stricken Billy, told him that Thomas and the American Cathy had driven a digger into the castle wall. Billy was being held in the tea room by the police, together with Cathy and Thomas.

The other passengers in the bus were shocked at the sight of all the police cars and the large clumps of earth and flowers scattered all over the grounds.

Angus staggered towards the tea room. In total disbelief, he stared at the remains of what used to be a statue of a lion. Pushing the door open with such vigor it crashed into the cashier desk right behind it, Angus barged in and was met by a tall broad-shouldered man who introduced himself in a booming voice as Detective Inspector Peter Duckett.

Angus saw old Billy sitting at one of the tea room tables with an untouched glass of water in front of him.

"What in Christ's name happened to my castle?"

"I think you better sit down, sir."

"I want to have a word with Billy," Angus bellowed, pointing at his doorman, who was looking at him with a desperate expression in his eyes.

"Sit down, please, Mr Macpherson, and I will tell you what we know."

Angus was led to a table and both men sat down. Inspector Duckett explained that they received a phone call from Billy requesting assistance.

"When we arrived, we found Mrs Catherine Stewart trapped in the JCB about six feet down in a hole she'd created using the machine."

"She shouldn't have done that," stammered Angus.

Inspector Duckett smiled thinly at the understatement. "Let me finish, sir. We also observed Mr Thomas Macpherson at the scene. When we arrived, he was trying to free Mrs Stewart from the cabin."

"I need to talk to him," Angus cried out, half-rising from the chair.

The police officer placed one of his large hands on Angus's shoulder and beckoned him to stay seated.

"We're not finished yet, sir. There's more you should know."

Staring at the policeman with a forlorn expression on his face, Angus sank back into his chair without a word.

"Sir, let me get straight to the point. We have cordoned off the area as a potential crime scene. We have found a body. It's clearly a body that has been there for a very long time. But, of course, we need to investigate. As we speak, our forensic team is on their way."

Lowering his head Angus thought, *Oh my God, he's been found.*

CHAPTER 55

Sunday, 7 August, 2011, Grantown-on-Spey, Morayshire, Scotland

David was lying in his hotel bed in Grantown-on-Spey. Even though it was only 5.30 am, he was wide awake and gave a deep sigh. Jet-lag was supposed to have kept him sleeping in the morning. All the impressions of the past few days in Scotland had jolted him more than he had expected and made him sleep lightly.

He now realized it was the funny scraping noise outside his bedroom window that had awakened him. Somebody was brushing a path or the driveway. He decided to get up and explore the local Speyside Walk. After that he could maybe work on his travel notes, before driving east to Ballindalloch to meet up with Cathy. Ten o'clock should be a decent time to arrive. The morning sun lit up his room as David pulled back the drapes and scanned the hotel lawn. A short chubby gentleman in his late fifties with a balding head and a grey stubbly moustache was indeed sweeping the path beside the flower bed under his window. After a long shower, he got dressed and made himself an "in-room" coffee from a packet of freeze-dried Nescafe. *Well, at least it's hot and wet*, he thought as he reluctantly drank half a cup while flicking through the television channels.

Ten minutes later he walked into the hotel lobby. Not a person was in sight. All he could hear was the ticking of the old grandfather clock close to the reception desk. Longing for some fresh air, he went outside and approached the man still sweeping the paths with great vigor.

"Good morning," offered David. "You're very busy for this time of the morning."

"Aye, well I'll be glad when I'm in my bed, I finish at seven," the man replied, without even looking up at David.

He must be the night porter, David thought, and tried again, as he knew locals often provided very useful information. "It's a lovely morning, nice clear blue sky. That was some rain yesterday afternoon, though."

As the busy man didn't respond, David asked, "Excuse me, sir, are you local to these parts?"

"No, no," the man responded, now stopping his sweeping and looking at David. "I was born and raised some ten miles from here."

David smiled, and thought, *My God, what does that make me?*

"Look at that." The porter pointed to a plant pot filled with old withered stalks. "They're meant to be marigolds, you know." He then pointed to another pot behind David. "Look, they were planted yesterday! Half o' them are already dead. Would you have planted them like that? It's a good job we have a full-time gardener here, don't you think?" he said with a hint of sarcasm.

David clearly understood that there must be some friction between the night porter and the gardener. Leaving the grumpy man, he set out to go on his Speyside walk. It took him just over forty-five minutes, to walk along the banks of the Spey that touched on Grantown. For most of the way, the river was covered on both sides with either trees or thick bushes. He spotted a couple of early-morning anglers seeking out the salmon. The older of the two waved a good morning. David thought how careful you would have to be wading in the river, given the rapid current.

On returning to the hotel, the lobby was now cluttered with Italian tourists and an excessive amount of luggage. He went to the dining room for breakfast. A young waiter, clearly under pressure, informed David he would need to wait until eight o'clock. "That is what you booked, sir and it's only seven thirty-five," he said triumphantly.

This annoyed David so much that he walked to the reception desk and cancelled his breakfast booking. He'd made up his mind to go back to the Garth. After a brisk ten-minute walk, he arrived at the charming hotel and asked a young lady at reception if he could have a table for breakfast.

"Yes, no problem. You're not staying with us, are you?" the receptionist asked. "I remember seeing you here last night."

He explained he was in fact staying at another hotel in Grantown. "I'm writing a travel guide on the region," he said. "I'm very charmed by the hospitality of the staff here and really impressed by the hotel."

The receptionist smiled at the compliment and volunteered that a famous Victorian British novelist, Marie Corelli,[18] used to stay in the Garth on many occasions to write her books. "'In the upstairs lounge." she added. "You could use it too, if you like."

"Corelli – that doesn't sound very British to me," he said.

The receptionist laughed and in the very distinguishable local accent said, "She was English and her real name was Mary Mackay. Her father must have been Scottish, I guess."

After a thoroughly enjoyable breakfast, David returned to his own hotel. He had planned to leave Grantown around 9.30. Dora told him it was an easy route to Ballindalloch Castle and gave him directions.

I do hope Cat has not been bored to death by the Macphersons, he thought as he walked to his rental car and put his luggage in the trunk. Now all he needed to do was to check out. While he stood waiting in a small queue at reception, his eyes caught the television that was showing the local morning news.

"... Ballindalloch Castle. The incident took place yesterday afternoon, where allegedly an American visitor destroyed a large segment of the four-hundred-and-fifty-year-old castle using an excavator. Let me pass you over to our reporter at the crime scene, John McKenzie."

"Thank you, Jackie. It was here behind me that two people, an elderly man and a woman in her thirties, deliberately destroyed a piece of this ancient building. Later, it was uncovered that the man in question was a respected member of the Macpherson family, Mr Thomas Macpherson, uncle to the present laird. The driver of the heavy machinery was an American tourist, we now understand from Raleigh in North Carolina, a Mrs Catherine Stewart. Fortunately, no injuries were reported and both suspects are being held by the police at Grantown pending their investigation. There will be a formal press conference at Grantown-on-Spey at noon today. This is John McKenzie, Ballindalloch Castle, BBC News. Back to you Jackie..."

"Mr Stewart? Mr Stewart, are you okay? Is anything the matter?" Dora asked with some alarm, from behind the reception desk.

Hands shaking, he put on his coat, went down the stairs as fast as he could, and made his way across the street that divided his house from the Grantown-on-Spey police station.

Still wearing his pajamas and slippers, he walked inside the police building towards the duty officer who was sitting behind a large counter.

"I w-want to report s-something regarding y-yesterday's B-Ballindalloch incident."

"Okay Mr Durie," the duty officer replied, looking rather surprised. "Take a seat, please, and I'll get an officer to meet you."

At that moment, a tall well-built man walked into the station. Looking anxious, he approached the duty officer. "Can I speak to my wife, please? Her name is Catherine Stewart," he asked in a strong American accent.

CHAPTER 56

Friday, 7 October, 2011, Inveravon Church and Burial Grounds, Banffshire, Scotland

"We are gratefully gathered here today for a special ceremony to lay to rest the bones of Gordon Ramsey Macpherson, Laird of Ballindalloch from 1868 to 1895, therewith closing a remarkable chapter in the history of the Macphersons…"

The meaning of the minister's words faded away as Cathy's thoughts overtook her. She still found it hard to concentrate on long sentences or people's chatter in general, even after two months. Memories of that fearful Saturday, when forces from outside had taken control of her, kept coming back in her mind. She still wasn't sure herself what had made her do it.

Sitting in Inveravon Church now, to give closure to the series of events, gave Cathy a challenging set of emotions to deal with. The touch of Thomas's hand on top of hers felt reassuring. Uncle T had become one of the rare people in Cathy's life with whom she felt she could let her guard down without putting up a fight first. She had completely lost her sense of urgency, the feeling that there was always something waiting for her to do. Even her job at the Raleigh PD, which had always been her main reason to get out of bed in the morning, seemed futile and unimportant now.

"…for thine is the Kingdom, the power and the glory, for ever and ever. Amen."

The minister's voice was now asking those present in the little church to rise and take a moment to commemorate the life of the former laird of Ballindalloch.

Cathy heard Angus cough nervously. *Poor man,* she thought, *it must almost be as if he is standing at his own funeral.* In his heart, Angus was a good man who only did what he felt was expected of him, sometimes lost in his own prison of obligations. She understood that now.

Respectfully, she stood up and looked at the coffin in which Gordon had finally been laid to rest. A church attendant opened the doors at the minister's signal. The three Macpherson sons, John, George, and Angus Junior, and five "cousins", positioned themselves in two lines flanking the coffin while a piper outside began to play *Amazing Grace.*

In his mind, Angus heard the opening words of the traditional Scottish hymn.

"Amazing Grace how sweet the sound
That saved a wretch like me
I once was lost and now I'm found…"

Angus flinched at the morbid truth the lyrics portrayed. He still hadn't come to terms with life without Gordon.

Looking at each other in an awkward moment, the eight men slid their shoulders under the coffin and lifted it from its stand. To the sound of the piper, Gordon Macpherson was slow-marched out of the church to be reunited with his beloved wife Elizabeth, in the family mausoleum.

Outside, the sun made one of its rare October Highland appearances. The select company of people was totally silent, while nature abundantly celebrated the sunny day, with birds chirping and the sound of a barking dog floating in from a distance. Except for the piper and slow footsteps grinding the gravel of the church grounds, none of the people present produced as much as a sigh. The ceremony seemed to be taking place in a bubble within time and space.

As the coffin was carried into the mausoleum, a light blue butterfly landed on the arrangement of flowers that adorned the top of the casket. Cathy smiled and thought, *at some point we need to forgive*.

EPILOGUE

A week after the dramatic happenings, Cathy had called her boss to tell him she was staying in Scotland a while longer and had no idea if or when she would return. She also spoke briefly to Steve Hicks. He told her the incident had been reported by CNN and they had shown footage of the devastated castle wall.

"It took some time to sink in, Cathy. I couldn't believe it was really you. The boys at the PD have taped it. Not sure what they'll do with it, but I've heard rumors they want to post it on YouTube."

When she'd called her parents, her mom confessed they'd been pestered by the media, but James was keeping the situation under control. Despite constant questioning from her father, Cathy had not really been able to explain her actions or why she was not coming home.

Thomas had hardly left her side since the cataclysmic afternoon when Gordon's remains had been found. Cathy remembered very little of the two days immediately after the discovery. David had told her she had basically slept for two days, sometimes tossing and turning in her dreams, at one point even sitting up with her eyes wide open, but in another dimension.

On the third morning she had surprised those gathered in the library of the castle – Angus, Uncle Thomas, John, David, and a police constable who had arrived to formalize the procedures of Angus dropping all charges. She'd suddenly stood behind them, showered and fully dressed, asking for a coffee.

It had been Uncle Thomas who'd arranged a coffee and some breakfast for her. David had stayed seated with Angus and the constable. Cathy had been fine with that.

After her breakfast Cathy and David finally had their showdown. They'd sat on one of the benches overlooking the lawn at the front of the castle grounds.

"I shouldn't have touched the cat, huh," David had said thoughtfully.

She'd asked him what he meant by that.

"I should never have forced you to come here. What on earth possessed you to drive a digger into a five-hundred-year-old castle?" he had said.

She had corrected him despondently, "Four-hundred and fifty and I don't know. It could be Gordon's ghost for all I care."

"But why did it have to be you, Cathy? It has always been about you, hasn't it?"

Cathy had no other explanation that David would understand nor had she the energy to care. She had told him she needed more time on her own. Their discussion had gone around in circles and in an attempt to end it, Cathy had looked at David and suggested, "Go home, David." To her surprise, he did.

Uncle Thomas and Cathy took long walks along the banks of the river Spey after David's departure, reconstructing what must have happened to Gordon, speculating on what had prompted him to leave his fishing gear behind and go to the old whisky hideout in the scullery. During one of their strolls, they had sat down on the banks of the river. Cathy had been tossing small pebbles into the water, not saying a word with Thomas observing her silence and studying her features.

"What happened to you, lass?" Thomas had asked. "I'm not talking about our wee demolition of the castle. I mean, there's something else, isn't there? Something happened to you before you arrived here. I can tell, I've seen the signs before."

For the first time, she spoke candidly about what had happened to her in Wake Forest. She didn't look at Thomas when telling her story, just stared ahead at the river. There were no tears, her voice crisp and clear.

She had turned to Thomas and said, "Quite a story, eh, imagine if Cameron had killed me…"

"Did you say Cameron?" the old man had asked.

"Yes, it was a Bobby Cameron."

Thomas had thought it best not to tell Cathy the Camerons were ancient enemies of the Macphersons.

Thomas and Cathy had also gone to Raigmore Hospital in Inverness, where a police forensics team held its facilities for post-mortem and DNA research. Uncle Thomas had stood behind the window that separated the mortuary's theatre from the observation room for medical students and had looked at the skeletal body one more time – the body he'd found in childhood seventy years earlier, now covered in white sheets; the body that had haunted his thoughts and dreams for such a long time.

PROLOGUE of "BLOODLINES -Traces"
(Sequel to Bloodlines - Touch Not the Cat)

Wednesday 22 July, 1896, Ballindalloch Castle, Banffshire, Scotland

The pain shot through her lower back like knives.

Around her, the servants were busying themselves bringing new warm towels and bowls of fresh steaming water, while the family doctor fumbled underneath the white sheet that covered her legs and the lower part of her body.

"For Christ's sake, help me," Katherine cried out angrily, her face reflecting the agony of pains that jolted her body. "How can a baby come out when this tent is built over me?"

Even though she was totally absorbed by the process of giving birth, she was distracted by the anger at the back of her mind. She kept thinking that in the old days, when woman were living in thatched houses and giving birth with the aid of wise women of the clan, things had gone a lot smoother than they were going for her now. She wished she could toss off her constricting nightgown with its long sleeves and high collar. She felt it was suffocating her. The Swiss cotton clung to her sweat-soaked body, exposing the shape and pink color of her breasts through the wet fabric.

Carried on the wave of the next contraction, the anger at her situation rippled through her body.

Katherine wished she could disappear into nothingness, free of the physical and mental agony that had been plaguing her since discovering she was pregnant, three months after Alex had left.

Had it not been for the knowledge that university was waiting for her and that her brother John and his wife, would raise the child as one of their own, Katherine would have given in to the call of the grim reaper.

She was not ready to be a mother. Every fiber in her being told her so. Even though she already loved the child that had turned her life upside down, she could never be like her own mother, Elizabeth.

She had traded in her rightful place as mother of the child about to be born, for her bothers consent and funding for her to go to the University of Edinburgh. The condition had been she would never disclose her identity as the real mother, not even to the father. The servants had been sworn to secrecy as well, at the threat of being expelled, should they ever breathe as much as one word. It was agreed this was the only way to avoid a family scandal. John had even anticipated that with his sister studying medicine, new gossip would replace anything else happening at Ballindalloch.

Talk in the county about the former laird's mysterious disappearance needed to be quelled.

ABOUT THE AUTHORS:

Thomas Neil McKerley (1952) is a consultant in the IT industry who has now fulfilled a longstanding dream to become a writer. Tom was born near Glasgow and presently lives in Troon, Scotland. He has spent over twenty years of his career living and working in Italy, Switzerland and the Netherlands.

Ingrid Schippers (1959) was born and presently lives in the Netherlands. She has traveled and worked in Europe, the USA, and Asia. Since 2001, she has been part of the international community of The Hague, working as a counselor and personal development writer with the portableyogacompany

Tom and Ingrid are both first-time mystery novel writers. By combining their fortes of consistent research and psychological analysis, they make a remarkably compatible team.

READER'S NOTES

[i] **Inveravon Church and Burial Grounds**; a church has stood in the grounds since the 12th century. The existing church was built in 1808 and four Pictish symbol stones are attached to the exterior south wall.

Source: personal visit.

[ii] **Inveravon Public School**; a school has stood in these grounds since 1633. The existing school includes the Victorian building erected in 1850.

Source: personal visit.

[iii] **Lady's Walk;** is a known trail from Ballindalloch Castle grounds to Inveravon Church and School. It was formerly known as the **Church Walk** in Victorian times.

Source: personal visit.

[iv] **Ballindalloch Castle;** is situated approx. thirteen miles east of Grantown-on-Spey. It has been the home of the Macpherson-Grants since 1546. The castle is often referred to as the "Pearl of the North". The castle opened to the public in 2005.

Source: personal visit.

[v] **Newtonmore**; is a town that is situated forty-three miles south of Ballindalloch. The town hosts the Macpherson clan gathering and Highland Games in August every year. The Macpherson Clan Museum is situated in the town centre.

Source: personal visit.

[vi] **Aberdeen Angus cattle;** ancient cattle and first bred in 1842. The early breeders of the Aberdeen Angus were Sir George Macpherson-Grant, Hugh Watson and William McCombie who carefully bred and selected the cattle in the Angus area of Aberdeenshire, Scotland.

Source: Internet research.

[vii] **The Tay Bridge Disaster;** a true event in 1879. However, the name of Edward Macpherson is pure fiction.

Source: Internet research.

[ix] **Lagmore Stone Circle;** a Bronze Age relic that lies in the Parish of Inveravon, walking distance from Ballindalloch Castle.

Source: personal visit.

[x] **Air Line;** this brand, was part of the New England Limited of 1891. In 1891, the Pullman Palace Car Company refitted the train with luxurious new cars described in the book. This inspired their advertising department to call it the White Train. However, folks along the line started to call it the Ghost Train as it sped through their towns after dark.

Famed author *Rudyard Kipling* memorialized the train in a popular verse:

Without a jar, or roll, or antic,

Without the stop to Willimantic,

The *New England Limited* takes its way

At three o'clock each day,

Maids and Matrons, daintily dimited,

Ride everyday on the *New England Limited,*

Rain nor snow ne'er stops its flight,

It makes New York at nine each night,

One half the glories have not been told

Of that wonderful train of white and gold

Which leaves each day for New York at three

Over the N.Y. & N.E.

Source: Internet research

[xi] **Alex Ledingham:** a famous photographer in Strathspey in the 1900s. He was born in 1883 in Forres and died in 1959.

Source: *Old Grantown to Aviemore, Upper Strathspey* by Ann Glen.

[xii] **Plessy versus Ferguson:** Homer Plessy was arrested for entering a "white only" railcar in 1896. The Supreme Court in Louisiana upheld the doctrine of "separate, but equal," and Homer was imprisoned. When Plessy was arrested he stated, "We, as freemen, still believe that we were right and our cause is sacred."

Source: Internet research

[xiii] **Ballindalloch Castle Dungeon:** the plaque depicted in the book is the actual inscription from the dungeon door.

Source: personal visit.

[xiv] **Spey angler is swept to his death:** an actual event from the Scottish *Daily Mail* published on Wednesday 18 August, 2010.

[xv] **The Bookmark** a book shop on the High Street in Grantown-on-Spey, owned by Marjory Marshall.

Source: personal visit.

[xvi] **Old Grantown to Aviemore, Upper Strathspey by Ann Glen;** is an actual book purchased by the authors in Grantown-on-Spey

[xvii] **The Garth Hotel** is in close proximity to the local Museum in Grantown-on-Spey. Friendly staff and the Scottish kitchen is recommended.

Source: Personal visit.

Lightning Source UK Ltd.
Milton Keynes UK
UKOW051148180412

190974UK00001B/2/P